THE CLEARING

For Gina.

THE CLEARING

Patrick Kanouse

This is a work of fiction. All of the characters, organizations, and events portrayed in this novel are either the products of the author's imagination or are used fictitiously.

Published by Walter Glenn Publishing.

ISBN-13: 978-1-5352-2983-8
ISBN-10: 1-5352-2983-7

ACKNOWLEDGMENTS

First and foremost, I want to thank Gina, who has supported my every writing endeavor, regardless of the topic or form. Without her encouragement, the task would be much more challenging. She put up with me getting early starts and cranking out words to reviewing and commenting on the novel multiple times—multiple times. And she patiently looked at numerous cover rough drafts. Her passionate and honest opinions have made every aspect of this book and my life better.

Thank you to Meg Magnusson, Peter Magnusson, Doug Bowers, Wes Herron, Larry Sweazy, Dan Parker, and Christina Wall for their encouragement. Having seen a different novel (soon to be published), they continued to request to see more of my fiction.

Doug Kanouse, my brother, provided early and valued feedback on this novel as well as taking a look a number of draft covers. For looking at covers and providing keen criticism, thanks to Carol Pogoni.

Last, but not least, thanks to my parents for encouraging—always—my writing and reading. They opened worlds to a young boy.

CHAPTER 1

January 2, 1979

The gunshot cracked across the snow laying a foot deep in the clearing in the woods. Snow fell heavy, in large, wet flakes. A rabbit, some distance away, perked its ears and stood upright, looking for danger. But as the sound of the gunshot dissipated and the sound of the snow landing on the trees replaced it, the rabbit returned to its exploration of the tree and hill, nudging its nose into the the clumps of snow into the underbrush for grass.

The bullet itself lodged in the ground near the man lying against the tree. He would have been running had he not twisted his knee a few yards back after stepping into a hole obscured by the snow. He shined a black metal flashlight up at the man who had fired the shot, smoke curling from the barrel.

The shooter, dressed in a thick coat with a fur-trimmed hood, light brown knit hat, and large light blue scarf, stared at the man on the ground.

The sitting man first grabbed his knee but then held his hands up in front of his face. Tears fell down his cheeks. How had he ended up here? When he first started meeting this close to the border, he not once thought he would find himself with a twisted knee in the snow with a gun pointed at him. He wondered if he could talk his way out of it, but he knew this was it. His short life gone. He had always wanted to see San Juan with Sarah. She had talked lovingly of the place. It sounded warm. And her arms—almost as if he could feel them now—felt warm around his neck. How had he gotten himself here? He knew, of course, but still the path one's decisions lead is obscure, impossible to predict with accuracy.

The shooter looked down at the man on the ground. He held the gun steady. Had anyone heard the shot? He looked around quickly, never taking his aim off his target. Clumps of snow weighed down the branches of the firs at the edge of the clearing. The trees were beautiful in the sliver of light from the crescent moon. They reminded him of the Christmas cards from a few weeks ago that showed happy families around campfires and through the windows, trees heavy with snow. He too wondered how he found himself at this moment training a pistol on another man.

The injured man dropped his hands. Tears ran down his face. "Please don't."

The shooter shook his head slowly. No way he could back out now. He was too far into this, but that did not make it any easier. No, he realized killing a man was more difficult than he could have imagined.

"Please don't. What do you want?"

The shooter pulled the trigger. The other man's head snapped back, blood splattered the tree trunk and snow behind him. His entire body relaxed and slumped all at once. The tree taking the full weight of his body.

The animals and the elements would take care of the body for him, so he dropped the gun and turned north and walked across the snow, across the clearing, and into the woods. He walked across that imaginary boundary from the United States to Canada. His car was parked off the side of a Canadian farmer's access road. He had done what needed to be done, but he would never forget the steam rising from the hot, fresh blood as it melted the snow.

CHAPTER 2

January 7, 1979

Lieutenant Dean Wallace turned off Route 23 and onto the driveway that led to the Pratt farm. A gravel driveway that Cole, the youngest Pratt son, had simply driven back and forth in a truck on to crush the foot of snow. The barn, which had been re-painted a cherry red the past summer, stood at the edge of the property as a signpost of civilization. The house, a white three-story built in 1902, was almost lost in the drifts of snow that receded backward to the tree line, three hundred yards away.

The Chevy Nova bounced over the uneven gravel. Dean's keys jingled against the dashboard and his coat scratched against the leather seat. The snapping sound of the turn signal clicked off. The radio cracked and spit, so Dean twisted the volume knob to low.

The Pratt's two Ford trucks were parked haphazardly near the house, and as he pulled into what seemed like a reasonable spot, Dot ran up to the car, her tongue hanging out. Dean put the car in park, turned off the engine, and opened the door. The cold rushed inward and slapped his face. The air had the sterile smell that only temperatures in the single digits or lower seemed to bring.

Dot jumped up and put her paws on Dean's chest, tapping Dean's name tag and the police logo.

"Hey, girl, good to see you. It's been a long time." He petted her head, scratching just below her jaw and toward the back, where she liked it. "Let me get my hat." He reached into the car and pulled out his campaign hat and pulled it on his head. When he looked up, Cole, his ex-wife's youngest brother, stood on the porch.

Cole looked the least like the male side of the family. Blond and skinny and tall, he stood a head taller than Dean, which meant a good foot and half taller than his father or brothers. A senior at Zion High School, Cole was a star of the Panthers basketball team. The boy raised his hand and waved before opening the screen door, peering inside, and stepping back out on the porch. "It's cold. Get inside."

Dean smiled. "If I go in now, I won't want to go out there." He pointed to the woods beyond the barn and the field.

The Pratt's farmed two hundred acres along the U.S. and Canadian border. According to Wayne, the eldest living Pratt, the farm had been in the family since the 1820s, when Elias Pratt bought two acres after working for three years in the slums of New York City. Dean had listened over the years to Wayne rattle on about the founding of the Pratt farm as if it were some mythological tale equivalent to the Olympians many times.

Wayne stepped out onto the porch. He was bundled up in a heavy, navy coat trimmed with a faux sheepskin tan fur and a John Deere knit cap. He waved and nodded his head, which Cole took as the command to go back inside. Wayne was archetypal for the Pratt male line: dark, nearly black hair, strong cleft chin, average height, and stocky with a five-o'clock shadow that was a several days' growth for many men. He wore a pair of fur-lined, black boots. He walked down the two steps and onto the small path of pounded snow to Dean's car. He held out his hand. "Good to see you, Dean. Sorry to trouble you on a Saturday."

"Good to see you. And no worries." Dean gripped his former father-in-law's hand and shook once. "It's damned cold."

Wayne nodded and breathed out, which condensed and the wind carried to the side and upward. "Is anyone else coming?"

"No. You weren't clear why you needed me out, other than I needed to be out here. Do we need someone?"

"Yeah. Yes. You'll need someone. Probably several."

"What's up?"

"Dot found a body."

⌥

After Dean called the station to have them send out a couple of officers and the coroner, Wayne led him behind the barn and back toward the tree line. Dot bounded alongside them, kicking up the snow in fine bursts of powder that were caught in the gusts of wind and carried easterly into the snow-covered field where last year the Pratts had grown potatoes and winter and summer squash.

Dean walked beside Wayne despite not having the proper footwear. He cursed himself for not thinking ahead. He also regretted not accepting Cole's offer and stepping inside to warm himself with a coffee. He refrained from pulling out the flask in his coat's inside right pocket. Wayne was no teetotaler, but he had always frowned on Dean's drinking.

The older man walked at a fast clip, and Dean kept pace, but they both kept their heads down until they reached the woods, their gloved hands buried in their coat pockets.

"Those are mine and Dot's." Wayne pointed to a trail of dog and human footprints leading through the trees, both to and from. "Dot came home a while ago and was spinning in circles. She didn't want to play. She didn't want to eat. She kept running out this way, so I let her lead. I hadn't seen her so insistent except when I hold her back from retrieving ducks. I followed her, and she led me to a body. So we came back, and I called the station."

"Did you recognize it?"

"Nope, but I can't say I looked at it too long."

"You found it this morning."

"Yep."

They followed the trail back for about fifteen minutes, walking among the stands of leafless maple, black ash, elm, and green and heavy with snow spruces and firs. The sun had begun to burn through the clouds and was a bright aura in the sky. Despite its presence, it seemed unlikely to alter the bitter cold. Rather, the sun seemed a taunt of its denied potential.

Eventually, they reached a small clearing. The trail ended in a swirl of Dot's prints from when she had discovered the body and after leading Wayne here. Wayne's steps were singular. They paused about where they were standing now—ten yards or so—made a one-eighty, and headed back to the house.

The body—a man—leaned against a large chestnut oak as if he had sat down to rest. A dark, hardened splotch fell on the right shoulder of the thick gray overcoat. The man's right arm rested along his side. His left hand laid on his stomach, as if he had reached for the wound in his head, stopped, and then relaxed. A pool of black, frozen blood had created a depression in the snow at the base of the tree.

Animals had gotten to him before he froze too much. Crows or some bird had gotten the eyes, leaving two dark recesses staring upward at the empty space above the trees. Probably a fox or coyote had gnawed on the face and neck. The coat—tufts of white lining poking through—and jeans were shredded and torn in places. Dried flecks of frozen blood clung to the tips of the threads where the animals had made their attempts.

"You can head back, Wayne. I'll take it from here. If you can, when the officer and coroner arrive, send them back this way. You'll need to answer some questions, too."

Wayne nodded.

"Make sure they know they have a hike."

"Sure."

Wayne whistled at Dot, and they headed back the way they came. He paused a few feet into the woods. "Oh, and Happy New Year." He gave a friendly wave and walked away.

CHAPTER 3

After the sound of Wayne's steps disappeared and his final, "Come on Dot," Dean remained standing where he was but took in the clearing. Perhaps a quarter of an acre, the ground rose at a small angle to a point in the center. Tips of tall, brown grass stuck through the snow, which was as fine and powdery as that in the woods itself.

The wind had blown the snow eastward giving the clearing the appearance of being tilted in that direction, like someone holding a glass of water and leaning it to one side.

He returned his attention to the body and then looked down at his feet before taking a step toward it. A number of prints—both human and animal—were visible around the body, so he decided for the moment to remember where he stepped and not to mess up any of the others, which would prevent his examining the corpse from all sides. But Dot and other wildlife had left tracks around the body so numerous they had contaminated the area in the snow.

He also knew the body was frozen. Snow and ice clutched at the ear lobes and the back of the head. The body had warmed up during the day in the sun, letting the snow melt and drip down before refreezing at night. Other than the smear of brightness in the sky, Dean was not sure when the last clear or partially cloudy day had been. A uniform grayness seemed to have dominated since before Christmas. Temperatures had not broken the freezing point since the day after Saint Nick's bounty was opened by families across the county.

He did not recognize the man, but that may have been because of the animal mutilation. No eyes and the missing pieces of flesh and the frozen state made visual identification difficult. Dean patted the outside pockets of the victim's coat. He could not feel anything, but his gloves were thick and the coat thicker. He pulled up on the top panel of the coat, which lifted, but then he stopped himself. No need to rush this. Wait for the assistance. He needed a camera to document the scene. A flood of to-dos and steps jumped up at him from his days in New York City as a homicide detective.

He knew it sounded strange to people, but he was fond of those days. He felt a purpose in life stronger than he had ever felt before and he did not understand that until it was gone. Only then did he comprehend what people meant when they said, "I just want to do something meaningful." Solving murders had been Dean's meaning.

Zion's crime consisted of petty theft, rowdy teenagers, some domestic violence, and speeding. He could not remember when the last time someone died a violent death at the hands of another person in the town.

He stood up and walked back into the woods to get moving again, to try to warm up. He looked northward. Canada was only a half-mile away. From this position, looking across the clearing, he thought he saw what looked to be impressions in the snow leading north. Perhaps footprints partially filled with blowing snow. Maybe not. It seemed that way, but he knew he might be trying to find a pattern where none existed.

He shook his head. He looked north toward Canada and thought back to his days in New York City and wondered how, despite all his efforts, his path through life landed him smack back in the middle of his hometown.

೫෬

Dr. Miles Cotton had been the coroner for the county for twenty odd years. He owned the Cotton Brothers Funeral Home on High Street, as well as ran a small family practice next door to the funeral home. Miles, in his early sixties, carried a few extra pounds around the waist, though wrapped in the heavy, brown coat with a faux-fur trimmed hood, it was not noticeable. His large, brown plastic-framed glasses seemed ever ready to slip off his small nose. He kept pushing on the bridge with his right index finger. His wavy light brown hair stuck out along the edges of the hood, which kept blowing back in gusts.

Officers Zach Adams and James Ridge were walking the edge of the clearing as instructed by Dean. Both had cameras and were taking photographs of the larger scene along with specific photos if they saw something of interest. Dean had said to take more photos than not enough.

The coroner stood next to the body in footsteps Dean had created. "Well, I can't say for certain yet what killed him, but it's either the bullet through the brain or the cold weather. Tough call, but I guess the people will expect the bullet done the killing."

Too focused on the scene, Dean missed the joke. "We'll need to know eventually for when this thing gets to court."

"Mmmmm. Do you want to help me move him?"

"Sure. Do you know who it is?"

Miles rubbed his chin. "He looks familiar, but I can't say for sure." He pointed behind Dean. "Let's preserve this as best as possible by putting him directly in the bag I brought."

Dean had ignored the thick, black plastic bag just beyond the edge of the clearing. He had seen plenty of them over the years in New York and even as a cop in Zion for car accidents and suicides. Of the many millions of things he wished he could forget about Vietnam, body bags would be near the top of the list. He also knew he could not forget, ever. He stepped over, grabbed the bag, unzipped it and took it back to the body. Miles seized one end, and they set it down where they had photographed and already disturbed the scene.

Miles walked behind the victim's head and waved Dean toward his feet. The sounds of rubbing fabric on the coats. The crunch of them stepping in the snow. "The back of his head is frozen to the tree, so let me loosen that." The doctor grabbed the head and applied a back and forth pressure, rocking the head sideways. What sounded like snapping icicles and a crunch of bark rose up. "Okay."

Dean lifted the feet, and Miles lifted the body by the shoulders. Rather than flopping legs and arms and a rolling head, the body remained fixed as they set it on the body bag.

Miles knelt down and opened the man's coat. Dean looked at the tree. Where the man's head had been, frozen blood and brain matter. Icicles of blood rose up from the tree.

"Here." Miles handed him a wallet before turning back to the tree. "I want to take this part of the tree back with me." He pointed to the tree where the man's head had been attached.

"Sure. I'll get Zach to borrow a chainsaw from the Pratts." He looked at the wallet. A black tri-fold. A generic looking brand. The smooth sheen of the leather rubbed down on the edges and corners. Part of the stitching was coming loose at the top inside fold. He opened it. A number of business cards filled the slots. A collection of photographs in clear vinyl sleeves. He skipped over those for now. In the fixed clear plastic window, a driver's license. "William D. Nimitz."

"Billy. Ah, I see it now."

"Billy?" Dean could not abide adult men being called by youthful versions of their name.

"Yeah, Billy. He worked down at McCord's Body Shop."

"So you knew him."

"Knew of him. Saw him when Sally got hit on the square, and we had to get some body work done. Damned insurance wouldn't cover all of the costs." Miles sighed.

Dean flipped open the money portion of the wallet. Three dollar bills and a slip of folded paper. He pulled that out. The paper was a torn piece of an envelope, the precise cut of the flap and a thin strip of dried glue, yellowed from use. On the surface that would have faced the interior of the envelope was written in nice flowing cursive, "I love you." On the backside, a partial address was visible:

mitz
ckson St.
, NY 55768

Dean slipped it back into the wallet.

"Well, that's interesting," said Miles.

"What's that?"

Miles handed Dean a thin book, which could have even passed for a pamphlet. "Found it in the front upper pocket of the coat."

Dean took two steps back. "Zach, come here."

Zach looked up, nodded, and started walking back. He and James had nearly completed their circuit around the clearing.

Dean looked at the book in his hand: *The Communist Manifesto*. What was this? He tried to open it, but his gloves were too thick. He shook his head and bagged it.

Dean took one more step back and felt something under his foot. Hard. Not natural. He lifted his foot up and looked down. Where he had crushed the snow down, he saw the exposed polished black metal of a pistol decorated with snow and slivers of brown grass.

CHAPTER 4

Dean recognized the pistol as a Remington M1911A1. The short trigger, the extensions behind the grip, the safety spur all told him it was the later model of the iconic pistol. One he had used himself in Hue and the bush, in places he could not pronounce the name of or had no sense of where he was.

He had Zach photograph the pistol before heading back to the farm for a chainsaw. Dean then picked up the cold gun, dropped the clip, and emptied the chamber. He held the pistol out and down toward the ground, looking into the chamber and through the barrel to ensure it was empty. He popped the bullets out of the magazine. Including the round in the chamber, he had five bullets. Assuming a fully loaded magazine, two shots had been fired—at least.

He stood and held the pistol toward the bloody spot on the tree, putting himself into the mind of the shooter. A few feet away. Up close, but cautious. Kept himself distant enough to avoid surprise.

He dropped the pistol, the magazine, and the loose bullets in a paper evidence bag and set it on a large tarp the officers had laid on the ground outside the clearing.

He looked back toward the clearing. All sorts of potential evidence could be buried under a foot of snow. Moving around without altering the scene was never possible in even the best of circumstances, but in these conditions, it was impossible.

Zach and James had found nothing around the edge so far. James, however, was certain a set of steps—covered by fresh and wind-swept snow—lead from the body northward. James pointed with his ungloved, thick fingers while leaning toward Dean. His breath foul with coffee. The same faint indentations in the pack Dean had seen when he walked into the clearing. With their condition, however, it was impossible to tell if the footsteps walked to or away from Billy's body.

He shook his head and bounced up and down on his toes. They may have to wait for spring and the snow melt before they could find any buried evidence, and that was at least eight weeks away, and this winter had not suggested any kindness in moderation. He had no way of sealing off the clearing or even monitoring it.

When Zach returned, Dean told him to help Miles. James and Dean walked into the clearing and began a grid search, looking and feeling for anything. The saw made quick work of the tree. While the coroner carefully wrapped the section of the tree with its brain matter and frozen blood, Zach assisted with the grid search. Miles left with the body and headed back into town. Dean, James, and Zach took turns warming up in the Pratt house while the other two searched.

What had happened here? What had brought Billy Nimitz to this clearing? Billy had walked in. Assuming this was not a suicide, had Billy walked in alone? Had someone met him? Was that Billy's gun or the killer's?

Dean called off the search as darkness approached. They had found a black flashlight near the body, almost directly beneath the right hand. They bagged it. Other than that and a handful of sticks and some rocks, they found nothing.

〜✿〜

Dean swung the car into the small parking lot to the north of the Shambles, one of the local watering holes. The restaurant and bar had been open since the early twentieth century, surviving two World Wars, the Great Depression, Prohibition, Korea, and Vietnam and now enduring the Cold War.

Designed to look like a log cabin from the last century, the wood had darkened over the years into a deep brown-red. Large glass windows punctured the facade. A paper Open sign with orange lettering hung on the door. Neon lights advertised Budweiser, Miller, and Pabst Blue Ribbon.

Dean parked the car, out of sight of the front windows. He took a deep breath, let it out, and turned off the Nova. He stepped out into a pile of slush left along the edge of the lot. The town was quiet that Tuesday evening. People were staying indoors, out of the cold. Still, the regulars of the Shambles or any of its other two main competitors braved the weather.

The front door creaked open, and Dean walked in, closing the door behind him. The bar proper was straight ahead, through the dining room, filled with four- and six-top tables and chairs with faded red cushions. Booths with the same red cushions formed an L pattern along the wall against the parking lot and the front windows. A hostess stand stood unattended by the door with a sign hanging from it: Please seat yourself.

The bar was separated from the dining room by a short, wrought-iron railing. A few bar tables with stools stood along it.

Three families sat at the tables and a half dozen regulars were already seated in their familiar locations at the bar. A waitress entered through the double-swinging door at the far end of the dining room holding two plates. She smiled at Dean. He nodded and walked toward the bar.

Joe Banks, owner of Banks Auto Repair on Elm Street and council man for the third ward, turned around in his stool, saw

Dean, and smiled. Using one of his too-thin arms for a person his age, he nudged the man sitting next to him, who was dressed in the full dress blues of the Zion Police Department. That man grunted and raised a glass to his lips before saying, "What's up son?" Eric Wallace turned around. The Zion Police Department badge spitting rays of light off its polished sheen.

Dean had not inherited his father's linebacker bulk, a mass waiting to surge forth and crush, a physique that never seemed to waver despite his fifty-two years. Dean had seen photos of his father when he joined the Marines at seventeen. A scrawny kid notorious for stealing apples from Faston's shelves. The Marines had transformed him, and then the Battle of Okinawa and transformed him again. The Marines had not transformed Dean. Not physically at least.

"Hey, Dad. We need to talk."

"What I'm hearing out at the Pratt farm?"

"Yeah."

"Have a beer and tell me."

Dean looked at Joe and hesitated.

"For Christ's sakes, you can talk in front of Joe. He and I just left the council meeting."

"Ah, that's why you're in your blues."

"Had to give the monthly update."

Dean pulled out the stool and sat down, his father between him and Joe. He saw his dad was drinking whiskey. Wild Turkey. He was tempted but ordered a Pabst Blue Ribbon instead.

On the TV hanging above the mirror behind the bottles of liquor, Walter Cronkite covered the unrest in Iran.

"So it's true?" Joe turned between Dean and the TV. "A body out at the Pratt farm."

Dean nodded. "William Nimitz."

Joe's eyes opened wide. McCord's Body Shop was the town competition for Bank's Auto Repair, though they tended to specialize—Banks more on fixing engines and McCord's more on the body—to avoid too much overlap. "Billy? Nice kid. I knew his family."

In Zion, a town just over three thousand, knowing someone or someone's family was a rather simple matter of getting out and about a bit.

"Details?" asked Eric.

Dean filled them in from the initial call from Wayne through the efforts of the day. Throughout, Eric nodded and asked for a few clarifying details.

"Suicide?" asked Joe, rubbing the underside of his nose.

Dean pulled out a pack of Camels, tapped out one part way, and used his mouth to pull it out completely. He said as he lit it, "Don't know."

"What do you mean, you don't know?" asked Eric.

Dean inhaled deeply, held it, and then let the smoke out in a long exhale. "Exactly that. The gun was close enough to maybe have been used, but maybe not. Seemed a bit far away. Usually in a suicide, the gun just drops right there. Might bounce or something if it falls and hits right. Maybe animals moved it somehow. We don't know if the gun was even fired. The coroner needs to do some work first. So it could be or it could be something else." He shrugged.

"Jesus, people'll flip out if they hear it was a murder." Joe said the last word in a whisper. "The last time that happened was in—"

"Sixty-eight when Freddie got smashed and killed his wife, Jeanine." Eric had been the Assistant Chief of Police at that time.

Freddie—Frederick Jarnkow—was thirty-two at the time and a notorious drunk and ne'er-do-well. Jeanine had put up with it for nearly ten years until he pulled the trigger on a loaded gun aimed at her chest. She was buried in Crown Point Cemetery just outside town off Route 23. Freddie was in prison outside Buffalo. When the murder happened, Dean had been in Vietnam several months into his tour witnessing and participating in sanctioned murder.

"Well, we don't know what it is yet," said Dean. "We'll find out and then deal with it." He looked at his watch: 7:12 p.m. "Shit, I need to tell his family."

Eric nodded. "If this is a murder, I don't want the state troopers here. Got it? It's your case."

"Okay. We really haven't gotten to that point yet."

"And we may not, but no troopers. Clear?"

"Sure. Yeah. The Sheriff'll be calling too."

Eric brushed the last fact aside. "I mean, this is what you did in the city down there, so do it here."

Joe took a drink and looked away. He knew as well as anybody that Dean's last homicide case in New York City had ended his career and his marriage. Like everyone else in Zion, he knew Dean was a cop in this town far from the big city because of his old man.

Dean hated Zion. Hated it. But he was stuck. He finished off the beer. "Yeah, Dad, yeah. I won't call the troopers or the deputies."

Eric nodded once. Joe kept looking away. Dean tossed five quarters on the bar and walked out.

CHAPTER 5

The Nimitz's owned a ranch house on Jackson Street. Red brick lined the bottom third, and white siding decorated the top two-thirds. Faded, red wood shutters hung on either side of every window. A row of evergreen bushes ran along the sidewalk from the driveway to the front door, obscuring a small porch. A large oak tree rose up from the snow that covered the front yard.

Through the front room windows, a TV flickered and cast a bluish glow. Archie Nimitz, Billy's father, peered through the window. As Dean walked up to the front storm door, Archie had already opened the main door. "What can I do for you?"

Dean took off his hat. "Lieutenant Dean Wallace. Can I come in?"

Archie's lip quivered. "This about Billy?"

Dean nodded once. "May I come in?"

"Of course, of course." Billy's father stood to the side, holding open the door, which he closed after Dean passed.

Archie followed Dean into the living room. A commercial for Irish Spring soap played on the TV. Emily sat on the plaid sofa. Jordy, a mutt by the looks of it, looked up eagerly at Dean but remained seated next to Emily. She looked up at him, anticipation visible in her shoulders, which rose as she sat straight up.

Archie said, "This is Lieutenant Dean Wallace."

She nodded. "Hello. What brings you here?"

After years of practice, with a serious but calm tone, Dean told them about finding their son out at the Pratt farm. They had reported him missing on the third of January when Archie had received a call from Charlie McCord, Billy's boss at the body shop. They had feared the worst, but the shock was still palpable. Archie asked for details, but Dean fell back on the too-early to know anything line, which was true but also allowed him to escape having to describe anything specific.

Large tears rolled down Archie's face. Some so big they caught at the rim of his glasses and ran sideways, wetting the bottom edge of the lenses. Emily put her head in her hands and leaned over into Archie's side. He rubbed her back.

"I know this is very difficult, but I have a few questions about when William disappeared."

Archie nodded once. He clicked off the TV with the remote and slipped it between his thigh and the sofa cushion.

"Tell me about that day, the last day you saw your son," said Dean.

Archie's chest rose with a heavy sigh. "I'm not sure what's to tell. He didn't get home before we went to bed, and we didn't see him that morning. We assumed he had gone off to work early. Charlie called around, oh, I think it was nine or something like that. Asked if Billy was coming into work. We told him he had left already. Charlie said he wasn't there yet. We gave it another hour in case he was doing something and was late. But when he didn't get to work by ten we started to worry. So I called the police about then. They said to wait a while. So we did. We waited through the day. Waited through dinner. We had a plate set out for him even. But we didn't eat. We were too sick with worry.

"We called Charlie at seven. Seven that night. Had to call him at home. Billy hadn't shown up to work at all. So we called the police again. That's when they sent one of you fellows down. Can't remember his name. We answered some questions, and we've waited ever since."

Dean knew that his dad had assigned fellow detective Jeremy Guthrie to work the case. "William lived with you, then?"

Emily pulled at her skirt at the knees, picking off imaginary lint. "He didn't make a lot at Charlie's, but he made some. And he worked overtime. He worked hard, really hard. He was saving and taking care of us."

"Had anything been bothering him prior to his disappearing or had he acted strange?"

Archie shook his head. "No. No. He was the same boy he'd always been."

"He wasn't married, right? Did he have a girlfriend."

Emily smiled. "No. But he had been dating that Sarah woman. Sarah, oh what's her last name. Sarah—"

"Esposito," said Archie.

"Yes, Sarah Esposito."

"Dating but not a girlfriend?"

Emily answered with a nodding shrug.

"Did he date anyone else?"

"No, not that I know of."

"Friends?"

"Corey and Josh and Alex," said Archie with a scornful tone on Alex's name.

"Last names?" asked Dean.

"Bender, Frasco, and Smith." He said "Smith" with a bite.

"Alex Smith?"

"Yes."

Alex Smith, son of the Clinton County District Attorney, was a regular at the station holding cell for public intoxication and less frequent bar fights. He had spent a month in county lock up the year prior for seriously beating a man.

"I don't like him," said Archie.

"Why?"

"He's a bum. Always getting into trouble. Always dragging Billy into trouble. But he and Billy have been best friends since grade school."

Dean nodded. "What kind of car did your son drive?"

"Oh, he had one of those fast cars. He worked on it a lot. A seventy-three Dodge Challenger. Canary yellow with a black hood stripe."

Dean had seen it around town. So that was Billy. But he had not seen it at the Pratt farm. He closed his notebook. "Can I see his room?"

Archie nodded and stood up. Emily lowered her head and started heaving. He looked down at her and put his arm on her shoulder. It was a small, effortless gesture that spoke of years of familiarity and fondness. "It's down the hall. Last door on the right." He sat back down, his arm wrapping his wife.

"Can I get you a water or start some coffee?" asked Dean.

Archie shook his head. He left them to their grief.

The hallway led straight off the entryway, and Dean walked it in the dark. He passed picture frames hanging on the wall, but assuredly photos of happier times, in happier days. He passed a bathroom, a closed door that he guessed was to the master bedroom. At the end of the hall, he stopped. The door in front of him was probably for a linen closet. He opened the door on the right. He did not know what he expected. Billy was still living at home so he thought he might enter the world of the teenage Billy, but he was wrong. He flipped the light switch, which turned on a lamp next to the bed. A twin bed with a solid blue bedspread and matching light blue pillows. The wall was an eggshell white. A tall dark wood dresser with five drawers stood in a corner near the closet. On top of it was a bowl with a few bits of change and a matchbook from the

Shambles. A photograph in a light wood frame of grade school Billy holding a baseball bat over his right shoulder. Orange t-shirt with Franco's Pizza spelled across the front. A black wood frame leaning on an easel held a photograph of a dark-haired, olive-skinned woman at a beach. Sarah Esposito Dean guessed.

A small desk with a desk light set against the wall beside the bed. Dean turned on the light and opened the drawer and sifted through the pencils and pens and rusting paperclips. He picked up the photograph leaning on its stand on top of the desk next to the light. Archie and Emily standing together with the Statue of Liberty looming behind them. With Archie's black frames and leaner build and Emily's darker hair, Dean guessed this was at least a decade old. Could have been while Dean was humping in the jungle and Billy was only fourteen or fifteen or so. Billy had just escaped the draft.

Dean opened the drawer on the nightstand, where the lit lamp sat. A small Bible—New Testament only—which he flipped through and found nothing. The dresser drawers exposed only clothes. Billy wore jeans and t-shirts. In the closet, two pairs of slacks hung on wire hangers with cardboard tubes. Two shirts with large pointed collars and decorated with some vague floral pattern hung along with three standard dress shirts in white, light blue, and a darker blue.

On the floor, Dean opened a shoe box to find a pair of brown dress shoes. He opened another and pulled out a manila envelope. He opened it and pulled out fourteen wads of cash folded in half and tied with red rubber bands. At the bottom of the envelope, a copy of *The Communist Manifesto* by Karl Marx and some loose bills.

He picked up *The Communist Manifesto*. The gray cover was stiff. It looked like the same copy they had found on Billy's body. The quote "Workingmen of all countries, unite! You have nothing to lose but your chains. You have a world to win" appeared below the title. Published by Charles H. Kerr Publishing. Samuel Moore translation and edited and annotated by Frederick Engels. He flipped through the sixty pages. No marks. Two copies of this book. Was Billy a radical?

The cash totaled nearly twenty thousand—two years' wages for Billy, Dean guessed. Fourteen bundles of wrapped ten-dollar bills and one unwrapped set. The remains of the rubber band in the bottom of the envelope. Dean contemplated where the money might have come from. Legally, saving. Otherwise, moving heroin or marijuana across the border made the most sense, except that it was across the southern border most drugs moved through. Besides, Zion's drug problem was not significant—it was there. In favor of moving drugs, New York was only a few hours south. But what do money and *The Communist Manifesto* have in common, in Zion of all places.

He put the money and the book into the manila envelope and debated what to do. He could leave it. If Billy was a suicide, then this money was his parents' and no one would care about the book. If, however, this turned into a murder investigation, that was evidence.

He pulled out his flask and took a swig. The warmth of the Wild Turkey rolled down to his stomach. He played it safe and grabbed the manila envelope. He walked out of the room and set the package on the entryway table and then walked into the family room. Archie sat holding Emily's hands, which were gripped together and on the top of her legs.

"One more question before I leave. You said William worked overtime. Was it a lot of overtime?"

Archie nodded. "All the time. He was working hard. They didn't pay him a lot there."

"Did he have any other job outside of McCord's?"

"No. He worked more than enough there."

"What were his politics?"

Archie squinted and thought. Emily looked up. "Why on earth are you asking that?"

"Just a question. I found some evidence where we found your son, so I thought I'd ask."

"What kind of evidence?" asked Archie.

Dean contemplated how to answer and decided to be straight with them. "A copy of *The Communist Manifesto*."

Archie squinted again and then his eyes opened and he looked straight at Dean. "I don't know why he would have that."

Dean nodded, said his thanks and condolences, grabbed the manila envelope, and walked out into the frigid January air.

CHAPTER 6

The police station was in the basement of the town council building, itself a modest two-story renovated home. Brick with thick, white columns at the front entrance. To get to the police station, however, Dean used the side entrance down a ramp of concrete that also served as an efficient channel for water during heavy rains. He swung the door open.

In New York City, the front desk was manned by a uniformed officer who controlled all access into the building, usually several floors. Here, during the day, the chief's civilian secretary, Laura Mannheim, took the calls, told people to wait, managed the chief's calendar and appointments, and handled dispatching. At night, one of the two officers on duty fielded any incoming calls. That night Reginald Hargrove sat at his desk reading a copy of *Sports Illustrated*, an issue from December that Dean had already read with Earl Campbell on the cover.

Reggie looked up and nodded. "Hey."

"Any messages?"

Reggie shrugged and went back to the magazine, licking the tip of his thumb, touching a corner of the page, and lifting it—pausing before turning it over.

Dean walked by the largest office in the basement, his father's, and past the hall that led to an interview room and a small evidence locker, which had a clipboard hanging from a string wrapped around the wire gate enclosing it. Dean's desk was at the far end of the room, where he had requested it, in the shadows. A gray IBM Selectric II sat on the left side of the desk and a desk light just behind it. On the left side, a beige phone beside a container full of pens, the blue and black end caps chewed up.

He tossed the manila envelope on the desk and sat down in the wheeled, cushioned chair, and pulled the plastic white ashtray toward him. He squeezed out a cigarette, tapped it on the top of his hand, put it in his mouth, and lit it with a red disposable lighter, which he stuffed back into his pocket. He inhaled and held before audibly exhaling. He pulled out the flask, took a swig, and refilled it from the bottle in the bottom drawer. He stared at the envelope.

He smoked the cigarette down to its end and stamped it out in the ashtray full of butts and ash. He scratched his chin and opened the envelope, pouring the bundles of wrapped ten-dollar bills onto the desktop. The unwrapped bundle and rubber band fell over the top of those followed by *The Communist Manifesto*. He recounted the bundles, fourteen and slid them and the book back into the envelope. He tossed in the rubber band. He counted the loose ten-dollar bills until he totaled ninety-five three times. He slipped two of them into his front pocket, watching Hargrove still immersed in his magazine as he did it. He slipped a blank evidence form in the typewriter and wrote up the contents of the envelope, noting only ninety-three loose bills. He slipped the envelope and the typed sheet into a larger manila envelope and grabbed the evidence locker key from his top, center desk drawer.

He grabbed the clipboard that hung from a string, looked at his watch, wrote his name and the time on the first blank line available, about two-thirds down the page. After unlocking the metal gate, he found the boxes Zach had brought back from the Pratt farm and tossed the envelope in it. He locked up and walked out, nodding to Hargrove as he left.

◈

Sadie Harper pulled the cigarette out of Dean's mouth, inhaled, and put it back in his mouth. She smiled as she let out the smoke. Underneath the diaphanous black robe, she was naked. He loved her body best this way. After the sex, when they were relaxed, but the sensuality of her body was just visible, fleeting, and surprising. She pulled her long, blond hair back into a pony tail, letting the band snap. "Light me one," she said, her native Georgia accent just leaking into the sentence.

He pulled out a cigarette, put it in his mouth, used his other one to light it, and gave the fresh one to her.

"What's this about the Pratt farm?"

"News travels fast."

She sat on the edge of the bed and smiled. "It's a small town."

"We found William Nimitz out there, near the border."

"Oh dear. Was he the kid at the body shop? McCord's?"

"Yeah. You knew him?"

She drank from the glass of water sitting on the end table. "I know some of the guys that work there. Not Billy though. But he seemed like a nice boy."

"Hmm." He leaned up on this elbow and twisted around. His watch was on the side table. Approaching midnight. "Does everyone call him Billy?"

She ignored his question. "Is Jenny still coming up?"

He nodded. Jenny was his ten-year-old daughter who lived with his ex-wife most of the time. "She is. I pick her up tomorrow."

"Is Cindy bringing her up?"

"Yeah. Going to see her old man while she's at it."

"Most men don't care, you know?"

He squinted at her. "What do you mean?"

"Like you, is what I mean. Taking your daughter for the weekend and days at a time. Most men, they want to forget about their kids. Wham bam, see you later, and all that. Not you."

"You're too cynical." He tossed off the covers and sat up. Shrapnel scars in the thick meaty part of his thigh and calf dotted down the outer side of his right leg. He slipped on his pants and buckled the belt.

"I'm not. And you're the cop. Aren't you guys supposed to be the cynical ones?" She cinched the robe around her tightly. "When will I see you next?"

As he stuffed his shirt into his pants, he said, "With Jenny here and this case, probably a few days. Can you handle that?" He half smiled, a touch of the devious in him.

She smiled broadly, letting all her teeth show, the smile that pleased him most, the one that seemed genuine. She walked over to him and put her arms around his neck. "I'll be lonely. I'll miss you. But I can handle that."

"I see." He wrapped his arms around her waist and pulled her tight, his arousal apparent to her.

"Oh, Dean, you know how to turn a girl on." She let go and stepped back, letting her hand fondle the front of his pants before stepping back and giving him a clear path out of the room.

He adjusted himself. "I think you tell that to all the guys." He laid the two tens from the shoebox and another ten on the dresser as he walked out.

CHAPTER 7

January 8, 1979

The alarm woke Dean at 6:47 a.m. Darkness still clung to Zion, and the way the wind scratched at the windows and the cold made everything seem more fragile than it really was told him it would be yet another bitter cold day. He rolled onto his back, felt a small tinge of guilt about the twenty he pocketed, and chased it away lighting a cigarette.

After he stubbed half of it out, he unrolled the heavy quilt over him and got up. He took a long, extra hot shower before wandering from the master bedroom down the hall past Jenny's room and a spare bedroom. The kitchen was small, but he did not need a big one for what little he did in it. He made a pot of coffee, grabbed the *Zion Beacon* from the front porch, and dusted off the ice crystals. He lit a cigarette and poured himself a mug of coffee, splashing in a finger of Wild Turkey.

The *Beacon* was informed of Nimitz's death too late to get it into this edition, but he expected it would have something the next day. Instead, the front feature story was about the fall of the Pol Pot regime in Cambodia and the victory of the insurgents and their ally the Vietnamese army, which had invaded just this past Christmas. The Khmer Rouge defeated. No surprise. He drifted back to his time in Vietnam, marching through the jungle and avoiding being killed. He poured another coffee. The local news focused on how the money for snow removal was disappearing faster than planned. The colder, snowier than expected winter was wreaking havoc with the city budget.

He threw the *Beacon* into the trash beneath the sink and tossed the dregs of his coffee into the sink. He set the mug in the base of the sink and filled it half with water. After he grabbed his coat and donned the campaign hat, he walked into the garage.

He lifted the garage door, pulling with extra effort to free up the edge that had frozen to the concrete overnight. He started the cruiser, pulled the car back, stepped out of the car, closed the garage door, and jumped back into the front seat. He waited a few minutes and then cranked the heat to high as he made his way into town, which was quiet. The few commuters drove their cars with months of winter plastered along the sides and snow gripping the back bumpers.

The Town Council house, which hosted the mayor's office as well, was two blocks off the main square, which functioned as a large traffic circle. From Dean's home, he entered and passed the first two turnoffs for the third. The square was dominated by the courthouse. The building, constructed between 1887 and 1890, was a two-story, red brick building dotted with cream brick embellishments. Four entrances, one on each side of the square, were covered by arches. A center clock tower, rising an additional two stories above the main building was added in 1902, though the bricks were not exactly the same, those of the tower a less vibrant red. A wrought-iron fence came out to the edge of the square's interior sidewalk. Dean passed the four-pounder Revolutionary War cannon that local history insisted turned a British platoon of grenadiers invading from Canada early in the war—an event celebrated with undue bombast and pride every June.

Outside the courthouse, the square consisted of two-story buildings with a variety of facades featuring a number of businesses, including restaurants, law firms, a dress and suit shop, the cinema playing *Superman*, and Gable's Hardware and Seed.

He parked the car at the station and walked to the Square Meal. The front door was frosted over, obscuring the Open sign he knew was there. The warm air hit him and he saw those sitting at the tables nearest the door shiver. Dean closed the door behind him and walked up to the counter. Mayor Conner Phelps and a few of the ward members, including Joe Banks and Eric Wallace, sat at their normal table toward the back. If you were lucky enough to get elected as a alderman in the town, it did not mean anything unless you were invited to the mayor's breakfast table. Rumor had it that Phelps purposively kept some on the outs just to demonstrate his power, which he had lorded over the city since the early Sixties, taking over after his father.

Debbie Josephs, chewing gum even at that hour of the day, sat a mug of coffee on the counter. Dean looked up and smiled. "Thanks."

She winked and carried the hot pot of coffee back to the machine. Dean lit a cigarette. He looked over at the mayor's table. He shook his head and turned away. A big fish in a very tiny pond was the mayor. He would be squashed by any Brooklyn or Bronx councilman's clerk. He picked up the copy of the *Beacon* sitting on the counter just so he would have something to read.

After finishing three cups of coffee and his normal breakfast of two scrambled eggs, bacon, and wheat toast, he walked back to the station, leaving the mayor and his cabal ruling over the city.

Laura, her shoulder-length brown hair at least a decade out of style, greeted him as he entered. He passed Etheridge Stone, the sergeant and supervisor of the patrol officers, at his desk. Stone, the only black man serving in Zion's government, had none of the bearings of a sergeant. Wiry and with an Afro cut just under the maximum length allowed by the chief, he was six years older than Dean. He had known drill instructors and Marines tougher than anyone else but none as skinny and seemingly benign as Etheridge. The sergeant was putting on his coat to head out to patrol. Dean stopped by his desk.

"Hey," said Etheridge.

"Morning, sergeant." Dean called him sergeant despite Etheridge's protests. "Did you hear about the body we found?"

"I did. I did. Kid named Billy Nimitz, right?"

"That's the one."

"Sad thing."

"It is. So we're not sure yet if it was suicide or homicide. The way the body was, where the gun was at, I don't think it was suicide. But we got to wait on Doc Cotton. Anyways, if you hear anyone talking about it or anything like that, take it down. Bring it back to me. Okay?"

"Sure thing. No one's been murdered in this town since sixty-eight."

"Yeah, Freddie. And keep an eye out for William's car. A seventy-three Dodge Challenger. It's canary yellow and has a black hood stripe."

Etheridge nodded and put his cap on.

Dean retreated to his desk, grabbing a cup of coffee along the way. At his desk, he looked around, and then poured a finger of whiskey from his flask into the cup. He took off his coat and took a drink before walking back and turning right near Laura's desk and into the records room. A wall of gray and tan filing cabinets stood before him. They were ordered by types of crime or reported crime. Moving violations dominated along with other misdemeanors. He found the cabinets for miscellaneous felonies—filed there because of how few a year occurred. The armed robberies, murders, stolen vehicles, and so on entered this corner of the records. Dean assumed that William Nimitz's disappearance would appear here.

He opened the cabinet and searched in the late December time frame, but did not find the file. He closed the drawer and walked back out and to Laura.

"Morning."

She smiled. "What can I do for you?"

"Two things. Can you put out an APB for William Nimitz's seventy-three Dodge Challenger. You'll need to call to get the plate number. Once you have that, make sure the sergeant gets it, too." Dean watched her write the information down and look back up at him. "Also, I'm looking for the Nimitz missing person file. Did Guthrie file it in something other than miscellaneous?"

"No, I don't know where he put it."

He looked down the room at Guthrie's empty desk. "Is he out someplace?"

"Yes. Some burglary out on Somers Avenue."

Dean nodded and walked back to his desk to await Guthrie's return. He took a small stack of paperwork that had been sitting on his desk's inbox. The top memo provided a few updates on legal changes. The next described a shift in policy for using the assigned police vehicle for personal use. The final was a thank-you letter from Gary Bent for assistance when his house was broken into while on vacation. He read through them all, killing time.

Dean's dad walked in around ten in the morning, handing his hat and overcoat in well-practiced form to Laura. He paused at the edge of her desk and looked down at Dean and nodded before disappearing into his office.

At eleven-thirty, Dean walked back to Laura's desk and asked her to get Guthrie on the radio. She turned around in her chair and grabbed the handset, turned up the volume, and said, "Unit 142?"

They waited a half minute or so. Laura looked at Dean and he nodded. "Unit 142?"

"142."

Dean waved for the handset. "142 this is 141."

"Go 141."

"Status?"

"Leaving scene now."

"Destination?"

"Follow up on potential suspect."

"Lunch?"

"What's that 141?"

"Lunch?"

"Copy that. I'll swing back to HQ."

"I'll be here 142. 141 out."

"142 out." Dean handed the handset back to Laura. "Thanks." She took it from him and smiled.

As Dean turned to walk away, he heard from his dad's office, "Goddamnit, this is not a county case. The Pratt farm—and you damn well know it—is in city property." Dean shook his head and walked back to his desk. If the sheriff or state police were calling about jurisdiction, the other could not be far behind.

CHAPTER 8

Dean returned to his desk and stood by it. He was anxious to get started. He lit another cigarette.

A rush of cold air swept in. Instead of Guthrie lumbering through the door, Paige McFadden strode in. Her long red hair flowed out from beneath her orange Syracuse University knit cap with a black pom-pom on top. Laura, always wary of the press, stood up, looked at Paige and then at Dean.

He frowned, shrugged, and sat down behind his desk. "Come on back, Paige."

Paige winked at Laura and walked toward Dean. She was short, had always been so, and was pale with green eyes that reminded Dean of ripe Granny Smith apples. A year older than Dean, she had been a journalist since high school when she wrote for the *Zion High School Gazette*. In sixty-six, she had penned an editorial condemning the build up of U.S. troops in Vietnam. The school administration refused to allow her to publish the piece, resulting in a several-week controversy that finally saw the *Beacon* print it, though the editor had made sure in a preamble that he printed it only to demonstrate the freedom of the press.

Paige stopped in front of the desk, leaned over, and said, "So, I hear Billy Nimitz's body was found in the woods near the Pratt farm. Care to comment?"

"We did."

"Did what? Find his body or commented?"

"Found a body."

"That's it? I can't write a piece using just that."

"What do you want?" He shrugged.

"Any details? Any information you can provide? I'm asking here."

Dean put his elbows on the desk and leaned in close to Paige, looking only a little up at her. "I can't comment on an ongoing investigation. We don't have official word from the coroner yet as to the manner of death."

"So we're looking at suicide or homicide?"

Dean leaned back, the chair squeaking as he did so.

"I know it was a gunshot. So don't bullshit me with accidental."

"Why are you asking me when you already know?"

"Could be an accidental gun shot."

She glared at him, but a friendly one.

"Will you call me when the coroner gives his report? You have my number." She waited for Dean to say something, but when he did not, she continued, "It's an awful long way to go for suicide. I mean, he hiked a good long ways."

"I'll think about it."

"Nice, Dean, nice. You know my number." She thrust herself up from the desk and flew out as quickly as she had stormed in.

Guthrie stepped aside at the door to let her pass. He looked down at Dean.

Dean shook his head. "Let's get lunch."

⚬

They drove separately to Dean's preferred pizza place near the high school, Brunetti's. As they waited for the large pepperoni, mushroom, and black olive pie, Guthrie told him about his current case load of minor thefts, burglaries, and shoplifting. He had heard about the Nimitz boy.

"That's what I wanted to talk to you about," said Dean. "I was looking for the missing person's report."

"Ah, yes. That's in my desk. I haven't filed it yet. I was still going over some of the details." He swept his hand over his balding head, the dark brown hair dotted with gray clinging over his ears. His mustache, however, was a dominating fixture on his face, its edges looping over the top lip and the sides arcing down toward the chin with a bit of a flare. He could stand to lose a few pounds, and Dean knew his fitness reports were marginal. "I was wanting to ask you—"

"Yeah?"

"Can I work this case with you?"

Dean cocked his head to the side. "It's probably a suicide and not much of a case." He did not need Paige, however, planting any seeds in his mind that Billy Nimitz did not shoot himself.

"Yeah, yeah."

The waitress, dressed in a red-and-white checkered skirt with a white button-up top, slid the pizza onto the table and set two plates and sets of utensils down. "You boys okay?"

They nodded.

"But if it's something else. That's what I mean," said Guthrie.

"If it's something else, we'll probably have the state troopers come in."

Guthrie snorted as he slid a slice onto his plate and offered to do the same for Dean. "Your dad ain't going to let that happen."

Dean nodded. Guthrie was right. The old man hated any interference. He would prefer to blow a case all on his own than get help and do it right. He always cited the Marine adage that the Army loses the hill and the Marines take it back. But if this was a homicide, the Zion police had little experience in dealing with that. "Maybe. We'll see. Not much point in talking about it now."

"Just a word man. Just tell me you'll include me. I want something other than—than—than shoplifting. You've done this in the big city, where it counts. I'd love to be a part. I mean, I'm not sure I'll feel like a detective otherwise."

Dean shook some red pepper flakes on his slice, bit into it, and said through chewing, "Okay."

❧

Back at the station, Dean pulled the folder from Guthrie's desk drawer, carried it back to his own desk, and poured himself a fresh cup of coffee before sitting down to read the thin sheaf of papers bound by a single paperclip. The top item was a photo of Billy Nimitz. He held a good size rainbow trout—twelve inches perhaps—at chest level with a broad smile plastered across his face. He still wore waders, a hat with a number of lures at the top. Behind him, the stream where he caught it and the forest.

Guthrie's narrative was no more and no less informative than Archie Nimitz's account. Guthrie had asked the right questions, probed for the right details. He, however, had only done a cursory search of Billy's bedroom.

Guthrie had separate reports for his interviews with the girlfriend, Sarah Esposito, and each of his friends: Corey Bender, Josh Frasco, and Alex Smith.

Sarah was twenty-seven and lived on Madison Street in an apartment. She worked the day shift at Adamson's, that historic, long-lived manufacturer of tables, cabinets, curios, and other furniture. Outside the mayor, Tommy Adamson, the fifth family owner of the business, was the most powerful figure in Zion. Sarah saw Billy the day before his disappearance, New

Year's Day. The notes indicated he gave his girlfriend a gift, but no note on what that gift was. No note on what they talked about or did.

Corey and Josh had been with Billy at the Shambles the night of his disappearance. They had a few drinks, ate fries and mushrooms, and that was it. Alex Smith said he and Billy had not seen each other for a week and could not remember the details of their last meeting.

No leads. No indications of where Billy had gone off to or that he was going anywhere. Dean lit a cigarette. No point in digging in more if this was a suicide. Billy's last moments would be his own. His reasons his alone.

He picked up the phone and called Doc Cotton. The phone picked up on the fourth ring. Tess Gibbons, Cotton's secretary, answered. "Doctor Miles Cotton, Family Practitioner and Coroner's office. How may I assist you?"

"Hey Tess, this is Dean down at the station."

"Hello and good afternoon. I bet you're calling about that poor Nimitz kid, right?"

"I am. I am."

"Well, the doctor hasn't gotten to him yet. But he will later today. Should I have him call you?"

"Yeah, please do. Probably best to call me at home this evening."

"I'll make sure he does."

"Thank you."

"Bye now."

Dean typed up a report regarding his interview with Nimitz's parents and finding the cash and book. He pulled it out of the typewriter, signed it, dated it, and slipped it into the folder, which he then filed in the records room.

At 2:49 p.m., a call came in about a break-in at a home on Elm Street. Dean and Zach, who had reported mid-day for the transition shift as the chief liked to call it, drove to the home and interviewed the victim and her neighbors. The thief had broken a window at the back of the house, unlocked it by reaching in, opened the window and then absconded with an heirloom pocket watch and jewelry of varied value, leaving the back door wide open to the cold. By the time they wrapped up at the scene, with little hope of solving the case, it was early evening.

Dean's ex-wife, Cindy, would be en route to her family home, the Pratt farm, from NYC to drop their daughter off. The last week of winter break. He stopped off at the Shambles to grab a burger and fries. He recognized Alex Smith at the bar. He had a beer and a shot glass in front of him. With his long, straight hair and small circular glasses, he tried to imitate John Lennon of the *Let It Be* cover. When Dean sat a few stools down from Alex, he gave him a cold stare and sucked hard on his cigarette. He crushed it out, waved at the bartender to get his attention, and held up an empty glass of beer.

Dean ate his burger and most of his fries watching the TV sitting up on the shelf above bottles of whiskey, vodka, and gin. The weather report was for cold days ahead, a prolonged winter. He left enough cash on the bar to cover his meal and a tip and walked out. He thought he heard Alex mumble as he did so, "Pig," but he was not sure. If so, he had been called worse.

CHAPTER 9

Dean had first turned onto the Pratt farm's gravel road the night he picked up Cindy Pratt for the school winter dance just after he had turned sixteen. He had been nervous, his palms so sweaty he had worried he would ruin the steering wheel he clutched so hard his knuckles were white. He had loved Cindy since before he could remember, though he was just a boy out there to her. Her original date to the dance, Tom Perkins, had broken his leg a few weeks earlier during basketball practice. Tom and Cindy were an item, but he had called on his good friend, Dean, to step in and take her to the dance so she would not have to miss it. If Tom had known Dean's feelings for her, he would not have made the suggestion. But he did not and he did.

Dean had not swept her off her feet at that dance, as he had dreamed of, but he was no longer just the boy who hung out with Tom and Eliot and Christian. Dean won her in the end. Lost his friend, but won her, and she was the prize. Tom got a football scholarship and disappeared from Zion shortly after. Eliot was a lawyer in New York. Christian died on some hill near the Cambodian border.

He bounced over the final ruts in the driveway as he pulled to a stop next to the S-class, light brown Mercedes-Benz, its wheel wells splattered with dirt and dirty snow. A familiar orange-warm glow emanated from the front windows of the house. He used to be a part of that cozy family, before he had dragged it to shit. He turned off the car and gazed into the glow for a few minutes before getting out and walking up the front porch.

As he got ready to knock, the door opened. Jenny stood there beaming. "Daddy." She hugged him, her thin arms wrapping around his waist, just above his revolver and radio. Her long blond hair was braided into pigtails that fell down onto her collarbones and the front of her shirt. She looked up at him with her green eyes and smiled again.

"Hey there, pumpkin." He hugged her back.

Cindy sat on the couch across from a well-stoked fire next to her mother, Eileen. Both shared a remarkable resemblance: the same chin and nose and eyes. Cindy, if she had been so inclined, was model material. Jenny's eyes and hair were her mother's. Cindy waved and returned to talking to her mother.

"Daddy, are we going to do anything fun?"

He had given this some thought. "How about some sledding?"

She beamed and hugged him again. "Let me get my stuff." She unclenched him and ran up the stairs.

"No running," said Cindy, who was now standing and walking toward him. "Hello." She stopped in front of him and slid her hands into her jean pockets. She wore a light cream colored blouse with red trim and buttons.

"Hi." He half smiled at her. "You look good."

She ignored his last statement. "School starts Monday, so I'll be back on Saturday to pick her up. Okay?"

He nodded. "How was the drive up?"

"Long."

"Well, be careful going back."

"Don't strain yourself over the concern." She said it without anger lacing the words. Matter of fact. Nearly monotone.

He closed his eyes and breathed in deep and reminded himself the toxicity in their relationship was his fault, or at least he blamed himself. That did not make putting up with any of it any easier though. "Geez, I was just trying to be nice."

"Save it for when it counts." She gave him a stern look, like a scolding from a parent.

He held up his hands in defeat.

Jenny came back down the stairs, slowing when she saw her mom. She sat her bag down on the floor and hugged Cindy.

Dean picked the bag up and watched the two of them. They had a familiarity he had forever lost with his daughter. He would be spared much of the difficulty of raising a teenage girl, but he would have preferred to have had that so he too could be embraced every day. He pinched his mouth to hold back the sadness.

"Behave, okay?" Cindy rubbed her daughter's head.

"I will Mommy."

Cindy pulled them apart and guided Jenny toward Dean and the front door. "I'm serious."

Jenny walked out to the porch.

Dean looked at Cindy. "See you Sunday."

Cindy nodded and turned back toward the fire.

❦

On the drive back, Jenny peppered him with questions about where the good sledding hills were and told him stories of slumber parties and school with her friends. He knew, by the time they pulled into his driveway, that Jessie and Connie were her best friends and that Christmas break had been fun but was getting boring.

While unlocking the front door of the house, he asked, "Did you have supper yet?"

She shook her head and ran inside. He turned on the light. "How about pizza?" Despite having eaten at Brunetti's for lunch and having had dinner, pizza sounded tasty.

"No mushrooms."

"Pepperoni?"

"Yes."

"All right, then. Let's get you settled in, and I'll have one delivered."

He opened the door to her bedroom, where two years earlier, he had set up the twin bed with a blue bedspread, white headboard, and a white, pine dresser. Jenny walked in. "What's that?"

"That," Dean said as he tapped the small desk he had bought a few weeks ago and placed in here, "I got for you so you can do your drawing and stuff."

"Oooh."

He sat down her bag. "Okay, I'm going to order the pizza now." As he walked out of her room, he said, "With so many mushrooms they'll think they're in a mushroom farm."

"Stop it."

He caught the door jamb with his left hand, leaned back, and smiled at her. After calling Brunetti's and ordering a large pepperoni pizza, he turned on the TV in the family room. *Little House on the Prairie* was on. The phone rang, so he turned down the sound of the TV and answered the phone. "Hello?"

"Dean is that you?"

"Yeah."

"Dr. Miles Cotton."

"Ah, yes, doc. Thanks for calling."

"Yeah. Look, I did the autopsy today. And no way it was a suicide. I'm ruling it a homicide."

"I thought it would come down that way. What makes you say so, though?" Dean covered the phone's mouthpiece and coughed quickly.

"—no powder residue."

"But the weather could have done that."

"Yeah, but here's the other thing. I didn't notice it at the scene. Neither did you. But it was cold and his coat was thick. I thought I reached in. But we had gloves on."

"I understand. We missed something."

"Yes. Yes. There was a pistol in his inside coat pocket. Small thirty-eight. Snub nose. Six bullets in the cylinder. Serial number is filed away."

"Yeah? So either he brought two guns or—"

"Right. Except, that's not likely. If this was suicide, he would have used the revolver in his pocket. Powerful enough. Simple gun to work."

Dean contemplated the idea. The coroner's logic was sound, though not all encompassing. Billy could have walked in with two guns. "Any idea how long he's been out there?"

Miles paused. "Could be two days. Could be two weeks. It's been cold since before Christmas. But with the way the birds had gotten to him and allowing for some thawing of the parts of the body exposed to the sun, I'd estimate, he's been out there at least a few days. Around New Year's or so. I can't be anymore precise."

"So since he disappeared."

"That's what I'd go with."

"All right. What else can you tell me?"

Miles yawned and mumbled, "Sorry," part way through. "He'd busted his knee and ankle. I'm guessing he stepped in a hole or tripped over something. But it wasn't long before he was killed. Inflammation but no healing. He would've been in pain."

"He couldn't have run from his killer?"

"Unlikely. Though I guess a jolt of adrenaline could have helped. But where he was when we found him was where he was when he was shot."

"Tripped. Hurting. Takes a seat against a tree. Bam. Killer drops the gun there."

"That's the short of it."

"Anything else doc?"

"Nope. That's it. My report'll be on your desk tomorrow."

"Thanks."

"Yeah. Have a good night." Miles hung up.

Dean sat the phone down.

"Something wrong daddy?" Jenny opened the refrigerator and grabbed a Big Red.

"Oh, nothing. Just work, pumpkin."

When the pizza arrived, he placed a couple of slices on a plate for Jenny and only a single slice for himself. After the TV show ended, he tucked her in, letting her read with the lamp next to her desk.

He sat on the couch. He clicked to the movie *A Small Town in Texas*. He ignored it mostly, though he paid attention when Poke barrels over the corrupt sheriff and sparks a chase scene featuring more pursuit vehicles than any small town had a right to.

When he turned in, he laid awake longer than normal. He had seen plenty of death and murder through the years. The cruelty of man was no philosophical puzzle to him. He had seen it. He had done it. But that was war and New York City. This murder in Zion, his hometown, the town he had fled to after everything crumbled, this place of solace—as much as he hated to admit that—felt different. A violation of that peace, that security he expected here.

He slept fitfully through the night.

CHAPTER 10

January 9, 1979

G randma." Jenny clasped her arms around Jessica Wallace. Dean's mom smiled and clasped back and then lifted her granddaughter off the porch a couple of inches and swung her back and forth. "Jenny, it's so wonderful to see you again." She winked at Dean standing on the sidewalk beside the porch, his hands in his pockets.

His mom seemed younger than her age by a decade, betrayed only by her quickly graying hair. Her dark brown eyes could be mistaken for black in the right light. Thin, tall, yet strong, Jessica was a Zion native. She worked part time at Willows Realty but spent most of her days reading, gardening, and "tending the home"—her phrase. When she had had three boys in the home, life had been different for her. Days of packing lunches, making dinners, seeing them off, volumes of laundry. To Dean's eyes, she did not miss those days, but she had never really gotten over the death of Nolan, the youngest of the Wallace boys. He had died in an ambush outside a village Dean could not remember the name of anymore. A mortar shell exploded in a tree above him. The wound was invisible, so fine was the splinter that killed him. Dean had thrown his Purple Heart into Monroe Lake when he found out. His mom had sprouted a sadness that never seemed to leave her. Her every smile tinged with mortality.

"We've got some fun things to do today, my sweet," said Jessica. "Now let's get in from this cold."

Dean leaned over and kissed his mom on the cheek. "Thanks. I'll see you this evening."

"No thanks needed."

As his mom and daughter walked into the house, Dean retreated to the warmth of the car. At the station, Laura told him to go into the chief's office. He was on the phone and wanted Dean in there. She grimaced, cluing him in on the chief's mood.

Dean rapped twice on his dad's door before cracking it open. Eric waved him in when he saw Dean and then gestured for him to close the door.

"Yes, I know," said his dad.

The chief's office was paneled with wood from floor to ceiling. The wood beginning to curl outward at the base. Carpet was long ago abandoned in the station because any heavy rain storm could send a torrent of water down the outside steps, so the floor was a light tan linoleum with darker dots and splotches to provide variety.

Eric paced back and forth behind his industrial desk, gray metal with a black highly varnished wood top. Photographs in small frames leaned on their easels. His three sons on a fishing trip in 1958. A snapshot of Eric and Jessica on Coney Island. A family vignette near Niagara Falls—the Canadian side. On the wall behind him, an official portrait of Eric with the mayor. Dean's official Marine photograph with his Purple Heart citation. Nolan's official Marine photograph. Only that one image from 1958, though, of Tony, the middle of the three.

Their father had always been an overwhelming presence in their lives. Chief of Police for many years of their youth, they lived not unlike many a preacher's child. Obedience, doing the right thing, all of that was presumed. It hardened Eric too—always being the chief. Never off.

"Look," Eric waved for Dean to sit in the chair across from the desk, "this is my city's jurisdiction. I've got a former NYPD detective here. We'll handle it ourselves. I've already told the sheriff it was on city land." The chief, whose fist pressed down on the top of his desk, shook his head at the voice on the other end and then bit his upper lip. "Look here, colonel, this is my jurisdiction. I don't want and don't need your help. Capiche? Mmm. Yes, a good day to you too, sir." Eric shrugged the phone's handset from his ear, tossed it lightly with his shoulder, and caught the shoulder rest attached to it, setting the handset in the cradle in one smooth motion. "How the hell did the state police find out about Billy?"

Dean grunted. "The news? The bullet Doc Cotton sent to the lab in Albany?"

"They say it's a homicide."

"It is."

"Why did I find out this morning?"

"Because I found out late last night and had Jenny."

"You should've called." Eric paced behind his desk, looking down at the floor.

"Okay." Dean rubbed the leather padding on the right arm of the chair he was sitting in.

"And now the state police want to come in and take it over."

Dean nodded. "I don't think that's a bad idea. They've got—"

"I don't care if it's the best damned idea since sliced bread. It's not their case. It's not their jurisdiction. It's mine. And it's your case."

Dean held up his hands. "Fine. But they've got more—"

"Zip it. I've already pissed off the colonel, so I ain't going back groveling for his help now."

Dean crossed his arms.

"So tell me. What's next?"

"We talk to the people we know Billy talked to before he disappeared. When Jeremy talked to them back a few days ago, he approached it like a missing person's case, which is what it was. So we go back now. We talk to them like what it is: murder. That usually shakes up the scenery. We've also got what we think are steps going north. Killer could have crossed into Canada. So I want to call the provincial police up there. I know someone there. It probably won't lead anywhere, but you never know."

"Good. Do it."

Dean stood up. "One thing, one of Billy's friends I'm talking to is Alex Smith."

"Henry's boy?"

"Yep."

"Just talking though."

"Right now, yes."

"You think he's involved?"

"At this stage, anyone could be involved. But, no, I have no reason right now to think he is. But you know what he's like. He'll raise a stink to his dad, probably. Just wanted you to know."

"I never liked that prick."

Dean nodded and left, not sure if his dad was referring to Henry or Alex.

CHAPTER 11

Beside his desk, Dean found Jeremy waiting for him. Dean nodded, grabbed his coat off the back of the chair, and pointed to the exit. Halfway toward the door, he patted his coat and realized his flask was still in his desk. He jogged back, slid open the bottom drawer and, with his back turned to the rest of the station, stuffed the half-full flask into his inside coat pocket.

When he turned around, Etheridge was wrapping his coat around the back of his chair, a small styrofoam cup of coffee on the desk. Jeremy was standing beside Laura's desk. As Dean walked back, Jeremy opened the door and stepped outside.

Once in Dean's car, Jeremy broke the silence. "So a homicide, eh?"

"Yeah. Here's the file." Dean handed it to him. He started the car. "We're still waiting on the Doc's report. Should have it today." A stream of cold air rushed out of the vents. Dean turned down the heater. "It'll warm up fast."

Jeremy opened the folder. "Where we going first?"

"Let's start at McCord's."

Dean pulled out of his parking space, crunching over the snow and gravel. He turned onto the square and kept on High Street for four blocks before turning onto Fox Street. Two blocks down, McCord's Body Shop sat back from the street. A half-dozen cars sat in front of the body shop. The mayor had long tried to adjust the ordinances to prevent the unsightly view, but Charlie McCord found a rare ally in Joe Banks, whose own business was a similar eyesore.

Dean parked the car in the lot. He left it running and looked over at Jeremy. "So you'll need to look at the photos and evidence we collected at the site. You will probably want to go out there to see it for yourself today or tomorrow."

"Makes sense. What do we have that you can tell me?"

"Right. Billy Nimitz walked into that clearing. We're not sure from where. We haven't found his car yet, and we're not sure when he got there. Obviously, some time after he was last seen by his friends on the second. Somewhere along the way in the woods, he jacks his knee and ankle. Doc Cotton says there's no way he was going to run. Painful to walk. So he leans against a tree. His knee's probably throbbing.

"Someone else comes into the clearing. Sees Billy. Puts a bullet in his head. Probably dropped the gun, but we need to wait on ballistics. Billy has a thirty-eight in his pocket. Was buried deep in it. Both the Doc and I missed it with all the coats and gloves. There's a copy of *The Communist Manifesto* in his front coat pocket. When I check Billy's closet at his parent's house, I find a crap load of cash and a copy of *The Communist Manifesto.*"

"He was a pinko?"

"Probably best to leave it as, 'We found a copy of the book.'"

"How much cash?"

"Nearly twenty thousand."

"Jesus." Jeremey rubbed his chin.

"So was he meeting someone out there?"

"Or did he come across someone?" Dean turned off the ignition. "No way of knowing right now. That said, I don't know why you'd go out there—no trails, nothing—unless you're meeting someone, right?"

"So he could've jacked his knee if he were running away."

Dean nodded. "Yeah, he could've. So let's go with the probabilities: he was meeting someone. But is that the killer or just the reason he's out in the woods?"

"Meaning, maybe the killer was not there to kill Billy but whoever he was meeting?"

Dean gave a thumbs up and opened the car door to a rush of cold air.

They got out of the car and walked up to the front of McCord's. Dean rubbing his gloved hands together while Jeremy stuffed his deep in his coat pockets and brought his shoulders in tight.

The garage doors were closed, but through the grimy windows, Dean could make out two cars and shapes of people. The brick facade had been painted white years ago and not touched since. They walked into the front entrance—the bell hanging on the inside dinging—and the smell of auto grease and oil hit Dean immediately. The concrete floor was covered in a film of black grime accumulated over the years. A small counter with a cash register sat on the right. On the left stood a set of shelves with Pennzoil, Havolene, Castrol, and Marathon oil cans. A door behind the counter led to the garage.

Jeremy pulled his hands out of his pockets and stood beside the counter. Dean stood close to the entrance door.

Charlie McCord—former tight end for the Zion Panthers—ducked as he walked through the door. He wore a gray coverall with the dark blue McCord Body Shop logo embroidered on the left chest. Stray black hairs from his balding head fell down toward the back. Thick sideburns were peppered with more gray than black. He held a thick, short cigar at the side of his mouth, the leaf wet with his chewing on it. "Ah, this 'bout Billy?" He wiped his hands on a grimy, red rag.

Jeremy looked at Dean and when he realized Dean was not going to say anything said, "It is Charlie. Did you hear?"

"I heard he was found out at the Pratt farm. That's it. Sad to hear. What happened?" He set the cigar on the edge of the counter.

"He was killed," said Dean.

Charlie's eyebrows lifted and he took in a short breath. "God, that's awful." He pulled a stool, silver with a red vinyl seat, over and plopped heavily onto it.

"It is. It is. And we're doing some follow up now that we know it's not a missing person's case."

"Sure. Sure. How can I help?"

"Tell me about Billy."

"Of course. Anything I can do. Billy was a good kid. He started working for me, um, let's see, it's probably been five years. Didn't know a thing when he started. But we were training him. Getting him up to speed. He started as a helper, basically. Cleaning up. Grabbing parts and tools. Checking people in and out. Calling them. That kind of stuff. Over time, we got him changing oil, which we do for a few of the ladies in town, you know. He started to learn how to fix dents and rust. He painted his first car not too long before." Charlie hung his head and shook it. "Damn. I liked that boy." He looked back up at Dean, still shaking his head.

Dean said, "How was he? I mean what was he like?"

"Nice. Nice kid. If I had a daughter, I'd let her date him."

"Anything odd the day he disappeared? Or the weeks prior."

Charlie looked down at the counter, frowned, and shook his head. "No. Everything seemed normal. I didn't talk to him much beyond work, mind you."

Dean grimaced and cocked his head to the side. "So when I talked to William's parents last night, they said he'd never shown up to work." He noticed the quick and focused glances between him and Guthrie.

Charlie picked up the cigar. "I think they, um, well, have it wrong. He did show up. Late. But he showed. He showed." He rolled the cigar from one side of his mouth to the other. "Yeah, I mean he was late."

"Okay. What time did he show up?"

"Hold on." Charlie held up a finger, stood up, and walked to the door that led to the garage. He opened it, leaned out and reached for something, his head and arm disappearing behind the wall.

Dean raised his hand casually into his coat pocket, hand on his pistol, unsnapping the button strap in a singular, practiced motion.

Charlie leaned back in, looking at a timecard in his hand. Dean dropped his hand.

The former football player looked over the card, tapped it with his middle finger. "He came in around nine. Clocked out at five-thirty."

"Why was he late?"

"I don't know. I'm flexible, you see. My boys put in their hours, they get the work done." He looked up. "I'm sorry if his folks got the wrong impression about him not being here. They were pretty upset though."

"Sure. I think they were."

Jeremy, who had been taking notes, asked, "What about his friends? You know them?"

"Nah. I didn't."

"Billy had a girlfriend, right?"

"Yeah, he talked about her. I can't remember her name. Susan. Sarah. Something like that."

"Sarah Esposito?"

Charlie snapped his fingers and pointed at Jeremy. "That's it."

"You know her?" asked Dean.

"Nah. I seen her around town I guess. But I didn't know her."

"Tell me about the day he went missing."

"Just a normal day. Except for that, of course. I got to the shop my normal time."

"Which is?"

"Six. Always been an early riser."

"Sure."

"So I get here and start to open up shop. The guys start coming in normal time. Eight. I want them here at eight. Well, Billy's as prompt as the rest of them, so when eight-thirty rolls around, I'm thinking he must be sick or something. So I called his home. He lived with his parents, you know?"

Dean and Jeremy nodded.

"Anyways, they tell me they hadn't seen him since the day before." Charlie stuffed the rag into his back pocket. "That's the last I know. Well, like I said, he did show up. Left on time. That's it. Then Jeremy here shows up with his questions."

"Were you guys working on anything before the holiday?" asked Dean. "Or did anything odd happen over the past few weeks?"

"Nothing odd. No. Not that—no. Hold on." Charlie reached down behind the counter and pulled out a battered metal box. He lifted the latch and started thumbing through a list of index cards. "I keep everything sorted here. Insurance, you know?"

"Yeah, sure."

Charlie kept flipping. "Ah, here." He pulled out an index card and gave it to Jeremy. "So this would have been that Friday before the weekend. The twenty-ninth. And the second, when we all got back. Mrs. Hendrickson's car." He reached over and tapped her name on the card Jeremy was holding. "She'd slid into a tree. Real light. She wasn't going fast or anything. But she banged up her passenger door. We were fixing that." He kept flipping. "And Mr. Davis. Chris. Yeah, he wanted to repaint his Corvette."

Everyone knew Chris Davis and his Corvette, a silver 1974 Stingray Coupe. Davis and his brother, Jack, ran the biggest law firm in Zion—anything from wills to injury lawsuits.

"Nothing odd about those, though," said Charlie. "I know you guys are wanting to find something odd, something that'll give you an answer or a direction or whatever, but I ain't got it here. Everything was normal. Absolutely normal."

"How much overtime did William work?" asked Dean.

Charlie tilted his head and squinted. "None. None at all."

"None?"

Charlie shook his head.

Jeremy looked at Dean, who nodded toward the door. Jeremy said, "Thanks, Charlie."

"Sure. Sure thing."

Just as Jeremy was getting ready to step outside, Dean looked back at Charlie and asked, "Did Billy have any money issues you know of?"

Charlie slid the stool back to its corner. "No, not that I know of."

"What about his political views? You guys ever discuss that?"

Charlie looked at Dean, one eye squinting in confusion.

"You know. Republican? Democrat?" Dean shrugged. "Socialist?"

"I don't know. We never talked about it."

"Thanks." Dean walked out into the cold air, followed by Guthrie. They got into the car and started it. It was still warm enough to start cranking out warm air.

"So what do you think?" asked Guthrie.

Dean leaned back in the seat, the vinyl creaking. "We'll see. Seemed pretty straightforward other than that he didn't show up, he showed up late discrepancy. But I can see upset parents making that mistake."

His partner, Dean did not know what else to call Guthrie now, shook his head and tapped the pen he still held in his right hand on the dash.

Dean smiled, sat upright, and put the car into gear. "Let's talk to the Canadians."

⟡

Dean sat at his desk, and Guthrie sat at his. Both were on there telephone, on the same line. Dean gave Guthrie a thumbs up and called Renard Desplains at the Sûreté du Québec. Renard, a longtime detective, also worked as the U.S.-liaison officer out of Montreal, a couple of hours north of Zion.

"Bonjour ceci est lieutenant Renard Desplains de la Sûreté du Québec," said the rough voice of the French-Canadian Renard.

"Renard, this is Dean Wallace of Zion. In the States."

A short pause. "Ah, oui, oui." Renard and Dean knew each other casually, having participated in several cross-border conferences, meetings, and an investigation since his return to Zion.

"Look, I'm calling about a murder down here in Zion. I have my partner, Jeremy Guthrie on the line as well."

"A murder?" The distinctive ticking of a lighter.

"Yep. One of Zion's folks got themselves murdered. Thing is, it was really close to the border. Less than a mile. We think there were footprints leading to the border, but with the snow, wind, and some melting, it was at best a guess."

"How long ago?"

"The person disappeared the day after New Year's Day. The second. He was almost certainly killed that night. A William 'Billy' Nimitz. Aged twenty-five. I'll send you a picture. He worked at an auto shop down here in Zion."

"I see. How can I help?"

"Well, thing is, I found a lot of cash in his home, tucked away in the closet. Way more than what one earns at a body shop working normal hours."

Renard took in a long drag. "You think drugs?"

"That's a possibility, yeah."

"Oui, that would make sense."

"So I'm calling, to see if you know or can keep an eye out for anything close to the border down here near Zion."

Renard muttered something quickly in French, covered the mouthpiece, and then came back. "Désolé. I will. I will ask around, but it is a long shot, you know, eh?"

"Yeah, yeah. What about drug trafficking?"

"We have seen the normal. Heroin mostly between here and there."

"Anybody or groups specifically?"

"The normal. You are aware of these, eh?"

"Yeah, I think we're on the same page there."

"Excellent."

"Hmmm." Dean put a cigarette in his mouth. "The only thing I can't figure is the copy of *The Communist Manifesto* with the cash."

"Pardon?" Renard covered the mouthpiece but less effectively this time. Someone was wanting to speak to him. "Désolé. What's this?"

"I found a copy of *The Communist Manifesto* with all the cash. And a copy of that book in his front coat pocket when we found the body."

"Oui, oui. Look, I must go. But have you spoken to the FBI? Ciao."

The line went dead.

The FBI? What was Renard talking about?

CHAPTER 12

Dean had Guthrie drive them to the Tracks Diner for lunch. The restaurant was beside the old freight-line railroad tracks. Guthrie asked him what the FBI line was about.

"I haven't a clue, other than we're talking a border here, so maybe he thinks the FBI knows something. Or he heard 'communist' and assumes the FBI knows something. That's a scratcher."

They stepped out of the car. Guthrie asked across the roof, "And what about the drugs question? You hadn't mentioned that before."

Dean stuffed the keys into his pocket and shrugged. "Seems only natural, right? How many of the B and Es around here are ultimately drug related?" Breaking and entering. People smashing open a window or door and grabbing the valuables. Sometimes they turned violent if a person were at home, but most often just a violation of property.

Guthrie shrugged. "I don't know. A quarter? A third?"

They walked across the poorly cleared parking lot to the restaurant, a small building on the edge of town. The restaurant was more a mobile home than a proper building. The poutine was the reason—at least in Dean's opinion—that the Tracks had survived the arrival of McDonald's.

"I'd bet you it's half." Dean held the door open for Guthrie. "I mean, most crime when it comes down to it," he continued as he followed to their table, "is about money or love. And drugs are a big part of the money factor. I want a hit, I don't have money, so I hold up a gas station for it. I sell drugs. You do, too. I want more money. I kill you I sell drugs to your clients. I make more money. Stupid, simple shit."

The waitress put two plastic cups of water on the table. Dean asked for coffee and ordered the poutine. Guthrie chose the meatloaf sandwich and a Coke.

They talked game plan over their coffee and Coke while waiting for the food. The diner was crowded, the noise of people talking, glasses and plates clanking and jingling, and the door opening and closing with a swoosh of wind were enough to make discussion challenging. They agreed they would talk to Billy's friend Corey next. Guthrie asked why not interview Sarah, the girlfriend, first. Dean wanted to get to at least one of the friends, see what his opinion of the girlfriend was.

The waitress set their plates in front of them and asked if they needed anything else. Guthrie tapped his Coke glass, which was two-thirds empty, and Dean shook his head. She turned and headed back to the counter.

Dean stuck a fork into his poutine as Guthrie eyed him before dousing his meatloaf sandwich in ketchup. He set the ketchup bottle down. "I don't know how you eat that stuff."

Dean smiled. "Like everyone else who eats it."

Guthrie frowned and shook his head.

"I love it. As good as you can get in Quebec." Dean watched Guthrie's lips thin and almost say something before winking at him. Dean stuck a forkful of curds and fries into his mouth. After he finished chewing, he said, "I keep trying to figure out why Billy was out there, at the Pratt farm."

"Who knows." Ketchup squirted out the backside of Guthrie's sandwich. He looked down at his pants to ensure none fell there. "I mean, we've got to figure that out. But if you ask me, the stack of money. That's the key."

"How so?" Dean thought it was key as well, but he wanted to hear what his partner came up with.

"Frankly, seems like he got involved with some people he shouldn't have. That's where drugs make sense."

Dean leaned back and wiped his mouth with a white paper napkin. The door to the restaurant opened and in walked Tony, his younger brother.

He looked around the restaurant, caught sight of Dean, smiled, and waved. He walked over and the two brothers embraced. The middle of the Wallace brothers still maintained his thin frame by running five miles daily—rain or shine. He wore a wool, gray peacoat and light blue jeans. A large gray scarf encased his neck and piled on his chest. He pulled off his Montreal Expos knit hat, revealing his full head of light brown hair.

"Join us?" asked Dean. "This is Jeremy Guthrie, my partner."

Tony shook his head. "Nice to meet you." They shook hands. Dean's brother looked back at him. "Was in town for some supplies, but I need to get back. You should come by. We'll share a beer." Tony patted Dean on the back and walked up to the counter, where Steven handed over a styrofoam container. Tony left cash on the counter and walked out.

Guthrie turned from the closing door back to Dean. "Can I ask you something?"

"Is it about my brother?"

"Yeah." Guthrie grinned. "It is."

"I won't stop you."

"What's the deal with him? Your dad doesn't have a photo of him in his office at all. Got yours and Nolan's everywhere."

Dean picked up the last gravy-covered fry with his fork and jammed it into the last cheese curd. "There is one photo with Tony." He paused before continuing, "Short or long answer?"

"I always prefer the long."

"Hmmph." He popped in the last bite and ordered two coffees, which he spiked with some whiskey from his flask. "You'll have to ask him."

The truth was, Tony had used college and other deferments—actions not unique or special during those years—to avoid the draft and active duty in Vietnam while Dean, the rambunctious thorn in the family's side, and Nolan, the youngest and favorite of Jessica, volunteered. Dean joined the Marines in an effort to impress his father and without much sense of purpose. Nolan joined out of a sense of duty. Dean still had the letter the youngest brother had sent him from Zion a few days before he officially joined. He read it on some blasted, forgotten, terrible hill. Read it between shouts of "Tubing" and huddling in captured NVA bunkers.

> Dean, I know you think I'm crazy for doing it. I know you're counting the days until you can leave. I know this. But I can't sit around here and do what Tony did or many of my friends are doing. I can't ignore that my brother is over there fighting a war his country has asked him to fight while I sit here, drinking cold sodas, enjoying walking out in the world, while you walk in terror. I can't not join. Duty calls.

And Nolan did.

"Seriously, man," said Guthrie.

Dean chuckled. "The old man has his reasons. Let's say Tony didn't land on the right side of the war."

Guthrie dug with his tongue into his teeth. "Fine. Does he live around here?"

"He lives out down Route 22 toward Plattsburgh. He works for the FBI. One of their lawyers." Dean slapped his forehead. "We had our FBI guy there. We could've asked him about what Renard said. I'll call him up later."

Guthrie folded up his napkin and put it on his plate. "He can probably help, yeah. So why did you move back?"

Dean squinted at him. The question was such a radical pivot from their conversation it held him up a bit. He did not like that Guthrie had asked it. "You know why I moved back."

"Only what they say on the streets. Is it true?"

"Is what true?" Dean ground his teeth.

"Did the guy get off? The one that killed those hookers?"

He stood up and put a dollar on the table. He leaned in close, putting his hand on the back of Guthrie's chair. "Then what you heard is probably true. Yeah, the shithead got away with it because I was too drunk to do anything right."

Guthrie looked at Dean's arm on the chair and changed the subject. "So besides talking to people, do we need to do anything else with Billy?"

"Yeah, we need to see who owned those pistols. The forty-five and the thirty-eight. Look up all the people we're talking to and see if they have a gun license."

"Hold on." Guthrie pulled out a notepad. "Let me write this down. Check gun licenses."

Dean tapped the table with is fingers. "While you're writing it down, note we need to talk to Corey, Alex, Josh, Sarah, and probably Paul Zorn."

Guthrie sighed. "You think he's the source of the drug money?"

"Who better to talk to than Zorn?"

Guthrie wrote it down and closed the notebook. "Let's get going."

They picked up their checks from the table and walked to the register.

"Detective Wallace."

Dean looked behind him to find her standing nearby, arms crossed. "Paige."

Guthrie turned back and looked at Paige as he handed his check to the waitress along with three dollars.

She smiled at the both of them and focused back on Dean. "So you got anything for me?"

He shrugged. "I'm a public servant. I can only afford my lunch."

"You know what I mean."

"I do."

The waitress handed Guthrie his change. Dean handed her his check and three dollars.

"Come on. You've got to say something."

Dean smiled at the waitress. "Thank you." He looked back at Paige. "Actually, I don't."

The two detectives walked back into the cold January air. Cold despite the shining sun.

CHAPTER 13

Corey Bender worked at the Farmer's General Store store at the east edge of town on Harrow Road. The building's facade was corrugated sheet metal in alternating dark blue and forest green. The place had started out in the nineteenth century as a seed and general store. Since the 1950s, it had expanded—and built the current building—to sell fertilizer, work clothes, toys, lawn furniture, and many other items no longer used by the farmer for his crops or herd.

A clerk filling candy bar boxes at checkout line three pointed the two detectives to the inventory room at the back of the store when asked about Corey. They followed the main open aisle toward sporting goods before turning left and finding the two large swinging doors that led to the inventory room from the lawn mower section. Jeremy eyed a Lawn-Boy push mower. "I need a new one."

"For mowing snow?"

Jeremy laughed. "No. But they're always better deals in the winter than in the spring, when you need them."

They walked through the double doors into a small warehouse. The back loading dock door was open, letting in the bitter January air. The driver of the truck was standing just inside the building, his hands shoved into his pockets.

A man, a full head of silver hair, a large silver mustache, and large gold-rimmed glasses walked up. He wore the bright green polo shirt with Farmer's General Store embroidered on the upper left chest. Below it the phrase, "More than seeds!" His name tag read "Joe," and he smiled and lowered the clipboard to his side. "How can I help you?"

"Detectives Dean Wallace and Jeremy Guthrie. We'd like to talk to Corey Bender."

Joe grunted. "He's that away." He pointed and fluttered his hand up and down toward the back of the inventory room. "He's loading the new shipment on the shelves." He walked away from the detectives and toward the truck's open door, waving at the driver.

They walked back in the direction Joe had indicated and found Corey jamming a pallet lift beneath a stack of boxes wrapped in plastic. Corey pumped the lift to raise the pallet up and then pulled back and pushed forward to maneuver the awkward stack from its narrow space. When he noticed the detectives, he stopped his effort and put his hand on the lift's handle.

Corey, the same age as Billy, was lanky but short. His dark brown hair fell over his ears and was parted slightly off center. It had a slight wave. He wore a thick, red turtleneck beneath a Farmer's General Store blue and green vest. His blue jeans covered the tops of his steel-toed work boots. He had stuffed a green knit cap into his front pants pocket. He reached into his vest and pulled out a pack of Salems and lit one.

"You okay to smoke when you're not on break?" asked Jeremy.

Corey waved his hand dismissively in the direction of Joe. "What can I help you fellows with?"

Jeremy said, "You remember me?" He pulled out his badge and held it up for the kid to see.

"Yeah, detective or something, right?"

"Yeah. Guthrie. And this is Detective Wallace." He stuffed the badge back into his inside coat pocket.

Corey inhaled and let out a large bellow of smoke.

"You heard?" asked Dean.

"Yeah, I heard." He let his cheeks bloom and slowly exhaled, a small stuttering sound.

Dean knew he had lit the cigarette in an effort to control his emotions. He could see Corey's eyes getting moist. "So you were with Billy the night his disappeared, right?"

"Yeah. The Shambles."

Dean waited for Corey to add more color, but when he did not, he asked, "Just drinking and stuff?"

"Usual night. We had a few beers. Called it. Left."

"Who?"

"Me, Billy, and Josh."

"What time did you guys leave?"

"We left around eleven-thirty. All three of us. Josh walked home. Billy and I got in our cars and drove away."

"That's the last time you saw Billy?" asked Guthrie.

"It is. I went home. Went to bed. Got up and came here."

"Anyone vouch for that?" asked Dean.

Corey's hand paused before he pulled the cigarette out of his mouth. "No." His eyes focused and looked and held Dean's gaze. "No."

"Anything going on with Billy's life we should know about?"

Corey ran his hand through his bangs. "The usual, I guess."

"What does that mean?"

"What do you think it means? People have shit going on in their lives."

With Corey's tone turning hostile, Dean wondered if he had gone too quickly to the alibi question. So he smiled, hoping to re-inject some friendliness into the interview. "Pretend we're stupid. What was going on with Billy?"

"The dude was unhappy. He was living at home, hated his job, and had a whacked girlfriend. But he was stuck in this town."

"He didn't want to live at home?"

"Hell no. Who wants to live at home? But his mom insisted on it. Said she needed help. So he did it. And he didn't like his job. No matter how much Charlie says he did. That guy pays as cheap as he can and screws them out of overtime. He needs to be arrested for something. It's criminal what he pays his employees."

"And the girlfriend?"

"Ah, man. She was just using him. Using him for his money but mocking him for living at home. Dude couldn't win. He'd buy her something, and she'd want something nicer. Like for Christmas, he bought her a diamond necklace. I don't know how much he paid, but those were some stones. But the month before, he'd bought her a bracelet with a bunch of stones. Sarah was like happy for a day and then started demanding more."

"Did you hear her demand more?"

"Nah. We didn't hang out with her. Billy knew we weren't keen on her, and, well, she would've been the only girl with us drinking. Not what we wanted."

"How do you know she was demanding stuff all the time if you didn't hang out with her?"

Corey scratched the back of his neck and then took a long drag. "You could just tell. And he'd like talk about her, so we knew he was buying her stuff. And Alex knew. He'd tell me and Josh all the time about how bad Sarah was."

"If McCord's pays cheap, how'd Billy afford these diamond necklaces and bracelets?"

"I wondered that myself. I don't know."

"He sell drugs or something?" asked Guthrie.

Corey snorted. "No. If you knew Billy, you'd know that's ridiculous. The guy was like a saint. No he didn't sell drugs. Maybe he saved well or something."

"What do you mean by 'like a saint'?"

Corey dropped the cigarette and crushed it with his shoe. "I don't know. I mean, the guy was an upstanding guy. He'd go over the speed limit a little. He'd help old ladies cross the street. Boy Scout stuff. He just wouldn't be part of something illegal like that." He bent down and picked up the crushed filter.

Dean had personally witnessed a paid killer for the mob help an elderly woman across the street in Manhattan. Boy Scout stuff there too. "Where was Alex the night Billy and you guys went to the Shambles?" asked Dean.

Corey shook his head and rolled his eyes. "Man, Billy and Alex got into it after Thanksgiving. Something about Sarah. I don't know the details. I felt like we were being made to choose sides."

"Between Billy and Alex?" asked Dean.

"Yeah. Alex can be a jerk, so I'm fine hanging out with Billy. But they were arguing—Alex and Billy—about Sarah. I didn't want to get mixed up in it. No way."

Dean turned at the sound of approaching footsteps. Joe was walking toward them.

Corey looked back and forth between the two detectives. "My boss is getting antsy. Can I get back to work?"

The truck pulled away from the loading dock, roaring in low gear as the driver gave it gas.

"Sure," said Dean. "If you think of anything else, anything at all, call us."

Joe stopped about ten feet behind them. "About done? I need to get these boxes put away." He sniffed the air and looked at the detectives. "You're not supposed to be smoking in here," he said to them.

Guthrie frowned a sorry and then he and Dean parted like the Red Sea and let Corey walk between them, dragging the palette lift toward a row of shelves with more pallets of boxes wrapped in plastic.

"What do you think?" asked Guthrie, scratching the back of his neck.

Dean made a sucking sounds between his lips. He looked at his watch, it was close to three. "Let's get back to the station and write up our reports. Tomorrow morning we talk to Sarah Esposito."

⟡

Dean picked Jenny up from his parents. A day of puzzles and crochet, which Jessica was intent on teaching her. Before they went home, they stopped at an ice rink the city set up just a block from downtown. Dean pulled out his hockey skates for the first time that season, got his skating legs beneath him, and joined the dozen people on the ice. Jenny liked to twirl, and they raced a few times. She seemed happy and oblivious to the murder and drugs her father had been investigating just a few hours earlier.

At home, he made them TV dinners. He despised the things, except for the overcooked mashed potato edges, but he could not argue their efficiency. A bit of television, and she was off to bed to read until she fell asleep.

He poured himself a tumbler of whiskey and sat down to watch the evening local news when the phone rang. He jumped up and got it just as the second ring was ending. "Hello?"

"Dean?"

"Yes." A heartbeat before he recognized the voice. "Tony?"

"Hey brother. Am I bothering you? I know it's late."

"No. No. Jenny just went to bed, and I was going to catch up on the news." His brother had not called him in months. They hardly spoke at all, though it was not because of any animosity. Just living their lives.

"Good. Good. Look, uh, I—" Tony paused on the line.

Dean let him gather his words.

Tony continued, "I just didn't want you to think I was rude this afternoon. At lunch."

"Huh?"

"When we saw each other and I was in and out. Didn't sit with you."

"Oh. That." Dean had forgotten about the encounter. "Think nothing of it. I wasn't offended."

"Good."

A pause. Neither knew how to proceed. They could talk about what had been going on in their lives, but they knew each would gloss over the details and offer generic statements. But to not ask seemed un-brotherly. So, instead, a pause. A pause Dean broke. "Hey, actually, I'm glad you called. I had a question for you." He gave his brother a quick summary of Billy's murder without using names and told him of his call with Renard, and particularly the Canadian detective's query about talking to the FBI.

Tony said, "Well, he's probably being thorough. The FBI would be involved if the crime crossed into Canada, though, frankly, we usually leave that to local law enforcement to coordinate with the Canadians. Maybe *The Communist Manifesto* prompted it. We do conduct counterintelligence. I can't think of any other reason why he'd say that. You're victim doesn't seem the spy type."

Dean scratched his chin. "He doesn't. Just a young kid working in an auto shop."

"There you have it."

They exchanged a few more pleasantries and hung up.

CHAPTER 14

January 10, 1979

Dean and Guthrie met at the station. After confirming with the Adamson's receptionist that Sarah had taken a personal day, the two of them drove back through town to the Ashbury Court Apartments. Three buildings with a red brick first story and Tudor Revival second story stood in a horseshoe pattern around a central parking lot. Four main entrances equidistantly spaced led to an open stairwell.

They climbed to the second floor in the building anchoring the horseshoe. Clumps of snow had drifted into the entryways and found corners of shadow to hide. Guthrie knocked on the door. After what seemed like a long enough wait, Dean pounded three times on the door. They heard shuffling inside. The slip of the chain. The click of the deadbolt.

In the half-open doorway, Sarah stood dressed in a long white robe. Her shoulder-length, black hair was parted in the center but strands stuck out at odd angles. Her nose was red and she held a tissue in her hand, crumpled and moist.

"What?" she asked. Then she recognized Guthrie. "Oh. You're the detective."

Guthrie nodded once.

Sarah stepped back from the door, pulling it open to let the two of them in. The entryway led directly into the living room.

A TV stood on a small stand. A coffee table sat between the TV and a tan couch with large dark brown throw pillows. A box of tissue and a mug with dark stains on the inside sat on the table. A checkered blanket of browns and tans was piled up on the couch. Beyond the living room, a small kitchen and a hallway leading to two closed doors. Bedroom and bathroom, Dean supposed. The room smelled of incense. Two sticks pointing at the ceiling in a small bowl sat on the coffee table. The pungent smell of marijuana lingered in the background.

Sarah flopped down on the couch and pulled the blanket over her. "Here about Billy, right?"

Dean stood across the coffee table from her. "That's right. Can we make you some coffee?"

She waved her hand in an I-don't-care fashion.

Dean nodded to Guthrie who walked to the kitchen. Dean looked at the TV stand, its antenna, and the wall behind it. A large picture of the moon and waves made with thread hung askew. A small framed photo stood on the only space on the TV stand—the TV had been shifted to the far right to offer the space. A palm tree and three teens stood near a beach. Dean picked it up.

"That's me and my two brothers." Sarah blew her nose. She sounded as if she had been doing that most of the morning.

Guthrie opened and closed the cabinet doors until he found the tin of coffee.

"Where's it taken at?" asked Dean.

"San Juan." She looked at him. "Puerto Rico. That's where my brothers are now."

"How long have you known Billy?"

"Since high school. Since we moved here."

"You been dating him the entire time?"

"No. Off and on. Mostly off."

"Recently."

"On. We'd been dating for a year now. Our longest stretch ever."

"What caused the break ups?"

She sighed and tucked her legs beneath her. "Many things. Nothing sometimes."

Dean pulled out his notepad and jotted a few notes. He tapped the pen on the metal spiral binder. "Did you see Billy the day he disappeared?"

"No. I was working. He went out with Corey and Josh after. We talked. He called me from the bar. I saw him the day before. New Year's Day."

Guthrie walked back in. "What'd you talk about?"

"I don't remember. Usual stuff probably."

"The last conversation you had with your boyfriend and you don't remember?" Guthrie sat himself in the chair beside the couch.

She glared at Guthrie. "I didn't know it was going to be my last conversation with him."

The clicks and knocks of the water heating in the coffee maker came from the kitchen. Dean studied her. She was distraught. Over the years, he had come to understand that every person reacts differently to death and that reaction was not indicative of anything, but something about Sarah's response troubled him. She seemed too distraught. He fought against his initial reaction, but he could not bury it.

"What happened to Billy?" asked Sarah.

"That's what we're trying to figure out." Dean walked toward the sliding door that led to the back porch. "Can you tell us about him? What was he like?"

"He was a great guy. He may not have been the sharpest knife in the drawer, but he was a good guy and he had a lot of common sense. He loved baseball. He was pretty good himself."

"What position did he play?"

"Second base mostly."

"Hmmm."

Sarah curled up her legs beneath her butt.

Guthrie asked, "Anyone you know want to hurt Billy?"

"No. No way. He was a nice guy. Nicest I ever met. I can't think why anyone would hurt him."

Dean walked back around and stood in front of her, interlocking his fingers and dropping his hands. "We heard Billy and Alex hadn't been getting along."

"Well, Alex is—. Alex is an asshole. Plain and simple. Spoiled rich kid thinks everything he does is gold. It'll catch up with him some day."

"So they weren't getting along?"

"Billy didn't talk about it, and I didn't ask. But yeah, I get the sense he was upset about something. So it could've been with Alex."

The sounds of the coffee pot sputtering the last of its hot water into the grounds called Guthrie back to the kitchen. He opened cabinet doors looking for a mug.

"Upset how?" Dean pulled his hand to behind his back. He walked over to the sliding patio door. The wood security rod was leaning upright against the frame. A small white bookshelf stood next to the door. A large plant with broad white and green leaves sat in the middle shelf. On the bottom shelf, *Salem's Lot*, *A Stranger in the Mirror*, *Chesapeake*, and *Eye of the Needle*. The covers looked worn. On the top shelf, a photo of Sarah, Billy, Alex, Corey, and Josh. Where were the photos of her and her girlfriends? He stared at the photo.

Sarah said, "I just knew. He seemed edgy somehow. Anxious."

"How long was this before he disappeared?"

"Not sure. Maybe around Thanksgiving or so. He was worried about his parents or something. But I don't know."

"Worried about them how?" asked Dean.

"It's all in my head probably. I mean, they didn't like me."

"Why not?"

Guthrie set a blue and white mug of coffee on the table, using John Travolta's face on *People Weekly* magazine as a coaster.

"Thanks." She looked at the steam rising from the mug and left it on the table.

Drexel said, "Don't thank him yet. It's probably policeman's coffee."

She let a smile flash across her face and then bit her lower lip.

"Why didn't they like you?"

"Look at me. I'm a Puerto Rican girl in a town without a lot of us."

"What does that have to do with anything?"

"They wanted Billy dating some nice Anglo-Saxon girl. Not me."

"They said something to you?"

"No. No, not directly. It was how they acted around me. Always on pins and needles. And his mom, I would catch her sometimes glaring at me. I stopped visiting him at his home. I don't need that."

"How'd Billy feel about this?" Guthrie picked lint off his pants.

"Said I was overreacting." She shrugged. "But what does he know?"

"How was yours and Billy's relationship recently?"

"Good. Really good. We were on a good path."

"Like getting married?"

"Yeah, I think that was in the future."

"And your parents?"

"My dad was more—." She bit her lower lip.

Dean kneeled down. "What about your dad?"

She let out a short breath. "Look, my dad is the Puerto Rican. My mom worked for the Navy for a while down at a base down there. At Roosevelt Roads Naval Station. Her parents got sick, so we moved up here. He thinks I should be dating a Puerto Rican. I know. Bullshit, right? And he definitely thinks I should be marrying someone whose parents at least are okay with my heritage. So he wasn't particularly happy to have me dating and thinking about marrying Billy. But where am I going to find another Puerto Rican around here? And who the hell is he to talk?" She held out her hand to emphasize the point.

Guthrie gave her a sympathetic shrug.

Dean said, "I don't see any photos around here of you with any girlfriends."

"So?"

He frowned and looked around. "Just unusual is all."

She shifted her feet beneath her. "I wasn't too popular in school. So I don't have any, really." She sighed. "I got into fights a lot. That's how Billy and I met. He jumped in one day to break up a fight between me and Tracy. Bitch." She shook her head. "And Billy and his friends became like my posse. They'd protect me."

"What about Corey and Josh?"

"What about them?"

"What was your relationship like with them?"

"Those four are thick as thieves, and I was allowed into their space. They'd protect me. But I was always Billy's girl."

"Corey says you were after Billy's money." Dean lifted the photo of Sarah and her posse. They were out at the Lance Field, where the Panthers played football, the large, unlit scoreboard serving as the backdrop. The balance was off. Off beyond the testosterone-heavy image. The boys were in front, kneeling or crouching down. Sarah was directly behind Billy. Her right hand was on his shoulder. Her left hand was on Alex's back, just at the neck.

"Billy and money? He didn't have any money."

"Did Billy buy you stuff?"

"Occasionally, yeah."

"A necklace and a bracelet, recently?"

Sarah shook her head. "Corey proves again he doesn't know anything. Anything at all. Yes, Billy gave me those. But." She looked to the side and shook her head. She grabbed a kleenex and touched the corners of her eyes. "I'm not sure how to say this."

"Usually it's easiest just to say it," said Dean.

"My mom got sick last year. Money was tight. So I pawned a bracelet and necklace last summer. They belonged to my grandmother—on my dad's side. I didn't tell dad about it. He'd kill me. Just gave him the money and told him it was from my savings. But it tore me up. Those had been in the family for three or four generations. Billy bought them back."

"With what money?"

"I don't know. I didn't ask. I was so happy to have them back."

"You didn't ask?" asked Guthrie. "Come on. You ain't stupid. You had to wonder."

"I did wonder, but I didn't ask. And he never told me." She swung her feet to the floor.

"Where did you think the money came from?"

"I don't know." She bit her lower lip and looked at Dean, who raised his eyebrows. "Fine. I thought he was stealing from Charlie."

"Stealing from the register?"

"Yeah, something like that."

Dean nodded.

Guthrie twisted his lips. "Okay. Thanks. So how much did you pawn them for? And where?"

"The bracelet I pawned for two hundred. The necklace for five. A place in Plattsburgh."

Dean asked for the name and address. He handed her his pen. She grabbed a copy of *People* magazine and wrote it down, tore off the corner where she wrote, and gave him the paper and pen. "Thanks. Where were you the night he disappeared?"

"You think—" She cut herself off. "I was here. I did my usual and slept."

"Didn't see Billy?"

"No."

"What time did he call?"

"I don't know. It was late. Probably midnight maybe."

Dean stood up. "Thanks. We'll check that against the phone records. How long did you two talk?"

She shrugged. "A few minutes. Not much."

"Anyone who would want to hurt him?"

"God no. No. He was a nice guy."

Dean pulled out the slip of envelope with "I love you" written on it, all still encased in plastic. "Yours?"

She leaned over and looked at it. She raised her hand to her mouth and tears welled up. She nodded.

Dean walked toward the front door. Guthrie stood up. "Thank you for your time and sorry for your loss."

She nodded.

Dean opened the door. "What were Billy's politics?"

She looked at him confusedly. "He said he voted Ford in the last election. Pretty conservative really. But we didn't talk about it much."

"Any reason why he'd have a copy of *The Communist Manifesto* in his possessions?"

"What?" She looked down at the floor, back up at them, and back down. "No, not really. He wasn't usually interested in that kind of stuff. Politics and whatnot. But—"

Dean squinted at her. "But what?"

"When he called that night, after I told him I had to go to bed, he said something odd. I just thought he was drunk." She paused and looked up at Dean, tears welling up along the outside edges of her eyes. "I only caught the first part. The rest of it sounded slurred. I thought he was drunk." A tear from each eye hurtled down her cheeks. "'Workers of the world.' That's what he said."

CHAPTER 15

Over burgers and fries at Burger Palace at the edge of town heading west, Dean and Guthrie reviewed their interview with Sarah.

"What do you think?" asked Dean before dragging two crinkle-cut fries through a dollop of ketchup in a small plastic cup.

Guthrie shrugged. "Now Billy's buying back pawned jewelry. Seven hundred worth. I don't know where he's getting his money." He scratched his cheek with the backside of his thumb. "But she seemed to care for him. Young love and all."

Dean let half a smile cross his face before dropping it. "Something's bothering me. She protested about Alex too much. Too quick to call him an asshole. The photo on the bookshelf—well—it was off. I don't know. But you're right. Where's this money coming from?"

"The way I see it, we've got more motives now." Guthrie raised his index finger. "He's doing something illegal to get the money. Taking it from Charlie maybe. He's crossed somebody. Bam." He raised his middle finger alongside his index finger. "There's also something going on in that circle of friends. Seems you're implying an affair. Perhaps Alex and Billy had it out and Billy came up short." He lifted a third finger. "You keep bringing up his politics. Maybe someone didn't like them."

Dean nodded. They finished their lunches, paid the waitress, and went back to the station. He had just taken off his coat, sat down, and slid a standard interview form into his typewriter when the phone rang. He picked it up to hear, "Bonjour, this is Lieutenant Renard Desplains of Sûreté du Québec."

"Renard, yes, this is Dean."

"Oui. So I'm calling about this case you, uh, called about yesterday. Something about a murder case, oui?"

"Yes. A young man, Billy Nimitz was murdered, and we think the killer might have come or went to or both from Canada. The scene was a half mile from the border."

"Oui. Usually your FBI handles these so I recommended them and that was that. I was not expecting to, ah, hear anything but it seems we do have something. Eh?"

"What've you got?"

"We got a call a yesterday ago. A man was shot and killed in a flat in Montreal. He had, ah, a collection of passports and cash. Seems he was going back and forth across the border."

"Okay, and where's the connection."

"Ah, oui, the connection is he had several passports for this William Nimitz. Among many others, but him. I thought I recognized the name."

"What do you mean several?"

"Un moment." Renard set the phone down and grabbed a folder, which he opened, flipped a few pages, and found what he wanted. He picked up the phone and held it against his ear with his shoulder. "We found four total. One Canadian, one French, one Spanish, and one Swiss."

"Why did he have them?"

"I do not have that information yet."

"Can I see these?"

"Oui. You can come up and look at the case file, if you would like."

"Very much."

Dean hung up the phone and walked to Guthrie's desk. He told him Josh would have to wait until tomorrow. Instead, he told Guthrie to drive to Plattsburgh and verify Sarah's story about the necklace and bracelet. "Take a picture of both of them and show it to the clerks. Leave copies if you have to. I want to know that the real Sarah and William were there."

⚬❦⚬

With the traffic, it took almost two hours to get to the Sûreté du Québec's station in Montreal. Despite the relatively short distance between Zion and Montreal, Dean had rarely ventured there. The big metropolis felt like a foreign country with so much in French.

The headquarters was a fourteen-story T-shaped building, just across the St. Lawrence Seaway on rue Parthenais. Dean parked in the visitor's parking lot and walked through the glass door main entrance and into the wide, sunlit lobby. At the main desk, he asked a uniformed officer where to find Renard Desplains. She looked up his name and directed Dean to the third floor.

The elevator dinged open, and he and a couple of other officers stepped onto the third floor, its light brown carpet and beige walls drove home the institutional feel. A string of like desks—silver legs and dark brown tops—stood in two rows down a lengthy part of the building. Dean paused and looked around, confused. A man spun in his chair next to him. "Puis-je vous aider?" But he said it so fast, Dean was not able to even begin to understand what he said. The man asked again: "Puis-je vous aider?"

Dean nodded and said, "Renard Desplains?"

The man squinted at him. "Pourquoi?"

Dean reached into his sport coat inside pocket and pulled out his Zion Police badge. The man looked it over and pointed in the direction Dean had been walking. He rattled off a couple of sentences that Dean could not comprehend. When the man had finished, Dean had the good sense to say, "Merci," and walk in what he believed to be the direction the officer had given him.

The place hummed with activity. People talking, phones ringing, walking to and from. It all reminded him of his days in the NYPD and that itch for that buzz crept into him. He had loved being an NYPD officer and then detective.

He reached the end of the desks and at a set of offices divided by a narrow hall. He walked down it, looking at the name plates, and passed a turn. When none of the rest had Renard's name, he went back to the turn and walked down it. On the fifth one down, he found Lieutenant Renard Desplains. The door was slightly ajar, so he knocked.

"Entrez."

Dean pushed on the door until it was fully open. The space was small and had no exterior windows and thus bathed in the bluish fluorescent light. A small desk that matched the ones in the open area, two chairs with a leather seat in front of that, and a short bookshelf with binders. A small green cactus sat on top of the shelf alongside a photograph of Renard and a young woman. On the wall, a certificate of some sort in French, an official portrait of Renard in dress uniform, and a photograph of Renard, the same young woman, and an woman nearer Renard's age, which seemed to be in the mid-fifties.

Renard stood up, setting his black-framed reading glasses on the papers in front of him on the desk. He had a full head of grey hair with wisps of the former dark brown color, a matching thick mustache that ended at the corners of the mouth, and a deeply lined face, the results of years of tireless work and gravity and time. He wore a pair of light red and yellow plaid slacks, a blue jacket, a light blue shirt with a long, thin collar, and a thick red tie loosened at the neck. "Bonjour, Detective."

Dean shook his hand. "Bonjour."

Renard gestured to Dean to sit and closed the door behind them. He then walked back to the desk, leaned down, and picked up a box, which he put on the desk close to Dean. "The case file and evidence. We processed everything, so ah, you can look at it."

Dean opened the box and found a manila folder, thick with papers.

"May I offer you café?"

"Yes, please."

Renard stepped out and closed the door behind him. Dean pulled out the folder and flipped it open. He looked at the blocks of French. No English translations. The evidence bag contained a variety of IDs, including passports, New York State driver's licenses, and Quebec driver's licenses. As Renard indicated, several of the passports were made out for William Nimitz. Several included his photograph and real name. Others had his photograph but listed him as William Conroy or William Sutton. The details of Billy's birth were accurate as well. All indicated different places of birth that conformed with the country of the passport. All also had the exact same issue date: 1 December 1978. Just a few weeks before his death. Passports and IDs for Julie Clarendon and Stephen Valosz were also in the box. He did not recognize the people in those photos.

Renard opened the door, set a cup of coffee in a paper cup in front of Dean, closed the door, and sat behind his desk, holding a steaming cup himself.

"This Julie and Stephen," said Dean.

"Oui?"

"Are they real people like my victim?"

Renard shrugged. "The Mounties are not telling us anything. We had to fight to keep that evidence, though they could swipe it up."

"Why are the Mounties interested? I thought this was a murder case."

"Oui, it is. They have not told us why they are interested. But with passports and IDs, we think—I think—they are doing counterintelligence work."

"Spies?"

"Perhaps. Or the Quebecois. But, ah, the FLQ is long gone." Noticing the puzzled look on Dean's face, Renard continued, "The Front de libération du Québec. The October Crisis?" Still not seeing recognition pass across Dean's face, he clarified more. "The kidnapping of James Cross and the murder of Pierre Laporte. These happened in 1970."

"Sorry, Renard. I don't remember. I was still in New York at the time trying to be a good cop."

"Trying?"

"Um, working at doing a good job."

"Ah. Oui. New York City?"

"Yes. I was an officer and detective there."

"And now in Zion?"

"Yes." Dean saw that Renard wanted more of an explanation, but he ignored it. "My apologies, I don't read French."

Renard said, "Bien sûr." He gestured for the report.

Dean handed it to him.

Renard flipped it open and pulled out the photographs, which he handed to Dean.

The first showed a man, dressed in light blue pajamas sitting in a chair, his head slumped forward, but his body held in place by duct tape wrapped around his chest, wrists, and ankles. Blood down the front of his pajamas and pooled at the base of the chair. Another photo of blood splatter on the wall behind the chair.

Renard licked his thumb and flipped a page. "The victim is Marcel Lorrain. Aged fifty. Former FLQ member. Ah, see?

Eh? Neighbor reported the gun shot. Found Monsieur Lorrain twenty minutes later. The passports and IDs were found in his closet. Witnesses recall a light tan or white or yellow sedan or sports car leaving the scene around the time the gun shot was reported. Eh?" He shrugged. "The Mounties showed up the day after. Since then, it is their case."

"You said cash was in the closet as well."

"Oui." Renard flipped more pages. Licked his thumb. Flipped more. "Here. Passports. IDs. Cash in American dollars and Canadian dollars. American was fifty thousand. Canadian was thirty thousand. And copies of *The Communist Manifesto*."

"What?"

"American dollars was fifty thousand."

Dean waved his hand. "No not that. *The Communist Manifesto*?"

"Oui. Found eighteen copies of it. There was other literature also. Pamphlets, ah, brochures. Some in French. Most in English."

Dean shook his head.

"Is something wrong?" asked Renard, setting the folder down on his desk, open.

"My vic had a load of cash and a copy of that book in his closet."

"Perhaps, he was a spy, oui?"

CHAPTER 16

Dean's plan had been to pick up Jenny and head home, making her a dinner of spaghetti and garlic bread and maybe a salad. He had a limited repertoire of cooking, but he could accomplish that.

Instead, he stopped at the Shambles, which was empty except for an elderly couple drinking coffee in a booth and Joe Banks at his barstool. The evening crowd, such as it was on a weekday, was not due for another hour or so.

Joe nodded and told the bartender something before Dean put his elbows on the bar and crossed his hands in front of his chest.

"How's it going Dean?" asked Joe.

Dean nodded. "It's all right."

The bartender, Gordon Vito, slapped a coaster down in front of Dean and then a bottle of Pabst. Dean looked up and Gordy pointed at Joe.

To Joe, Dean said, "Thanks."

"Any time."

"How's the case going?"

"Actually, that's why I'm here. Gordon, were you working the night of January second?"

Gordon had been tending bar at the Shambles since after Korea where he had flown a Chickasaw helicopter, flying front-line medical missions, helping to pioneer the use of helicopters that would save so many lives in Vietnam. He kept his hair cut in the high-and-tight style, graying along the sides. "Yeah, I was here."

"Did you remember Billy and his friends? Guthrie's report says you do."

Joe looked at Gordon.

Gordon nodded. "If that's what it says, then that's what I said. Billy, Corey, and Josh. They were drinking."

Dean lifted his beer and held it as he asked, "Anything seem odd?" He took a drink.

Joe put his hand on Dean's shoulder and leaned over. "What's with the questions of Gordy?"

Dean pushed Joe's hand off. "Just part of the job. Gordon, anything odd?"

Gordon looked at Joe, shrugged, and looked at Dean. "Nope. Normal so far as I could tell. They talked and drank. The only odd thing was Alex showed up after they'd gone."

"He did, did he?"

Gordon nodded once.

"What time did he show up?"

Gordon twisted his lips and looked up at the ceiling.

Joe shook his finger. "It was after I left. 'Cause I didn't see Alex after. I didn't. And I left right after the game. The Knicks lost."

Gordon gave a thumbs up to Joe. "He's right. Alex showed up after Joe left and right after Billy, Corey, and Josh left, but not long. Before midnight that's for sure."

Dean took a drink and gazed up at the mirror above the bottles behind Gordon.

After a significant pause, Joe put his hand on Dean's shoulder and quickly withdrew it. "That answer your questions?"

Dean shook his head to clear his mind. "Yeah, I think so."

He looked at Gordon and cocked his head to the side. "One last thing. I know Sarah and William were an item, but you see anything between Sarah and Alex?"

Gordon shrugged. He picked up a wet cocktail glass and wrapped a white towel around it, rubbing it dry. "I don't know. Maybe? She was friendly with all of them. More so Billy, but yeah, I'd see Alex's arm around her when Billy wasn't around that I wouldn't like if I were him." He slid the glass into the slot hanging above the bar and grabbed another.

Joe asked, "So what does that mean?"

Dean took another drink. He smiled at Joe. "Not sure yet. Thanks for the beer." He placed a dollar on the bar and walked out. As he drove to his parent's to pick up Jenny, he replayed the discussion with Gordon in his head, trying to understand why Joe was so odd during it. He had not come to a satisfactory answer when he pulled into his parents' driveway. When he opened the front door and walked a couple of steps in, the smells of cooking charged forth: Cherry pie, potatoes, and hot oil.

Jenny ran up and hugged him and told him grandma was making dinner for all of them and a pie for dessert.

Dean hugged his daughter back. "Did you have fun today, pumpkin?"

She smiled and nodded vigorously. They had played board games and worked on a puzzle together—half completed on a living room card table.

"What is that?" he asked.

"Castle New-shwa something."

"Castle Neuschwanstein. The Walt Disney castle is based on it," said Jessica, her voice coming from the kitchen. "Your father's in the family room. Jenny, dear, why don't you help me mash these potatoes?"

Jenny said, "Coming," and darted out of the room.

Dean walked into the family room, where his father sat in his dark brown recliner. On the end table between the recliner and matching sofa sat a pipe cradle—cigars were reserved for work—with three pipes, all bent stems, along with a pack of pipe cleaners in a Ziploc bag, and a pipe lighter. The kitchen's smells were defeated by the cherry tobacco. A cream and light red striped wallpaper put up many years before covered the walls. Dean had assisted in the process. The lamps were his mother's touch. Light red, almost pink glass bases with cream light shades. *Time, Newsweek,* and *Sports Illustrated* fanned out on the pine coffee table. The Zenith console TV was encased in a dark, reddish wood. Family photos sat in a mixture of gold and wood frames. One photo was of a younger Eric and Jessica in San Diego just after his father's return home from Korea, where he had been stationed after Japan surrendered.

"How'd it go?" asked Eric, looking up at Dean. He held a copy of *The Shining,* corners of the pages bent showing his progress through the book.

"It was a day. We've got some context for what happened up to about eleven-thirty the night of his disappearance." Dean updated his dad on what Renard had told him, including the passports, cash, and copies of communist paraphernalia.

Eric re-fired his pipe tobacco and took a couple of heavy puffs. "Hmm. What's next?"

"We still need to talk to Josh and Alex. And I think we need to make a visit to Zorn."

Eric set the book down beside the pipe stand. Zorn and the chief had long known each other, indeed, had been rivals since high school. Zorn joined the Navy and saw action supporting MacArthur's drive through the south Pacific to the Philippines. After the war, he founded the Grim Devils motorcycle club, which he had run since. To most people, Zorn ran a trucking company most notable for hauling Adamson's furniture south to New York and served as president of a club of war veterans.

The Wallaces, however, knew better. The Grim Devils were an integral part of illegal drug distribution in Zion. For years, Eric had attempted to get enough evidence to prove it but had failed. "What the hell does he have to do with this?"

"William's cash. I can't think of a legitimate reason to have that much. Nothing we've found yet at least. The obvious answer is its drugs, and we know where Zorn is with that. Just want to cover all the bases."

The chief grunted. "What about that commie—"

Jenny jogged into the family room. "Dinner's ready." She smiled.

"What'd I tell you about running in the house?" said Eric as he wrapped his hands around the recliner's armrests, lifting himself up.

"Sorry grandpa."

"Don't be sorry. Do what I asked."

Jenny nodded and looked at her father, he shrugged, though Eric could not see that.

The chief paused by Dean as he was standing. "You got to talk to the reporter."

"Paige?"

"Yeah, but I don't care what her name is. If the paper sends over a reporter, you talk to her. I can't have you getting the department on their bad side."

"I think—"

Eric stared hard at Dean, running his tongue across the inside of his cheek and across his bottom lip. "This isn't a debate."

After a plateful of fried chicken, mashed potatoes, and creamed corn casserole, Jenny excused herself from the table to work on the puzzle. Dean complimented the chef on the meal. She smiled and said, "You're welcome."

Dean tapped the top of the table next to his plate and then pushed the fork around before setting it down. "I saw Tony today."

Eric's eyes opened wide and he screwed his mouth sideways. Jessica smiled. "How'd he look?"

"Good. He looked good. Didn't have time to talk, though."

"Probably too busy dodging," said his dad.

"Eric." Jessica was the one person who could scold the chief. Not even the mayor dared to. "He's trying to make up for it." She too had been disappointed by her son's skills in avoiding the draft, but her sense of duty to country was less rigid than Eric's. She accepted Tony's job working for the FBI as his belated attempt to serve his country.

"Let's not talk about him. Not while there's pie to eat."

"Pie sounds good," said Dean.

After, the two men sat at the table, coffee cups in front of them, crumbs of pie on the plate. Eric said, "Keep working this case hard. Like you been doing. The drug angle could be right. Just don't press Zorn too hard. He's tough."

"I will. I did follow up with Gordon."

"Gordie at the Shambles?"

"Yes. He said Alex came in after the others left. About midnight."

"Hmmph. Be careful with that one."

Dean pulled out his flask, twisted it open, and started to pour a shot into the coffee.

Eric put his hand over Dean's coffee cup. "Don't do that son. You're driving that angel home." He pointed to the room from which the combined laughter of Jessica and Jenny emerged.

Dean looked at his dad, tried not to glare, but put the cap back on. "I plan on finding out who did this to Billy. I'll follow the evidence."

CHAPTER 17

Dean and Guthrie met at McDonald's for breakfast. They discussed the previous afternoon's activities. Guthrie had found the pawn shop in Plattsburgh Billy had visited: Earl's. The owner recognized Billy from the photo but not Sarah. However, his records indicated Sarah had pawned two pieces of jewelry, a bracelet and necklace, in July of 1978. Albert, one of his employees, had made the deal. Sarah did not pick them up in the agreed upon ninety days, so Earl's took possession of them. Billy bought them in November. Guthrie handed two Polaroids to Dean, one of each piece of jewelry. The bracelet, a tennis bracelet is what Cindy would have called it, was studded with clear, small stones around the entire gold band. The necklace was a less gaudy affair. A thin gold chain with a triumvirate of clear stones wrapped in whorls of bent gold. The center stone was the largest, and the two either side of it were the same size. Billy had bought them back for double the amount of the pawn, five hundred and a thousand. Everything about the items looked legitimate and corroborated Sarah's story. So the real question was where did Billy get the money?

Dean gave Guthrie a run down of the trip to Montreal. The two detectives shook their head at the meaning of the passports and copies of *The Communist Manifestos*. As they were talking, Dean wondered for the first time in a meaningful way, Renard's question was a realistic one to ask. Was Billy a spy? But why would a spy be in Zion instead of New York or Washington? Or near major military bases? He filed it away for now so he could focus on the investigation by ticking off the more likely possibilities, starting with friends and family and connections with the drug trade.

The two detectives finished breakfast and walked across the street to Bridewell's Grocery, where they found Josh sacking groceries for a young mother, whose child sat in the front of the cart, blue-booted feet kicking. Josh had worked at Bridewell's since high school and now helped manage for Gary Bridewell, who was in his seventies and had no children but had taken Josh under his wing.

They waited as he lifted items with his right hand and placed them in his left, which was hidden in the standing sack. He put cans of peas and corn at the bottom and built his way up, placing bread and bags of chips on top. All very practiced and efficient.

Josh offered to assist the woman out, and she accepted. Guthrie looked at the magazine rack near one of the four check out lines. The check out clerk, one of the town's Pentecostal women identifiable by her long hair wrapped into a bun, no make up, and modest, ankle-length denim skirt, asked if Dean needed help. He said he was waiting for Josh.

A few minutes later, Josh came in, pushing three carts, which he stacked with the others. He looked over at the clerk, who gestured toward Dean. "How can I help you?" asked Josh.

Up close, Dean could see all the freckles on Josh's face. His red hair and pale-complexion meant the boy burned in the summer. Tall and thin as most twenty-somethings are, he could still have been in high school for all Dean could tell. He held out his badge. "Detective Wallace. That's Detective Guthrie."

Josh raised a single hand to wave at Guthrie. "Ah, yeah, now I remember you."

Dean said, "Can we talk someplace? It's about Billy."

The clerk raised her hand to her mouth.

Josh nodded and walked past the counters to a brown door hidden behind racks of candy, greeting cards, and magazines.

The door led to a few offices, one of which had Josh's name in a fake-gold plaque with black lettering on the door. Josh's office consisted of an industrial desk, two hard plastic chairs—one red, one blue—and a book shelf lined with large, three-ring binders with tags reading "Produce," "Canned Goods," and "Frozen Foods." Three citations for employee of the month were framed and hanging on the wall next to the shelf. No windows. Josh gestured to the two plastic chairs and sat down in the cushioned one behind his desk.

"Terrible news," said Josh.

"It is," said Dean as he sat down.

"What can I do?"

"Tell us about the night he disappeared."

"If Billy hadn't gone missing, I probably wouldn't remember it. Just a night really. Corey and Billy were at the Shambles. I had to work late—dealt with some mistaken orders. So when I got there they were already two or three beers in. But we ate some food, and I had a few myself."

"How often did you guys meet up?"

"We tried to get together once a week at least. Sometimes more. Sometimes less. Depended on what was going on with work and stuff."

"Always at the Shambles?"

"No, not always. Most of the time, but sometimes at Tracks. Sometimes at my place. Wherever."

Dean scratched the side of his jaw. "So you're having some food and drinks with Corey and Billy. Then what?"

Josh shifted in his chair, grabbed the edge of the desk, and dug at it with his thumb. "Then we left. Nothing really. It was a complete shock when we heard about Billy not showing up to work. Being missing and all."

"What did you guys talk about?"

"Stuff. The playoffs. Work. Movies. I mean, we talked for a couple of hours. So lots of stuff."

"What time did you leave?"

"Eleven-thirty-two." Josh's answer was too quick, too specific, and he knew it. "Something like that."

Guthrie looked at Dean, but he kept his focus on Josh. "That's pretty specific. Why do you remember it so clearly?"

"I don't really. Well, I mean, I thought about it after I heard he was missing. So I talked to Corey to make sure we both remembered it the same way." Josh dug at the desk's corner with his thumb. "I don't mean it that way. I mean, we talked after. Recalled. We thought the police would want to know."

Dean nodded and frowned. "What are you not telling us, Josh?"

Josh stood up. "Look, I really need to get back to work."

Dean remained sitting in his chair. Guthrie did not move.

"Come on, I need to get back to work." He walked over to the door and opened it.

Dean stood up, took two steps toward Josh, and stood close to him. "All right." He pulled out one of his business cards. "If you remember something, call me." He placed the card into Josh's shirt pocket, patted his chest, and walked out, followed by Guthrie.

As Josh started to the close the door, Dean put his right forearm to it. He looked at Josh, whose eyes were open wide. Dean bobbed his head from side to side. "So answer me this. Did Sarah and Alex have a thing on the side?"

The question surprised Josh, and he could not hide it, but he shook his head. "No. No. Absolutely not."

Dean smiled, winked, and eased his arm off the door. He turned around as the door closed behind them. Back out into the store proper, the clerk walked up to Dean. She smiled and stood before him.

Dean smiled back. "Yes?"

"That Josh is a good boy."

"Okay," said Guthrie.

"You should know that. He's a good boy."

"Any reason why I would think differently?" Dean crossed his arms and tilted his head toward her.

"People talk in this town. But you shouldn't believe everything you here is all." She looked back to the register, where a man walked up cradling bread, peanut butter, and milk. "He's a good boy." She walked back to the check out lane.

The detectives sat in the car as it warmed up and lit cigarettes. "What the hell was that?" asked Guthrie.

"Which part?"

"Amy telling us he's a good boy." Guthrie saw the look on Dean's face. "It was on her name badge."

Dean nodded once. "Means something's going around town about Josh. Or." He inhaled deeply and blew the smoke out through the crack in the window. "Or about him and his buddies."

"What do you mean?"

"I've no idea, but we should find out. When you were doing your investigation after he disappeared, any rumors pop up?"

"No. Nothing. They seemed like close friends is all."

"I think they probably are. Maybe Sarah's father will tell us something."

"Him next?" Guthrie stabbed the cigarette out in the ashtray.

"No. Let's talk to Alex like we planned. We'll talk to Sarah's dad soon enough."

Alex Smith worked at Adamson's in the packaging and shipping department. That department broke the furniture down into its pieces and then boxed, wrapped in plastic-wrap, labeled for shipping, and loaded it all into trucks. The foreman told the detectives Alex's shift was almost over and hoped they could wait. They did, sitting in the running car smoking. About thirty minutes after talking to the foreman, Alex walked out of the factory.

He bore a striking resemblance to his father. Short with a smallish nose that bent along the dorsal edge. He was wrapped in a heavy parka and knit hat. Dean rolled down the window. "Alex."

Alex looked at him, surprised at his name being called.

Dean showed him his badge. "Get in. We need to talk."

Alex shook his head and mumbled something lost to the cold. The door opened with a screech. He flopped himself heavily into the back seat and slammed the door closed. "What?"

Guthrie turned sideways in his seat and draped his arm along the top. "You don't want us finding who killed your friend Billy?"

Dean looked back.

Alex pulled off his knit cap, revealing a full head of blond hair. Definitely did not get that from his father. "Course I do. But I already told you everything I know. What else do you want?"

"Missing is different than murder. So we have other questions," said Dean.

"Shit man, I don't know nothing."

"Anything."

"Hell, I don't need or want a grammar lesson from you." Alex pulled the door handle, letting the cold rush in through the crack.

"Where were you the night Billy disappeared? That's a lot more important now. In your earlier statement, you said home. No alibi."

"I need an alibi?" Alex jerked the door closed.

"It'd be helpful."

"I don't got one. I was home."

"Why weren't you at the Shambles with your buddies?"

Alex stared at the floor.

Guthrie tapped the top of the car seat. "We hear you and Billy had some sort of falling out. What's up with that?"

"Can I smoke?"

Dean nodded.

Alex pulled out a pack of Marlboros, shook one loose, and lit it. Cracking the window. "He and I argued about Sarah." He kept looking out the window, talking to it instead of Dean. "He was really falling for her, but she was just taking his money. Only interested in jewelry and expensive clothes."

"That's it? Corey said the same thing, but he and Billy were still drinking at the Shambles."

"It got heated between us, okay? You know me, I've got a hot head sometimes."

Dean almost praised him for his self-awareness. "So you two argue over Sarah. You were home the night of Billy's disappearance. That right?"

"That's right."

"Who'd want to hurt Billy? Did he have any enemies?"

Alex stared out the door window. "Billy was a good guy. But he was gullible. Believed what people told him. Couldn't see the darker side of folks."

Dean waited for Alex to continue, but he did not. Guthrie raised his eyebrows. Dean said, "What does that mean? You think he was friendly with someone who hurt him? Someone besides Sarah?"

Alex sat in silence.

Guthrie snapped his fingers. "My colleague asked you a question."

"Do you know what goes on in this town?"

"What are you talking about?"

"Shit." Alex shook his head and flipped his cigarette out the window.

Dean sighed. "Look, a lot goes on in this town. But if you want to say something, say it. Stop beating around the bush." He lit a cigarette.

"That body shop he works for, they're big-time drug guys. They're moving H coming in from Canada to New York."

Guthrie looked at Dean. "Most of the drugs come from Miami up to the northeast."

"Yeah, most, but not all. There's money to be made."

"How do you know this?" asked Guthrie.

"Rumors. People talking. McCord's got a nice house. Really nice."

"So, what? You think Billy found out about this and was killed?"

"Maybe. You wanted to know if he had any enemies."

Dean breathed in and out deeply. "You hear this from your dad?" He knew that most of the drug investigations work fell to the State Police, despite his father's efforts to keep that state agency out of Zion. But the District Attorney would know of any activities.

"Shit, I'm trying to be helpful. To know about McCord, you just have to have ears."

"So back to you and Sarah."

Alex looked back out the window.

Guthrie rubbed his thumb on the steering wheel. Dean watched Alex as Guthrie asked, "You and her have a thing?"

Alex turned to look at the back of Guthrie's head, and Dean saw his jaw clench. Alex opened the door and slammed it behind him.

Dean leaned over the front seat and said out Guthrie's now open window. "You want to tell us?"

Alex took two steps and stopped. With his back to the detectives, he turned his head. "Fuck you." He walked away, lifting his hood over his head as he did so.

Dean flicked his still burning cigarette out the open window before Guthrie rolled it up.

Guthrie twisted himself back around in his seat and grabbed the steering wheel. "So?"

"Let's get back to the station." He turned on the radio. The solo from Talking Heads's version of "Take Me to the River" crackled through the speakers.

"You think there's anything to what he said?" He put the car into gear and pulled forward into the cars of the employees leaving work.

"It's more than we had before. Frankly, makes more sense if Billy was shot because of drugs than because Corey or Alex thought Sarah was screwing him over. Or if Alex and Sarah were a thing and something happened because of that."

"Or if Alex thought he could have her to himself by taking out his competition."

"Definitely a possibility. But why would Billy go out to the Pratts to meet with Alex?"

"If it were drugs, there'd be a reason to meet."

"Right, and for my money, it makes more sense if it's McCord than if it's Zorn dealing in drugs."

"You think Billy was a part of it? Dealing drugs I mean?"

"Like I said, we know more than we did before. Let's see where it leads."

Guthrie drove them back to the station in silence except for the radio.

☙❧

Dean typed up his reports for the rest of the afternoon, taking nips from his flask the entire time. In New York, fellow officers had often complained about report fatigue, that they spent most of their days writing reports. Dean, however, had found the activity helpful, therapeutic even. It had started in Vietnam. One of the great misconceptions of soldiering was that they spent all their time fighting or waiting to fight. Broadly true, but the military was a report hungry machine. And one of the more important reports in Vietnam were after-action reports. Whenever they got into a fire fight—no matter how small—they radioed back the initial confirmed kills and probables and casualties. Those made their way up the chain, getting inflated to ensure the ratio of casualties and confirmed kills and probables was palatable to the commanders and politicians back in Saigon or D.C.

But the after-action reports, the ones written by the soldiers in the fight, were the history of the battle, the basis for medal citations, the path of promotion. Those reports entered the official record. They became history. For Dean, they helped him contextualize and, eventually, accept what had happened. Friends saved him. Luck was on his side. But those reports, the act of writing down what happened kept him sane.

By the time he was a detective in New York, he used reports to help him think, to sort through the mental clutter of the interviews, to reflect on truthfulness and logic. Sort the good from the bad.

So when he rolled the paper into the typewriter, a sense of calm descended over him. Every press of the key and its hard slam against the paper and the appearance of the letter as it slid into view made, somehow, permanent the conversations. Brought them into history. Like all history, it was more perception of facts than objective context. Another thing he had learned in Vietnam, reading over dozens of his officers' reports: History is one person's context in time and place.

And what he was getting from the interviews with Corey, Josh, Alex, and Sarah was exactly what he would have expected. Different emphases. Different interpretations. Different truths. One person's truth did not falsify another's. It might, but it might not.

Five interviews essentially covering the same span of time the night Billy disappeared. Billy goes to work and then to the Shambles. Around eleven-thirty or so, Corey, Josh, and Billy leave, and Billy is not seen alive again. Except by the killer.

What was particularly interesting were the different interpretations of what Billy was like. Some general remarks as to his kindness or being a great guy—not uncommon from those trying to not sully the memory of the dead. Then Billy's attitude toward work. Did he or did he not like it? Was he or was he not being used by Sarah?

Dean was inclined to believe Sarah regarding the jewelry. His friends had a wrong impression, but Corey's wrong impression seemed genuine and Alex's forced. He could not explain why, other than he felt that Alex was purposively leaving details out, and his hunch was Sarah and Alex had slept together at least. Perhaps during one of the breaks between Billy and Sarah. Perhaps not. It could even be more meaningful than a roll in the sack. But Alex had shown up shortly after Billy left the Shambles.

And then Billy's pile of cash, which was not from working hard at McCord's every day. *The Communist Manifesto* still stumped him. Pile of cash and communism? How did those fit in. Something was going on, and Josh—just by how the interview went—seemed like the weak link.

He twisted his chair around, opened a blank page in his notepad, and wrote down his next steps. Visit Paul Zorn. Follow up about McCord. Visit Sarah's father. He tapped his pen against the paper. Bring in Josh to the station to talk. He put a question mark at the end of that last one.

After stacking all the papers together and bouncing them on the desk to align the edges, he put them in a folder labeled interviews and stuck them in a larger, gray-green folder holding the autopsy report and crime scene photos. He slid the report into the bottom drawer of his desk, refilled his flask, and locked the desk drawer. He looked at his watch and saw it was after five, so he put on his coat and drove over to his parents. His mom met him at the door and said she and Jenny had had fun that day and had not eaten yet. Dean smiled and escorted his daughter to the car, where he suggested they get tacos at La Jolla restaurant, a place that had opened in the last year, and go see *Superman*, which he knew she wanted to see. She smiled and agreed. The tacos were disappointing, but the movie thrilled Dean. He told Jenny about *The Adventures of Superman* when he was young, how he would watch it every week. As he reflected on this conversation later, he sensed that Jenny was indulging her father by listening to his memories much as he indulged his own father's.

As they walked into Dean's house, Jenny said she saw Uncle Tony earlier that day. Even she noticed the surprise look on his face. "He came over. He said he knew I was visiting and wanted to see me at least once."

Dean smiled and said that was great. Perhaps the thaw between Tony and Eric was indeed occurring.

CHAPTER 18

January 12, 1979

Dean dropped off Jenny with his mom the next morning and drove to the station. The chief was meeting the mayor for breakfast, so only Laura and Etheridge were in the station. The winter so far had been brutally cold, but at least not like last year's blizzard. Still, it kept even the limited crime of Zion down to a minimum. Accidents, however, were more frequent. Slide offs mostly. Last night, a businessman traveling through Zion on Route 23 had hit a patch of ice or fallen asleep, slid off the road, slammed into a tree, and was thrown thirty feet into the field. Etheridge described how he could follow the blood trail across the snow to the crumpled up body.

Dean nodded his understanding of that grim scene. He had seen plenty of such accidents during his days on patrol.

After settling in at his desk, he asked Laura to call the State Police and get any info they had on Charlie McCord. He then picked the phone up from the cradle and held it. He dialed the number for the *Beacon* and asked the person who answered to be connected to Paige.

After a couple of minutes being on hold, Paige picked up the phone and said, "McFadden."

"Detective Wallace."

"Ah, so the chief talked to you?"

He was glad he was on the phone so she could not see him flush with anger.

"He's savvy about the press and my boss made a call," she continued. "I'm doing my job's all."

"Right. So—."

"Sorry. Didn't mean to bust your balls."

"Yeah, you did." He smiled.

"You're right. I did." She chuckled. "So this Nimitz thing. It's a homicide?" And he gave her most of the details. He left out *The Communist Manifesto* but told her about the cash. On the question of did he have any suspects, he said they did, but not enough evidence at this time to do much about it. She agreed to not phrase it so harshly but still get the point across.

He promised he would keep her in the loop.

"You know, we can be friends," she said. "You never know, what I write might prompt someone's memory."

"Might," he said.

They exchanged good-byes and hung up.

When Guthrie came in a few minutes later, they met to discuss the plan for the day. Dean wanted to talk to Zorn in the afternoon. They decided to split for the morning. Guthrie would interview the Pratts as well as get a look at the crime scene. Dean had spoken with Wayne Pratt the day they found Billy, but a more thorough interview was necessary. Given Dean's connection with the Pratt family, Guthrie needed to do it. Dean, however, would talk to Billy's parents again, asking specifically about the money and book and using the recent interviews with Billy's friends and girlfriend to elicit more information about their son. They agreed to meet back at the station at lunchtime.

Dean knocked on Billy's parents front door. Archie answered and led him to the kitchen table. He motioned for the detective to sit before doing so himself in front of a cup of coffee going cold. Emily was cleaning a stack of dishes from the food friends and neighbors had brought over. Many casseroles and what looked like the remnants of a ham.

Archie took a sip of his coffee. "Have you found out anything, Dean?"

"We're re-interviewing some people based on the, the fact that this is a murder investigation now. And we have information, but we're trying to make sense of it. I'm hoping you can help there."

Archie nodded. The tink of dishes from Emily placing plates in the drainer.

"We interviewed Sarah Esposito. From her statements, she and Billy were more than friends in recent months."

"He didn't talk about her much, really. It seemed to be an up and down thing, and it seemed down at the time."

"Why do you say that?"

Emily placed the hand towel over the top of the drying dishes. "Because he acted the way he always did when they were broken up. He started worrying about money. He was very keen to give her nice things, but he wasn't a lawyer or a doctor. She expected too much."

"Any nice things in particular?"

Emily grabbed Archie's cold mug. "No. Not anything he told me specifically." She threw the cold coffee down the drain and refilled his cup, adding two Sweet'n Lows.

"Anything else that indicated they were back to the just-friends stage?"

She set the mug in front of Archie, who said, "No. That was it. And he was moping around. Not sad like. I know some think he—"

"Neither the police department nor the coroner think it was anything but a homicide." He said it with more force than intended, and he frowned at the bluntness of the remark.

Archie patted his left hand. "Thank you."

Emily set a mug in front of Dean and poured hot coffee into it.

Dean wrapped his hands around the warm mug. "So when I looked in William's room when I was here last, I found something. And I'm hoping you can shed some light on it. On the floor and in the corner of this closet, I found thousands in cash."

Emily raised her hand to her chest. Archie's eyes opened wide.

"From your looks, I take that as a surprise?"

"Yes," said Archie. "How did he get that kind of money?"

"I was hoping you could help explain that."

"How could we do that?" asked Emily. She pulled a chair out and sat down.

"I thought perhaps you had found it in the past or he had talked about it."

"He never mentioned it. I knew he was making decent money from McCord's, but I thought it was all the overtime he was working."

"According to Charlie, Billy didn't work that much overtime."

A tear moistened the edge of Emily's eyes. "News to us. Why didn't you tell us when you found it?"

Dean scratched his chin. "If it had turned out to be a suicide, I wanted to be able to give it back to you quickly. Now it's evidence. I'm not sure when—"

Emily teared up and waved her hand at him. "That's okay. I don't need to know any more. I don't care about the money."

Archie put his hand over hers. They shared affection in ways that Dean had never seen his parents do. He did not doubt Eric and Jessica loved each other, but it was not what he had seen between the Nimitz's. He imagined they still held hands while walking, something he had never seen his father and mother do.

Dean said, "I found another item with the money. A copy of *The Communist Manifesto*." When both parents looked at him blankly, Dean said, "Did William read any political philosophy?"

Archie snorted. "You saw his room, sir. He was interested in baseball and cars. What he read matched those interests. I think the only philosophy he read was what was required at school."

Dean let go of the mug. "Thanks. It's probably nothing, but I wanted to ask."

Emily asked, "How's the money and the book got anything to do with Billy's—with his—our son's—?"

Dean stood up. "Maybe nothing. Maybe everything. It's something we need to explore." He left them, with more questions than answers and a reminder their son had been murdered. The frigid air outside seemed warmer than the Nimitz's kitchen.

❧

Dean closed the door of the car and turned it on, cranking the heat to full. A blast of cold stunned him before switching to warm then hot air. If he turned it up high enough, he knew the heat could be too much, but it felt so good, he let it go for awhile.

The radio crackled, and Laura's voice filled the car. "Unit 141?"

Dean lifted the handset and turned up the volume. "This is 141."

"Victim's car has been discovered."

"Nimitz's?"

"Confirmed."

"Where at?"

"Old Range Road. Two miles north of 23."

"Acknowledged. 141 is heading up there now."

"Tow is already on its way."

"Tell them to not touch anything until I'm there."

"Acknowledged."

"And can you tell 142 to meet me there?"

"Yes."

"141 out." Dean put the car in reverse and backed out of the Nimitz's driveway and drove toward Route 23 and the Pratt farm. A mile west of the Pratt farm turnoff, Dean turned his car north on Old Range Road. The road led to a number of homesteads that ran along the Canadian border. Cattle and crops.

The road curved east near the border. As he approached the two-mile distance, he saw a familiar car pulled alongside the road, a set of tires on the road and the other on the grass to the side. Tony's blue and white Oldsmobile Cutlass S.

Dean stopped the car behind Tony's and stepped out. Tony got out of the driver's seat. "Hey."

"Morning. What are you doing out here?"

"I found a car off the side of the road." Tony gestured over the top of his car. "I think it's the one you and dad were talking about."

Dean stood on his tiptoe and looked. In the woods, he could make out Billy's yellow Dodge Challenger. "How'd you find it."

Tony rubbed his gloved hands together. "I do my running out here sometimes. There's a spot another mile down to park. I was heading there today to do that."

"How often do you run out here?"

"All the time. All the time. Anyways, I saw it and drove to the house down the road a bit and called the station. I came back to make sure nothing happened in the meantime."

Dean walked past Tony and the front of his car and down a slight embankment into the lightly wooded stretch before a snow-covered field. In the summer with the full bloom of the trees, the car would have been well hidden from the casual passer-by. The trees denuded of leaves and the snow offered no cover. Only the lack of traffic and curiosity by those who did see it prevented it from being reported earlier.

Billy had backed the car off the road. Dean noted the deep tire tracks in the snow. The tires had made contact with the surface of the field. Bits of grass, small rocks, and dirt lined the tracks and the small mounds of snow either side of them.

No tracks from the road to the car, but from the driver's side a set of faded tracks entered the field.

A car squeaked to a stop and Dean walked up the embankment and watched Guthrie get out of his car. He looked at Tony. "Hey."

Dean waved him over. "Tony spotted the car on his run."

Guthrie nodded at Tony and walked over to Dean. Both walked down toward the car.

Dean pointed at the tracks in the snow. "Those lead to where we found him." A light layer of grime coated the hood and wheel wells. "You didn't touch anything, right?" asked Dean.

After a pause, Tony realized the question was directed at him. "Of course not. I know better."

Tony was not a field agent, but he did know better.

A car pulled up followed by a tow truck, which passed by Billy's car, stopped, and then put the truck into reverse.

"Tell him," Dean waved at the truck, "to wait."

Tony nodded and disappeared along the driver's side of the truck.

Reggie walked up, his right hand draped over his holstered pistol. He took off his large mirrored sunglasses. "That Billy's car?"

"Yeah. Well, I think so. Still looking it over."

"Right. Sweet ride."

Guthrie walked behind the car and wrote down the license plate, gave the paper to Reggie, and asked him to run it.

Dean tested the driver-side door. It opened, so he bent down and looked in the car. Black leather seats. Chrome and leather steering wheel. Box of cassette tapes. Led Zeppelin, Deep Purple, Lynyrd Skynyrd. Pink Floyd's *The Dark Side of the Moon* was open on the seat. Dean pushed the eject button on the dash's cassette player. He saw *The Dark Side of the Moon*'s label.

The front and back seats were clean and free of clutter. The dash's bright shine and lack of dust suggested to Dean a recent

Armor All wipe down. He reached under the dash and pulled the trunk release. Other than the spare tire and jack, the trunk was clean.

Dean told Reggie and Guthrie to get the car towed to the station's locked lot on the west side of town. "I'll meet you back at the station before we head over to Zorn's." Guthrie casually saluted.

Dean thanked his brother for calling it in and started to walk out into the field, following the tracks, which had melted at the edges. Tony stomped down behind him. "Care if I join?"

Dean smiled. "Why not?"

Tony followed Dean, who walked alongside the tracks. Billy had crossed the field heading south and when he reached a line of trees about a half-mile from his car, he had turned east and kept to the boundary of woods and field until he walked into the wooded area at the eastern edge, where the tracks became elusive. The snow was not as deep. Dean gave up a dozen yards in. Walking over the underbrush had effectively hidden whatever tracks Billy had left behind.

Dean stood in the woods, hearing his brother breathing behind him. "He came out here to meet someone. One set of tracks. So he wasn't forced." He faced—as best he could tell—the direction of the clearing where they found Billy's body. "At least, not at gunpoint."

"What do you mean?"

"I don't know. It's possible, I guess, that someone had something he wanted or threatened his family to force him out here." Dean shook his head. "Just thinking is all."

"Whatever it was, it didn't go well."

"It did not. But did the person he met end him or was there someone else?"

"Most likely, the person he met."

"It's the simplest answer, that's for sure." Dean sighed. "It's cold as hell. Let's get back."

CHAPTER 19

As Dean drove down Van Buren Street toward the Grim Devils clubhouse at the edge of town, Guthrie updated him on his conversation with the Pratts. All of them had been home the night of Billy's last sighting: Wayne, Cole, Eileen, Joshua, and Kevin. Joshua and Kevin were home from university. The other Pratt children, including Cindy, were not in town for the New Year's holidays. According to those that were there, all stayed in and did not hear anything. He finished as Dean turned left off Van Buren into the gravel parking lot of the clubhouse. Two pickup trucks, one shiny and new and one rusted along the bottom of the door and from the Sixties, sat near the entrance.

The building itself looked like one big, dark gray corrugated metal building punctuated by two doors at the front and several square windows. Two large garage doors with a single door between them were farther down from the entrance. The gravel gave way to a concrete patio at the front door.

Dean parked the car just beside the patio. He looked at Guthrie and said, "I'm not planning on getting much out of this. But I figure it can't hurt to toss a grenade in the bunker and see what happens."

Guthrie pushed the car door open. "Let's hope that grenade doesn't come flying back out at us."

At the front door to the clubhouse, Dean knocked and then twisted the door knob, which was locked. He pounded on the door. Zorn pushed aside the blinds covering the front window, shook his head, and let the blinds swing back as he unlocked and opened the door. The thin, lanky man held it open, gesturing for the two detectives to enter.

Guthrie followed Dean in. Zorn wore blue jeans, a Led Zeppelin t-shirt from the 1977 tour, and a black leather jacket with the edges showing wear. Despite his thinning hair on top of his head, his long blond hair fell to just below his neck, and the goatee ended in a point a couple of inches below the chin. AC/DC's "T.N.T." roared from out-of-sight speakers. "Well, well, well, if it isn't Dean Wallace come to pay me a visit. Your dad tired of harassing me so he sends his kid?"

Zorn had been a notorious bully to a number of freshmen who had crossed him. Dean's dad had defended a number of fellow students from the swirlies, circle games, and nipple cripples Zorn had his gang—even then he had a gang—inflict on a dozen other kids. His bad reputation and antics had grown up with him. After serving in the Pacific, Zorn had been arrested for a number of petty crimes, but nothing serious. Eric Wallace was convinced Zorn and the Grim Devils were major drug distributors, smuggling heroin coming from Montreal, which had originated in Sicily, down to New York or over to Boston. The Grim Devils ran most of the prostitutes in Zion and the surrounding area along with running illegal gambling sessions. He had blackmail material on dozens of city, county, and state officials, and he washed the money through the town's small, four-lane bowling alley. Even darker rumors circulated. In the early Seventies, two state troopers were found decapitated on the Plattsburgh to Buffalo railroad, rope, duct tape, and their own handcuffs bound what was left of them. They had been investigating biker gangs ties to a series of bank robberies in small towns across the northern part of the state, robberies with strong circumstantial evidence pointing to the Grim Devils. The robberies and the murders remained unsolved.

"Hey Paul," said Dean.

"And Jeremy." Zorn shook Guthrie's hand. "Where do you want to search now?"

Dean cocked his head to the side. "Not here to conduct any searches. Here to talk to you about William Nimitz."

Zorn closed the door. "I see. He's the one you guys found out in the woods?"

"Yeah, him."

Zorn walked past the two detectives into the clubhouse. Two pool tables sat to the north, a makeshift bar just to the right of it, and a set of couches. Nothing matched, and the floor was left as bare concrete. A closed door in the middle of a wall led to the garage, a couple of small offices, and storage space. The Grim Devils president walked over to the Pioneer HiFi and turned the volume down before sitting on one of the couches. "How can I help you?"

"Did you know him?"

"This Billy kid?"

Dean and Guthrie nodded. Guthrie took a seat in the couch opposite Zorn.

"Knew him in passing. I mean, I could identify him on the street, but I wouldn't say I knew him, no." Zorn pulled at his goatee. "I'll admit, I'm a bit confused why you think I can help."

"We found thousands in cash in his closet."

Zorn's eyes narrowed, focused on Dean, and his hand stopped, gripping his goatee. "Did you now? And...hmmm...let me guess. Your dad says that the only reason someone has a lot of money is because they deal in drugs? That I couldn't have earned it by working hard, saving, doing the good old American raising myself up, eh?"

Dean let a thin smile cross his face. "My dad didn't say it. And when the money is found in a shoebox in the corner of a closet, one does indeed wonder where it came from."

Zorn threw his arms out. "So you think of me first? I should feel honored? Tell me why you're here, why you think you need to come talk to me?"

Dean paused before responding. He knew this visit was a long shot. In fact, he expected nothing to happen other than to rattle Zorn's cage and see if anything fell out in the coming days. So how best to rattle him? "Simple really. Billy was working for you, stole your money or cut you short or something—there's always something you bosses don't like. So you killed him. You or one of your brothers on bikes." He raised a finger to cut off Zorn from interrupting. "And you didn't know where he had hidden the cash. Or you did and were waiting a bit."

Zorn smiled and shook his head. "Detective, I'll tell you what I tell your old man. I run a legitimate business and this club— despite our name—is just that. A club of motorcycle enthusiasts who like to spend some time riding in each other's company. This Nimitz kid wasn't a member of the Devils, he didn't work at the lanes, and he didn't bowl, so I didn't pay him much attention."

Guthrie scratched his head. "Look, Paul, we're not all that interested in your business. We're just trying to find out what happened with this kid. So he has a lot of money stuffed in a bag in his closet. Makes you wonder, you know?"

"Not really."

"Well it does us."

"Good for you."

Dean crossed his arms. "Let's try it this way. Can you think of any reason why Billy Nimitz, employee of McCord's, would have that kind of money. Have you heard anything in your rides?

"Maybe he saved it. Maybe he worked hard for it. I don't know."

Guthrie stood up. "Nice to see you care about the town you live in."

Dean said, "He loves this town."

Zorn leaned over and put his hands together. "And I love my club. But you've got me all wrong. Talk to Quentin Trask. He and I were here the night Billy was killed." He stood up. "If you're so worried about this town, maybe you should check out the DA's kid."

"Alex Smith."

"Yeah, that punk."

Guthrie sat back down. "Why him?"

Zorn smiled and leaned back in the chair.

To Dean, this was beyond even the practiced confidence of a man often at odds with the law. This was a man confident because he was telling the truth. "Is this about McCord?"

"Charlie. I got nothing against him. Shit mechanic, but, well." He shrugged.

"So answer Jeremy's question, 'Why Alex?'"

"Look fellas, I'm not too interested in bad-mouthing folks in this town. Let's just say, I've heard things about Alex. Things that, well, seem like a reason for investigation."

"Anything specific about Billy."

"No." Zorn shook his head vigorously. "No." He stood up. "I think that's all I can do, boys."

☙❧

Dean drove them back into town, and without asking his partner, straight to McCord's Body Shop. Guthrie followed him into the shop, where they rang the bell. Dressed in the same gray coverall of the other day and perhaps the same cigar and red rag, Charlie ducked as he walked into the reception area.

"Hey there. What's it today?"

Dean rubbed the back of his neck. "We've been conducting our investigation, and your name keeps popping up."

Charlie squinted, and Dean saw the man's fight or flight instincts rise to the surface. But Charlie fought them back, though he had stopped wiping his hands on the rag—they gripped the rag in front of them, stopped in mid motion. "How so?" He tucked the rag into his front pocket. "I can't imagine why that would be."

"Seems some people think you're distributing drugs, part of the illegal border crossing of cocaine and heroin."

Charlie shook his head and chuckled. "You've got to be kidding me. I've seen *Capone*. Do I look like a gangster, here with my hands dirty." He held them up. Dirt darkened the lines of this fingers and palms.

"The movies aren't real life."

"Yeah, whatever. I've got work to do."

Guthrie asked, "So those rumors?"

Charlie paused at the door leading to the garage. "I'm not bothering to answer stupid rumors." He went through the door.

Guthrie looked at Dean, walked to the door leading to their car, pushed it open, and said, "Well, that got us far."

Dean followed him out. Once in the car, he said, "We hit something though. When we said his name keeps popping up, something was there. You seen his house?"

"What? What Alex said we're paying attention to?"

"I'll take that as a no." Dean radioed in to Laura and asked for McCord's home address.

"I know it's north of here." Guthrie cracked the window and lit a cigarette.

Dean pulled out of McCord's and headed north. Within a couple of blocks, Laura responded with the address, in the Highland Estates housing division. The same division as the mayor and the Adamson's family. After a few minutes, they arrived at the entrance, designed with two large brick walls with Highland Estates plaques in limestone either side of the road. Long driveways, spacious yards, and very large houses, with everything longer, more spacious, and larger the farther into the division they drove. Dean made a couple of wrong turns down cul-de-sacs. Guthrie mumbled, "Jesus," a few times even though he had seen a number of these houses on the inside as victims of burglary and theft.

The McCord house, when they found it, floored them. Designed along federal style neoclassical lines, the rust brick, two-story house had the appearance of a squat rectangle on which sat a large cube. On the first floor, white-framed windows with black shutters. On the second, large Palladian windows. The double-door entry was covered by a flat-roof portico supported by four Doric columns.

Guthrie whistled. "I've only been back here once, I think, in this part of the division. I don't remember that."

"Hmm. It's a palatial estate. Think what you want about Zorn, but he's doesn't show off his wealth. At least like that. That's begging for attention."

Zorn sank his money into the clubhouse and motorcycles. The Zorn house was a modest half-brick, half-wood siding house just south of the downtown circle.

"This sure as hell means McCord is up to something dirty or something we don't know about. Legal that is."

"If it were legal, we wouldn't have people asking us to check him out. They would've just complained about it."

CHAPTER 20

Dean and Guthrie stopped at Tracks to grab a beer. The sun was already creeping low in the sky, its bright smudge its only notable trait. Dean was ready for spring, to see some green beyond the firs and spruces and white pines. Anything besides unrelenting gray.

Guthrie poured his Budweiser into a glass and rubbed his chin before taking a large drink. "What the hell is Zorn doing? Why's he throwing Alex at us like that?" He took a drink. "Hell, why'd Alex throw McCord at us?"

Dean leaned back in the chair, rubbed the back of his neck, and looked at the ceiling. "The question is, what does this have to do with William's murder?" He leaned forward and put his arms on the table. "If we assume it is drug related, then William—from what we know so far—was killed because of his proximity to Alex. Either he knew what Alex was doing or he helped Alex. So that presumes Alex is doing something illegal. But I don't think Alex just gets into the drug trade alone. No. So he's working for one of those two, Zorn or McCord."

"Zorn, right, if he threw McCord at us?"

"Maybe. But Zorn threw Alex under the bus." Dean waved his hand. "We're getting ahead of ourselves. We don't know if Alex was involved in anything illegal or not."

They finished their beers and ordered a second round. Guthrie asked who Dean liked in the upcoming Super Bowl. Given the drubbing the Cowboys inflicted on the Rams, Guthrie was convinced Dallas were going to win. Dean cautioned that in a fight between the Steelers and Cowboys, he would pick the Steelers. They paid their bill, returned to the station, and typed up their reports. Dean read Guthrie's quickly, counter-signed the document, and they slipped everything into the growing folder. After Guthrie left the station, Dean called the *Beacon* and left a message for Paige that Billy's car had been found but revealed nothing interesting. He pressed the hook switch and cradled the handset. He dropped the handset to his other hand and put it on the hook.

When he picked up Jenny, his mom sent him home with a container of turkey tetrazzini, piling in extra bits of the burnt cheese crust that he favored. While he heated up the casserole in the oven, he found a bag of frozen peas and dumped them in boiling water. While sucking in spaghetti noodles, Jenny regaled Dean with the day she spent with her grandmother. Another puzzle, but she had also begun to learn to sew dresses for her dolls. Dean let his mind wonder how soon his daughter would grow out of playing with dolls.

They played scopa—a game Dean had learned from Eugene Deluca during a rainy day on base in sixty-eight. As he considered which card to discard, Jenny asked if he was mad at Uncle Tony.

"Why do you ask about Uncle Tony?" asked Dean.

"He was over at Grandma's again today. Grandma said you and him haven't seen each other for years." She emphasized the last word, stretching her hands wide.

"You can't take that four-of-coins and two-of-cups 'cause a six-of-clubs is there."

Jenny replaced the two cards and picked up the six-of-clubs.

Dean looked at his cards. He shook his head at what his mother had said. It was not accurate even if it had the sense of accuracy, but it was not as if they spoke of Tony often. "I'm not mad at Tony, but it might've appeared that way." He discarded his knight-of-coins. "But we don't see him often, that's for sure."

"Why don't we?" Jenny showed her knight-of-clubs and swept up the knight-of-coins.

"It's a grown-up story." He led with that, not knowing what else to say, praying she would accept that and move on. But it was his daughter.

"So we're not allowed to see him?"

"Mmmm…that's not it. I mean, you've seen him a couple of times now. Nothing wrong with that." He paused, unsure of how to talk about the history, the context. "You know you had another uncle, right? Uncle Nolan? Mom's told you that?"

Jenny shook her head, and Dean almost cursed Cindy aloud. But then he had never brought up Nolan either.

He set his cards down. "Hold on." He walked to the kitchen and poured a tumbler of whiskey. "Milk?" He looked over the counter at Jenny, who nodded. He poured a tall glass of milk and pulled out the chocolate syrup, which he squeezed in and stirred around with a knife. He handed her the glass. "So you know I was in a place called Vietnam, right?"

Jenny nodded.

"Well, you had an Uncle Nolan who was there, too. But he didn't come home."

"He died there?"

Dean took a drink. "Yeah, he did. It was after I left there. Well, Uncle Tony didn't go to Vietnam. And that upset some people. So it makes it hard to be around him sometimes."

"Are you mad at him?"

"Mad at him? No. I don't think that's it. I think it's hard to see him and not think of Uncle Nolan. So it's easier to just not see Uncle Tony. Does that make sense?"

She put her finger to her lips—a gesture so reminiscent of Cindy that he thought he was looking at her twin. "I guess so, but can I see Uncle Tony, right?"

Dean took a drink. "Of course." He smiled at her. "But I want you to know. My not seeing Uncle Tony wasn't the right thing. Just because it's easier that's, well, that's not a good enough reason."

In the end, Jenny beat Dean at scopa. They watched some TV. After he tucked her in, he sat on the couch with the volume turned low and drank whiskey, thinking of Tony and Nolan and the war. And how he hated to think of the war but he could never not think of it. He had brought it home and, like a delayed-fuse bomb, it had gone off years later, severing limbs but leaving him alive—if barely.

Once he was in homicide at the NYPD, his drinking really took control. Cindy put up with it far longer than he had any right to expect, but even that bastion of strength had fled—or he had exhausted it, forced it away. She had found him too often on the couch in the middle of the night with an empty bottle in his hand, raging at the shadows of the war. He could never tell her. Or he could never find a way to tell her. Tell her how excited battle made him, the frenzy of killing, the explosions, the guns, the adrenalin. In those moments, fear washed over him with ecstasy and he imagined this was what the saints in the desert found as they approached God. How could he explain that to his wife? To anyone who had not been in battle? And then follow that up with how awful he felt about the NVA boy-soldier he shot from six meters. The three blood-spattered bullet holes rising up from the right-lower gut to the left shoulder. Killed as they stormed a hill. Kill or be killed. He did the right thing, but that boy haunted him. Those three growing spots of red and the swaying of the tree leaves behind him as the bullets rose up from the repeated recoil. He could never explain it, so he drank, but the drink stopped numbing it. And Cindy left him. And she needed to. He did not deserve her. He trudged on, but then he had messed up the Kerensky investigation, and the brass could not ignore the issue anymore. Sacked him. And he came crawling back home to his dad, who pitied him and gave him a job. And Dean could not forgive himself for his fall. So he drank, knowing it could not bring light to the darkness.

CHAPTER 21

January 13, 1979

Dean and Guthrie arrived at Zion First Baptist Church thirty minutes before Billy's funeral was scheduled to begin. The orange brick building's parking lot was sparsely filled, which was reflected inside the sanctuary. The closed, black glossy casket rested just below the pulpit and choir. A large, ornately framed photo of Billy sat on an easel beside the casket.

From the front pew, Archie stared at the casket, raising his hand to his cheek throughout to wipe away tears. Emily held a crumpled tissue in her hand, holding it up to her nose like a nosegay.

Behind them sat their family. Archie's younger brother, and Emily's two sisters. Pastor Rob Manson sat in a chair behind the pulpit, reading his copy of the Bible, bookmarked and dog-eared. He took off his large, gold-framed glasses to rub the bridge of his nose frequently. Charlie McCord and one of his employees sat on the opposite side of the aisle, toward the front. Charlie's wife, Eleanor, sat beside him.

Behind the family and Charlie sat Corey, Josh, and Alex filling half a pew. Alex wore sunglasses in a failed attempt to hide a black eye. Sarah and her mother and father, Alice and

Carlos, sat several pews behind Charlie. A few others sat in the pews, which Dean guessed were former classmates of Billy's given their apparent age.

Pastor Rob looked at his watch, stepped up to the pulpit, and said, "Thank you for being here today."

Dean slid out of the pew and through the main doors into the sanctuary, closing them gently, and then exited to the sidewalk. He would let Jeremy observe the grieving families and friends for any clues.

From the car, Dean grabbed the *Beacon* and lit a cigarette. He looked at the blackened snow. Unrecognizable from what had fallen out of the sky. The whiteness had been drained, leaving only clear frozen crystals coated with the grime of human activity. He shook his head, wondering how humanity always managed to mess up everything it touches. He shook off the thought, debated how much longer he could stand the cold, and crushed out his cigarette on his sole. He looked for a trash can, but, finding none, he stuffed the butt into his coat pocket as he walked back into the entryway. He sat on a chair and flipped through pamphlets, *The Christian Science Monitor*, and stacks of *The Daily Verse*. He wondered if Pastor Rob realized the *Monitor* was a Christian Science founded newspaper or had little to do with religion. Perhaps the "Christian" in the title was sufficient.

When Dean had read enough of those, he pulled out the *Beacon*. He had seen the top half earlier. "Murder in Zion." Paige's name was prominent just above the story, which led with Billy's senior class photo in black and white and the line, "His body was found by dogs in the woods near along Route 23." Dog, not dogs, he corrected her mentally. He read the story over the muffled voice of Pastor Rob. The article read very much like the articles about car crashes that took young lives too soon. Slipping into details about the victim's life. Boring details, but they mattered. They revealed the differences between people. Billy was into baseball but this person was into football. Did they go to college or not? Had they escaped Zion or stayed or, worse, returned? He tossed the paper in the trash.

After three more cigarettes, the organ music came on and the double-doors leading to the foyer where Dean stood opened. Pastor Rob nodded at him and then turned to face the exiting attendees. Guthrie walked up quickly, casually saluted the minister, and said to Dean, "So what're we doing?"

Dean leaned over and whispered in his ear, "Let's talk to the Espositos. If you can, talk to Sarah separately, I'll talk to her parents."

Guthrie smiled and gave a thumbs up.

Several people Dean did not recognize walked past him. Alex was the first of those he had interviewed. Dean said, "Hey Alex," as he walked past. Alex looked at him and then back to the doors and the street. He had severe bruises. Several on the face, including some scratches. Dean looked down at the young man's hands and noticed they were cut up, swollen.

Josh and Corey were not far behind. Charlie walked up to the pastor and patted him on the back. "Good service. Good service."

Rob nodded and frowned. "Sad day when we have to bury one so young."

Charlie nodded in agreement. He walked farther into the foyer and noticed Dean and Guthrie. "Gentlemen."

Dean extended his hand. "Charlie."

Charlie reached out and shook Dean's. When Dean gripped it, the body shop owner cringed, realized he had, and smiled. Dean let go of his hand and noticed it was red and swollen around the knuckles.

"What happened?" asked Dean.

"Oh, that." He held up his hand and looked at it as if it were some tool. "Dropped a wrench on my hand yesterday. Hurt like hell." He looked back at the pastor. "Sorry." He used that to escape out into the street.

Dean rubbed his chin. Josh's caginess and Zorn's statements suggested Alex was up to something beyond his usual rowdiness. Charlie had been labeled as a good boss and a bad boss, and Alex had implied Charlie's house was too nice for his salary, which—after seeing it—Dean was inclined to agree.

Sarah walked past Dean and brought him back to the moment. He extended his hand out to the dark-skinned man with a full head of dark hair and large sideburns. "Carlos Esposito?"

Carlos extended his hand. "Yes."

Dean lowered his voice. "Detective Dean Wallace. I'd like to talk to you a bit. Not here of course, but now."

Carlos nodded. Alice, a tall woman who stood several inches taller than Dean, and had long, brown hair wrapped into a ponytail, stepped from beside her husband to in front of him. "What's this about?"

Guthrie touched her shoulder. "Not here. Let's go to the tea room? After the cemetery service?"

Alice looked at him and nodded once. The Espositos walked out, and Dean and Guthrie followed. Too cold to walk the four blocks from the church to the Hardy Tea Room and Bookstore, the detectives got into their car and watched the Espositos get in theirs. A few minutes later, the parade of cars followed the hearse to the cemetery. When the last car had left, Dean turned on his car and drove to the tea room.

The Hardy Tea Room was founded a few years prior by Missy Hardy, a widow whose husband had made a fortune making fertilizer in the AgGroPro factory in Jasper, a town forty-five minutes southeast. When he collapsed at the grocery store one day, victim of a massive heart attack, he had left her that fortune, which she had used to open the tea room because she wanted to bring what she and him had loved about their travels to

Europe to Zion. The place was deserted most of the time. She kept its doors open despite the financial losses. She refused to let go of the dream and memory of her husband. Dean wondered why she did not just move to Europe.

Guthrie liked the place because it was not a bar and because it was empty most of the time, making it a good place to have a conversation. He interviewed witnesses and suspects if he could there. His wife was some distant relation to Missy. They sat and waited beneath the high-ceilinged parlor with small tables covered by rose-motif tablecloths, and each decorated with a small crystal vase with a single flower, Missy looked up and smiled.

When the Espositos entered, Guthrie diverted Sarah to a table with him, while Dean led Carlos and Alice to a table along the windowless wall butting up next to the Ace Hardware Store where a long bench served for seating. Carlos and Alice sat in the bench and Dean in the chair across from them.

Missy walked over with a tea box and explained the specials of the day. She took their orders—coffee for all—and left to prepare them. Dean said, "Thanks for meeting with me. I just had a few questions for you that will help in our investigation into who killed Billy."

"I'm not sure how we can help," said Alice. "We barely knew the boy."

"But you knew him?"

"Yes, yes."

"Sometimes, those who knew the victim the least are the best windows on his life." Dean scratched the back of his head as Missy set down three delicate looking tea cups. After she had stepped away, Dean continued. "Did you like Billy?"

"Like my wife said, we hardly knew him." Carlos grabbed the carafe of coffee and poured some into Alice's cup, then Dean's, and then his own.

"But you certainly had an opinion. He was dating Sarah."

Carlos grimaced. He pulled his cup of coffee toward him. "I didn't approve. Not because he was a bad guy really. Well, not a bad, bad guy. Just a guy who wasn't right for Sarah. Not at all. She could've done better." He grabbed two sugars from the holder on the table.

"What do you mean by not a 'bad, bad guy'?"

Alice leaned forward and her voice dropped to a whisper. "He stole from us. I don't think he would ever be violent. But he stole."

"Are you referring to your mother-in-law's bracelet and necklace?"

Now it was Carlos's turn to whisper. "How did you know that?"

Dean interlocked his fingers and bounced them against his lips. "Whenever we talked to Billy's friends, they kept referring to something about jewelry and Sarah. So we asked her about it."

"Those were heirlooms. My grandmother brought them from Spain, where they were made by one of my great-great uncles. They were priceless to me. And now they're gone."

Dean's eyes narrowed. "What makes you so sure Billy took them?"

"He's the only one who had access to them that would've known and could've taken them. They were taken out of the jewelry chest in my room." Alice took a sip of her coffee. "Only those were taken. And we don't have maids or anything."

"When did this happen?"

"I noticed they were missing this summer. July."

"I was furious," said Carlos. "Furious. I told Sarah I never wanted him to step foot in our house again. Ever."

"And did he?"

"Not that I know of."

Dean looked at Alice, who shook her head. "So Billy took priceless heirlooms, but you didn't report them stolen."

"Sarah begged us not to, saying we'd never get them back anyways. Only the money, and it wasn't the money we were upset about."

"Okay. I understand you were ill last year," said Dean, looking at Alice.

"I'm not sure what that—" said Carlos.

"Yes. Cancer. Breast cancer," she said, the corner of her mouth quivering.

Carlos set his cup down. "What does that have to do with Billy?"

Dean ignored Carlos's question. "Are you—are you better?"

"Look here—"

Alice patted Carlos's shoulder. "I'm cancer free. Radiation, then surgery, then chemo. It knocked me out of commission for a while. The chemo did a real number on me."

"Was money tight?"

"Have you had cancer or anyone in your family had it?"

Dean shook his head. "My grandfather, but I was young."

"It's expensive. And insurance doesn't like paying for it. And I didn't want to go to a VA hospital."

"I understand that." Dean raised a cup. "Knew a lot of brave Navy pilots back in Nam. Saved me a couple of times, I'm pretty sure."

Carlos tapped the table top. "I don't understand what any of this has to do with Billy."

Dean looked at Alice and pursed his lips. Watched as she thought through the conversation and teased out the implications of his questions. Carlos looked at her with an intensity he hoped he had had with Cindy years ago and knew that Carlos probably did not kill Billy. Not that he was not capable, just that the man was more concerned with his wife and not why a detective was questioning them.

Alice's eyelids flickered and her mouth opened when she understood. "Oh my God." Her head dropped.

"What?" asked Carlos.

"It wasn't Billy, was it?"

Dean shook his head.

Alice looked at Carlos. "Do you remember the money Sarah gave us last year? The money that helped us stay afloat."

"Yeah."

"Know that she did it for a good reason."

Dean thanked them and stood up and walked over to Guthrie's and Sarah's table. He put his hands on the back of the chair beside Guthrie and asked, "Why haven't you returned the heirlooms?"

Sarah looked down and then up. A tear welled up in each eye. He knew, knew how embarrassed she was and how as the time had passed it was easier and easier to avoid the topic. She had them, but she could not bring herself to tell her parents. He nodded and patted Guthrie on the shoulder.

Dean and Guthrie left the Espositos and drove back to the station. They agreed that Carlos was not a good suspect given the spacing between the disappearance of the jewelry and Billy's death, but how long had the anger of that simmered before it boiled over—if it did. Regardless, he seemed the only suspect with a clear motive. However, Carlos's alibi for the night of Billy's disappearance was his wife. They were at home. More importantly to Dean's thinking was Carlos's reaction to the questioning of Alice and then to finding out his daughter had take the jewelry. He had been angry about the jewelry. If he had killed Billy, he would have expected regret, anguish, some other emotion as it dawned on him he had killed an innocent. Anger was a legitimate reaction, but an unlikely one.

Too many other questions hung around Billy's disappearance, and Carlos did not come near enough to answering all of those.

CHAPTER 22

The Chief called Guthrie and Dean over the radio and asked to get an update on the investigation. They drove the short distance back to the station and dropped off their coats at their desks before entering Eric's office. He sat in his chair tamping the tobacco in his pipe. He only brought the pipe with him on weekends. "So I just talked to the mayor boys. He wants a status on this Nimitz investigation."

Dean nodded to Guthrie, who sat up straighter in his chair. "We've re-interviewed the witnesses from when this was a missing persons case. His friends. His family. His employer. We've interviewed additional people, including his girlfriend's parents and Paul Zorn."

Eric grunted at the name and chewed more vigorously on the pipe stem.

Guthrie continued, "Even interviewed the Pratts. Regarding physical evidence: We have the pistols found at the scene. The thirty-eight, fully loaded, deep in the victim's coat pocket and unfired. The Remington, a forty-five, and likely the weapon that killed Billy—I mean our victim. That gun and bullet are at the crime lab downstate waiting to be examined. We just found the victim's car, which is in the impound lot. Interior was clean as a whistle except for some cassettes. It's been exposed to the elements. We'll lift some fingerprints if we find them, but I wouldn't hold out hope. Even if we found them, could've been anyone that touched the car. My gut tells me Billy parked it there and that's the end of the story for the car. We don't yet know what the stash of cash in the closet or the copy of the commie book mean to the investigation, if anything. Though that much cash seems connected."

"I fought to stop those commies."

Dean did not bother to correct his father, who had fought with those commies against the fascists. Nor did he remind himself of his own war's convenient lies.

Guthrie nodded. "Yes." He paused to see if the Chief had anything to add and looked at Dean when it seemed he did not.

Dean leaned forward in the chair. "There's almost no physical evidence right now that leads us anywhere. The serial number on the gun led us to the license. It was purchased in 1952 by Dennis Kowlowski. He died in sixty-three—same day as Kennedy. The trail stops there. We think there were steps in the snow leading north. There were steps from the car back in the general direction where the body was found."

"One set?"

"Yeah. Lost them in the woods. Got a call from the Quebec police—"

Eric looked at Dean. "That Renard fellow?"

Dean nodded. "They landed on a murder there of a former terrorist. Had a bunch of cash, copies of *The Communist Manifesto*, and passports. Some with William's photo under different names. Other passports too with different people. That's pretty much it in the way of evidence."

"That's it," said Guthrie, wiping his hands on his pants.

"That's it? That's squat. That's less than squat." Eric held the pipe in his right hand and rubbed his neck with his left. "What the hell boys?"

Dean lowered his head before looking directly at his father. "It is what it is. Almost no physical evidence to speak of.

A body left exposed for days. The day he disappeared seems to be the day he was killed. No one knows where he went after eleven-thirty that night. No one knows why he was out in those woods. Or why he had that kind of cash. We've got a ton of dead ends. He did buy back some of the pawned jewelry his girlfriend took from her parents. Until today, they assumed the vic stole it. The only other thing we know is that Alex showed up sometime before midnight but after Billy and his friends left the Shambles."

"The girlfriend's father, Carlos, right?"

Guthrie gave Eric a thumbs up.

Dean said, "Motive…but a long time between knowing of the supposed theft and the killing. His wife alibis him anyways."

"Shit, that's about as good as no alibi. A sliver above when a parent provides an alibi."

"Yeah, but there you have it. Carlos seems good but doesn't account for the cash. Doesn't account for the book."

"It's drug money. We know it is." Guthrie held his hands in front of him and gestured something akin to "this is obvious."

"Probably," conceded Dean.

"So that's Zorn." The Chief stood up and started pacing behind his desk, his hands clasped tightly behind his back.

"Maybe," said Dean. "I know you've been after Zorn for a while. I know and you know that he's running H down from Canada. But we don't have evidence. As far as we know, he didn't even know Billy. And he's not the only peddler of drugs in town. Smaller time guys, but others. Alex fingered Charlie McCord. Zorn pointed to Alex."

Eric grunted. "Charlie wouldn't know the sharp end of a butter knife if you asked him. So where does that leave us?"

"Have you seen his house?"

Eric shook his head.

Guthrie whistled. "It's a beaut. A palace out in Highland Estates."

"If that's the kind of money he's making," said Dean, "we may have gone into the wrong business."

"Charlie's a respected businessman in this town." Eric leaned back and crossed his legs. "That's a pretty big accusation."

"No more than calling Zorn a drug dealer. But it doesn't matter. Given what we know, Alex is the center. We know he showed up late at the Shambles. Josh and Corey tell us he's not getting along with William. I think there was something between Alex and Sarah. I think that's the rift. You've got Paul fingering Alex. Alex fingered McCord. The common name in all of this is Alex. We've got to take a closer look at Alex."

"The DA's boy?"

Guthrie and Dean nodded.

"Hell."

"I think…and it's just a hunch…but I think Alex is running drugs, as well," said Dean. "Small time stuff. But enough to piss off Zorn or McCord. Maybe both. Josh, Corey, Alex, and Billy were a group. If Zorn knows Alex was doing something, he might have gone at him by going after William. And Alex was all beat up today at the funeral. And McCord's hand was red and tender."

"The cash?"

"William was holding it for Alex?"

"Or Billy was a part of the operation," said Guthrie. "They seemed tight. At least until the falling out over Sarah."

"So back to love and not drugs?"

Dean shrugged. "Maybe it's both. Maybe Alex is in love with Sarah and had started using William in his drug thing. And Sarah did mention she thought William was stealing the money from Charlie."

"Damnit boys, this or that. Drugs or love or revenge. All you've given me is a bunch of maybes. This is squat. I can't go back to the mayor with this."

"It is—"

"Yeah, I know the goddamned phrase." The Chief dropped into his chair. "We've got a murder. A murderer on the loose, and nothing." He pulled at his right ear. "What's next? Tell me how you're going to solve this."

"I think we need to probe deeper into Alex. And Josh and Corey. But Alex primarily. We'll dig deeper into McCord as well." Dean caught the glare from his father. "But nothing invasive. Light touch. I'd like to get surveillance on Alex as well."

"What? This isn't New York City. Surveillance?"

"If we can follow him, we can see what he's up to."

Eric waved it away. "We don't have the money for that kind of operation and no way the DA approves surveillance on his son."

"I think it's our best bet."

"Ain't happening boys."

"Then I say we bring all three of them in. Make it formal."

"Do it."

Dean drove to his parents' house, going over in his head the plan the three of them agreed to. Get Billy's three friends into the station and push a bit harder and see if something pops. They did not have much leverage; that was clear. Dean agreed with his father, at least in the bureaucratic reasons for not conducting surveillance on Alex: Money and the DA would not allow any surveillance, especially since it was an intuition unsupported by facts.

Jenny slid into the front seat with a large sheet of thick paper covered with a light blue mat. Without prompting, his daughter explained grandma had shown her how to paint with watercolors. Dean recognized the location. The long boarded walk to a pier and deck extending onto Lake Tonga. His parents' summer house. Jenny's version of it was very pastel and diaphanous and awkward in proportion and perspective. Still, she had done a good job for her first time at it. His mother was more accomplished, though far from professional—a hobby as she liked to point out.

Dean drove them to Burger Palace for dinner. The chain of six restaurants had opened its second store in Zion in the early seventies. It seemed like a treat for Jenny to go into the brightly lit building and sit across from her dad with her kid's meal and vanilla milkshake. He asked her if she was having fun with grandma, and she said she was. And they talked about how she liked history at school. The past semester they had been studying the Revolutionary War and the War of 1812. They were due to learn about the Civil War this coming semester. And science class was okay, but she preferred history. Her stepdad, Spencer Jackson, was making her take piano lessons, and she hated practicing. She asked Dean if she could get her out of it.

"The lessons?" he asked.

"Yes. Urrrr. I hate them." She sucked on the straw.

"It's good for you." He smiled at her look of surprise. "I mean it. Face it, you're not going to get any culture from me." While she was in the bathroom, he let his mask fall and sighed. Sometimes he hated what his life had become, despised that he had so little influence over his daughter, that he was a bit of decoration at the margins of her life. And here she was, staying with him during the worst time he could think of: the first murder investigation since Sixty-Eight. He consoled himself that he had his evenings with her, and she was able to visit with her grandmother.

He drove them to the Pratt farm, where Cindy was waiting with her mother. Cindy told Jenny to use the bathroom before they began the long drive home. While in there, Dean updated Cindy on what Jenny had done all week. "We even saw *Superman*."

"You did? She's already seen that. With Spencer right after it came out."

He could not hide the crestfallen look on his face. Cindy might as well have punched him.

"Oh," she said. "She probably just didn't want to tell you. Wanted to see it with you. Did you only get to spend evenings with her?"

He felt tears welling up, but the tone of her last question bothered him enough that he forced them away. "You know what happened earlier this week. I had a job to do."

Cindy shook her head. They both heard Jenny come at a fast clip down the stairs.

Cindy said to Dean, "Being a father is your job." She turned and said to Jenny, "Slow down. Say bye to your father."

Dean knelt down and he and his daughter embraced. And tears, this time, did come. Not many, but enough. He told his daughter he loved her and they would go to an Expos game this summer. He walked out of the warm Pratt home into the January cold. He felt like a husk ready to be blown into the waiting fields.

On the way home he noticed the car tailing him. At least, he thought it was tailing him. Too distant to determine the make. A pair of lights that followed him—not a difficult task in the town. When he turned into his subdivision, they did not follow him, but he still triple-checked the locks on the doors and windows and sat in the living room, his revolver on the end table until early in the morning.

CHAPTER 23

January 14, 1979

The station had only one usable interview room. The wooden table legs were bolted to the floor and the top of it was a rich tableau of nicks, cuts, and scars from years of subjects, often left alone, or cops themselves. Three wooden chairs, one with a short leg courtesy of Sergeant Benjamin Sidesdale, now retired. In it sat Josh, his forehead beaded with sweat and him thumping his foot lightly, occasionally forgetting the lopsided chair and catching himself.

Dean was pleased with the orchestrated arrival of Corey, Alex, and Josh. Etheridge had picked up Alex, while Zach picked up Corey. Both were brought to the station and seated across the room from each other. Guthrie and Dean walked in a few minutes later with Josh, who they marched into the main area before turning into the short hall with the file room and the interview room beside it.

Dean knew, with what they had, it was their best shot for rattling anything loose.

"What do you want?" asked Josh. He put his hands on the table. "Why did you have to drag me out of work?"

Guthrie slapped the table, not hard, but enough. "We're trying to solve your friend's murder."

"You've already talked to me. I told you everything I know."

"Did you?" asked Dean, his arms across his chest. "Did you?"

Josh blinked at him.

"See, we've got this issue. We talked to you, but you were, well, a bit cagey. I mean, why are you making sure you remember your story the same as Corey?"

"What's that about?" Guthrie lit a cigarette, shaking out the match and tossing it into a styrofoam cup with water.

"I've been thinking about that. I think you guys misunderstood me."

Guthrie looked at Dean and shrugged. They both looked at Josh, who blinked his eyes rapidly.

"You misunderstood me," he said. "I mean, how often does something like that happen in this town. That's big city stuff. And he was our friend, so we compared notes. 'When did you last see him? Same as you.' That kind of stuff." He rubbed his temple. He looked pale, like he would pass out at any moment.

"You seem awfully nervous," said Guthrie, who stood up. He walked toward the back wall, forcing Josh to look back and forth between him and Dean.

"My partner has a point. You're acting like you did something wrong. You look terrible."

Josh shook his head. "I didn't I'm telling you."

"Hmmm." Dean tapped his chin. "Would you be willing to take a lie detector?"

Josh looked at Dean.

Dean scratched the back of his neck. "I mean, let's clear this up real quick. If you've got nothing to hide that is. If you're telling the truth."

Josh looked back at Guthrie. Looked back at Dean. The kid somehow went even more pale. "Yeah. Yeah. Yes."

Dean held his surprise back and instead nodded. "That should clear things up. It'll have to come from a town over. Let me make the call." He left Josh and Guthrie in the interview room and walked out to his desk. Usually when police bring up a lie detector, the suspect goes on the defensive, and those defenses can take time to break down, if lawyers have not been brought in. He had not expected Josh to embrace the idea so quickly, though it fed into the plan he had. Did that mean Josh was innocent, that Dean had gone down the wrong path? He shook his head. No, Josh was weak, he told himself.

Alex and Corey were still sitting across the room from each other. Etheridge was sitting in his chair, typing a report and giving both of the men accusatory glances every once in a while. Dean picked up the phone and dialed the number of Barry Archer, the area's primary lie detector provider. He worked many of the towns in northeast New York.

"Barry Archer Security Services," said the woman who answered the phone.

"This is Detective Dean Wallace with the Zion police. Is Barry in?"

"He's not. May I take a message?"

"Yes," said Dean, who then elevated the volume of his voice, hoping that Corey would hear it at the far end of the room, "Tell him I'd like him to give me a call. He has my number. I'm in need of his lie detector. Today if possible." He had to hold back from looking at Alex's and Corey's reactions.

"I'll let him know. What's the number?"

"He has it. Thanks." Dean hung up and walked back to the interview room, smiling at Corey and Alex as he went. He found Guthrie still standing against the wall behind Josh, who was leaning over with his hands around his stomach. Dean looked at Guthrie, who shrugged. He told Josh he had called the lie detector services and it would be a while, so he needed to wait out in the station while they talked to his friends. Josh stood up and walked through the door Dean held open. Guthrie followed them out and called Corey to the interview room. Josh and Corey passed but did not acknowledge each other. Dean patted Josh on the shoulder after he was seated. "Officer Stone here will get you a coffee or water or soda if you want it."

Dean walked back into the interview room, where Guthrie had set Corey up much in the same way they had Josh.

Corey glared at them and ground his front teeth together. "What's this all about?"

"What do you think, numbskull?" asked Guthrie.

"Billy?"

Guthrie punched Dean in the shoulder and pointed his finger at Corey. "What a bright young man we have here. He figured out we wanted to talk to him about his murdered friend."

"He's the smart one," said Dean.

"What else can I tell you? What did Josh say?"

"Did Josh have something to tell?" asked Dean. Interrogations were like the shell game, he thought. When in New York City, he would play with the young boys on the streets, knowing it was a hustle but feeling bad for them and letting them take a dollar here or there. Detectives want the people on the other side of the table to feel they are honest brokers but not see the trick. In this case, Dean knew he was playing the game with a hand tied behind his back.

"I don't know, man. This is bullshit."

"You're free to go," said Dean.

Corey froze in surprise. "What?"

"You're not under arrest, so you can go anytime."

"But you picked me up."

"Yeah, that was a courtesy. We can get you back to the store." Dean rubbed the top of the table with his thumb. "But I got to tell you, if you do leave, you'll seem uncooperative. I mean, Billy was your friend, right?"

Corey nodded. "He was my friend, but last I saw him was about eleven-thirty the night he disappeared."

"Hmmm. Seems that's the last anybody saw him. Where was he going?"

"He didn't say. I presumed home. He usually went home. We all did."

Dean looked up at the ceiling, rubbed his neck. "So you're out drinking. You guys decide to call it a night. And that's it."

"Yep."

"What's this about having to compare your stories and get them to match up?" asked Guthrie.

Corey twisted his lips and looked at the detective. "Josh tell you that?" Guthrie shrugged. When Corey looked back at Dean, he received no acknowledgement. Corey sighed and looked down at the table. "It sounds worse than it is. We were just comparing notes. Seeing if Billy said something or did something that was odd. Nothing came up."

Dean nodded once, clasped his hands together, and set his elbows on the table. Both Josh and Corey had given the same explanation, and it made sense. "So tell us about Alex and Sarah and the fighting between them and Billy."

"Fighting's too strong a word. Sarah was after his money. I let it be known I didn't like that. Alex? Well, I'll let him tell you what his issue was."

"Did Billy own a gun?" asked Guthrie.

Corey shook his head. "I loaned him one."

Dean leaned backward. "Thirty-eight?"

"Yep. I've had it for years. My grandpa gave it to me to kill raccoons."

"Why'd you loan it to him?"

"We took the thing out in the woods occasionally and shot bottles and shit. He asked to borrow it. So I gave it to him."

"When was this?"

"After Christmas. Why?"

"We found it in his coat pocket when we found him in the woods."

Guthrie and Dean talked to Corey for another hour but obtained nothing more than he had already told them. He scratched his chin, repeated himself, and said he hoped they would catch Billy's killer. Still, Dean thought he was hiding something. Maybe not related to Billy's murder, but something, and he could not put his finger on it, but his instincts had helped him get out of Vietnam alive and survive the New York streets on patrol, and he trusted them here. He considered bringing up the cash found in Billy's closet, but stopped himself. He decided to wait to spring that on Alex. Guthrie walked Corey out and escorted Alex in.

After he was seated across from Dean in the interview room, Alex maintained a casual, relaxed air, often twisting his thumbnail into the table. His face looked worse than the previous day, the bruises beginning to turn ugly colors.

"So tell us your issue with Billy and Sarah. Were you sweet on his girl?" asked Guthrie.

"Please. She's not that hot." He tapped a finger in the air at Guthrie. "But she's got some fine features."

Dean leaned forward. "We talked to Sarah first, you know?"

Alex's eyes darted away from Dean's. He brought them back but could not hold them there.

Dean continued, "We know. And if we don't know something we will. Hiding information, not cooperating—"

Alex brought his fist down on the table. "Goddamnit!" He breathed in and out once. "Fine. Fine. We slept together. Happened a few times."

Dean was pleased his instincts were still on. "When?"

"Ah man. You got to believe me. The first time, they weren't together. They had broken up. It was a couple of years ago. They were always breaking up."

"And getting back together," said Guthrie.

"Yeah, I'm an asshole. I get it. I already knew it."

If Guthrie took the moral high ground, Dean decided to sympathize with Alex. "But she is that hot. I've seen her. She's a fine piece of tail. And that Puerto Rican vibe. I can see why you fell to her seductions."

"She did start it." Alex paused and gazed into nowhere, living in his memory palace, seeing her body. Dean did the same with Sadie. Imagined her in various states of undress.

"When was the most recent?" asked Dean.

"October last year. A few nights."

"Did Billy find out?"

Alex shrugged.

"What does that mean?"

"Means, 'I don't know.' Maybe he did. Maybe he didn't."

"That the reason you weren't hanging out with your friends the night William disappeared, right?" Dean crossed his arms. He watched Alex frown and knew he had gone back to the reason they were in the interview room too quickly.

"And because I wasn't there, you think I had something to do with his death? Over a girl?"

"I've seen murders for a lot less. Decided you wanted to be the lone man in Sarah's life? Or William found out. Confronted you. You had to defend yourself?"

"No man. No."

"Was there something else you were arguing about? Money perhaps?"

"Money. Hell, man, Billy didn't have any money."

Dean smiled. "Oh, but he did. Found nearly twenty thousand in his closet. Cash."

Alex's eyes darted a look at Dean and then Guthrie. He pushed and rubbed his thumb on the table. "News to me. I should've had him pick up the tab more often."

The knocking on the door broke the conversation. Guthrie got up, opened the door, leaned out, and then leaned back in. To Dean, he said, "We're needed."

Dean nodded. He looked at Alex. "Something's still not right about your story. I'll find it out." He got up and walked out into the hallway, closing the door behind him. He found himself face-to-face with tall and heavy-set District Attorney Henry D. Smith, Alex's father.

A full head of dark brown hair, vibrant green-brown eyes, and a mustache that cascaded down the side of his lips, Henry wore a gray suit, white shirt, and red tie with tiny gray anchors. He gestured to the door. "Let my son out. He's not to talk to you without a lawyer. Me. Did you read him his rights?"

Dean looked at his father, who stood beside Henry. Eric shrugged. Guthrie had taken up a spot outside the triangle. Dean scratched his head. "Your son's not under arrest. He's cooperating in the William Nimitz murder investigation."

"So that's a no."

Dean nodded. "Are you here as the DA or as his father?"

Eric said, "He's here as a concerned father."

"Okay, then, but Alex is an adult, and he can talk to us if he wants."

Henry's eyes narrowed. "Then I'm here as the DA. Let him go. He's not your guy."

"Have you reviewed the case file?"

Henry ignored the question and walked past Dean and opened the interview room door. "Come on. You're done here."

Alex walked out and down the hallway, followed by his father. Dean grabbed Alex's arm as he passed. "What happened to your face?"

He pulled his arm from Dean's grip.

"So why'd you show up at the Shambles the night of Billy's death at near midnight?"

Alex's eyes snapped up and met Dean's. Henry grabbed his son's arm and jerked him away.

Dean felt the cold January air rush through as father and son exited the station. Josh and Corey were absent. Etheridge shrugged and pointed in the direction Henry and Alex had just followed.

To Dean, it felt as if his case—as meager and absent as it was—walked out behind them.

CHAPTER 24

A s the door closed behind Henry Smith, the case ran out of paths to follow. Dean could continue to poke at Josh's and Corey's statements, but the threat of a lie detector, the whole staging of the three at the station at the same time had not produced—had never had time—the necessary cracks to wedge open the wider story. The detectives would not be able to shock them again, and now they had practice.

Dean wrote up his reports on the interviews, answering Barry Archer's return call during that task and telling him not to bother. Guthrie and Dean looked through the small amount of information Laura was able to obtain. McCord had a few speeding tickets over the years but no other arrests. The State Police had never investigated McCord or McCord's Body Shop. After a quick lunch from Burger Palace, Guthrie and Dean extended their working Sunday and drove over to McCord's estate. They pulled into the the long driveway and walked to the covered porch. As Dean raised his hand to knock, the door opened. McCord held it with one hand and smiled at the two detectives. He wore gray slacks, black dress shoes, and a white button up shirt, loosened at the collar and exposing the white undershirt.

McCord coughed into his hand and then said, "Good afternoon. What are you doing here?"

Dean extended his hand and held it for a second before pulling it back. McCord had not even thought about shaking it. Dean said, "Sorry to bother you, but we wanted to ask a few more questions about William."

"Okay."

"May we come in?" asked Guthrie.

McCord's eyes brightened and his smile changed to a smirk. "I'm afraid not. We'll have to do it here." He gestured back into the house. "The wife's cooking Sunday dinner, and some family are over."

Dean glanced back at the driveway. His Nova was the only car in it. "It's damned cold out here. We can be quiet."

"Sorry fellas." McCord stepped onto the porch and closed the door behind him. "I'll stand out here with you though."

"Sure. Sure. We'll try to make this quick." Dean had to go along with it. It turned up his suspicions of McCord, but he got the sense that did not matter to the body shop owner. "I'll just come out and say it, then. Were you aware of any illegal drug activities that William was engaged in?"

"Billy and drugs?" McCord tilted his head back and looked down at Dean. "Seriously. Billy was about as clean as they come. Nice kid. Tried to do the right thing. If that kid was involved in illegal drug stuff, then my mom's the godfather of Zion."

"What about Alex, Alex Smith?"

"What about him?"

"Do you know him?"

"Course I do. Small town. He's a brat."

"Did he ever stop by the shop?"

"Yeah. He and Billy were friends. Why I don't know. I guess when you're making friends at that age, you don't think of what assholes they'll become later."

Guthrie started bouncing up and down on his toes. "Seems like you know Alex a lot better than just in passing?"

McCord looked over at Guthrie. He sniffed. His nose was turning red. "You remember jerks like that."

"Was he in the drug trade?" asked Dean.

"Why all these questions about drugs?"

The authenticity of McCord's question fell flat. Dean was convinced right then and there that Zorn was not the only trafficker in town. He may not have had anything to do with Billy's murder, but he had bought this mansion with drug money. Dean ignored McCord's question. "When we saw you a few days ago, we forgot to ask about where you were at the night William disappeared. So where were you?"

McCord raised his hand and pointed to the door behind him. "I come home every night. The wife and I were probably watching TV. We usually do."

"Did Billy have any trouble with any of the other employees?"

"No. We all liked him."

Dean knew the momentum in the interview had shifted to McCord, and he was not going to get it back. "Did you have a fight with Alex on Friday?"

"I'm done. I'm cold, and I need to get inside." McCord turned his back on them and took two steps to the door. He looked back and said, "Be safe out there."

Dean knew he had scored a hit of some kind, but what it meant was still a mystery. The door closed, the weather stripping sliding across the stone entryway. The two detectives hustled back to the car and drove away.

As he warmed up, Dean was even more frustrated. He had learned new information, but how it meshed—if at all—to the murder of Billy was unclear. They had the car. The gun, which the lab confirmed launched the bullet lodged in the tree behind Billy's bloody skull. The money. *The Communist Manifesto.* Pawned jewelry. Two drug traffickers. It all added up to a bunch of questions.

And the days passed. Winter's clutch loosened, and Jenny went back to her mom's and her "real" life in the city. The town quietly forgot about Billy, except his parents, who called every Wednesday at nine a.m. to see if any new developments had happened since the last call. Dean told them every time, "No." He said it wearingly, worried that he would always have to say, "No," to answers in this case. He drank extra on Wednesday mornings.

As the town thawed, so too did the crime. Guthrie investigated several more break-ins as they entered March. Dean pitched in, but his heart was not in it. He kept going back to Billy, his body left just after the new year began out in that clearing at the Pratt farm.

He drove by the farm at least once a week, slowing down and contemplating the lonely death, knowing all deaths were in the end lonely, but not being any sadder by that fact. He walked and searched the spot and the clearing where Billy died, hoping for a new clue, a new thread that might lead him to the killer.

He had driven by the Pratt farm in high school, when he was courting Cindy. One night, she had even snuck out of the house and met him, and they drove to a teenage hideout in the woods. They may have even been in Canada, which they joked about for years until their marriage fell apart. They made love—the first time for both of them. They were young, amateurs, awkward, but it was the best night of his life. Everything after was compared to that. He learned only years later that the site was not secret from the police, and Cindy had confessed to her parents within days. Wayne turned cold to him, but never told him he knew or why.

Then the war wrecked it. His life, his marriage, his country. Like the huts of nameless people in Vietnam, his life caught fire, and he was left with only ash.

He buried his grief in drink and Sadie. She smiled at him and told him he was perfect, and he ignored that he paid her, tried to believe what she said was real. The drink helped with that.

Tony visited one night. They sat on the front porch in the first evening warm enough to be comfortable, or force themselves to be comfortable wearing jackets and hats.

"I'm surprised to see you," said Dean. "I mean, it's what, weeks since you've been here."

Tony shrugged. He seemed much younger to Dean than he actually was. He still had his athletic build. His face unmarked by gravity, where Dean's had begun to show, if only just. Tony smiled and drank from the Pabst Blue Ribbon can. "I avoid Zion if I can." The age difference was not about the churn of time, the incessant pull of gravity, or blind luck. Instead, it was in their experiences that told on them somehow, that served as a map of their paths through life.

Dean nodded. "I wish I could." He rocked in the aluminum, blue and white plastic lawn chair. "You avoid Dad, though, that's what you're doing."

"Isn't he Zion? But you know we have détente there." A thaw had been underway for some weeks.

They talked about work. Tony was cryptic, as most FBI guys are about their cases. He was a lot like the other G-men Dean had worked with in the past, particularly New York, but he lacked the superiority complex. "Do you know what I do?"

Dean cracked open another beer he pulled from the cooler beside him and handed it to Tony and then opened another for himself. "You're a lawyer for the FBI."

"Well, yeah, dip shit. But do you know what I do for them?"

"I assumed you helped ready the cases they brought to trial."

"Yeah, that's the gist of it. But I guess I'm not making myself clear. I work with the counter-intelligence team. I help prepare cases against Americans or foreign agents working on American soil. Make sure they get to the prosecutors ready to go."

"Huh. Does it keep you busy?"

"More than you'd like. But I wish I were in the field."

Dean sat with this, wondering about how many foreign agents—spies—were in the U.S. "Like spy stuff?"

Tony nodded. "We've got more than enough people in this country willing to betray it to the Soviets."

"No surprise there."

"Maybe." Tony got up and walked inside.

Dean sat there until he returned, contemplating his brother. The middle child scorned by his parents, though the scorn was really only their father's. Now working for the government, living not far from their hometown, but far enough. After Tony came back out and sat down, Dean asked, "Seriously, though, why today? Why are you on my porch right now?"

Tony took a drink. "Last week, a mentor of mine at the Bureau had a heart attack in the office."

"Jesus. I'm sorry."

"Thanks. It was awful. Died right there on the spot. Died surrounded by work and broken relationships. I thought to myself that's not how I want to go. I don't want broken things in my life." Tony tugged at his pants. "I don't want that."

Dean waited for his brother to continue, but the pause was long and he began to think about it in terms of a police interview. He decided to ride it out, to let Tony tell him whatever it was that was still lingering there at his own pace.

Tony downed the rest of the can. "Another?"

"Only if you spend the night here."

Tony nodded and Dean opened the cooler and grabbed another, which he handed to him. His brother cracked it open. "Thanks."

Dean acknowledged the thought by raising his can.

"So I've got broken relationships. Some bad. Some worse than that. I started trying to fix them with Mom and Dad, but I want to get there faster. So you're next."

"Me? Why me?"

His brother laughed.

"Ours is the least broken." Dean leaned back in the chair.

Tony tipped his can in salute. "Glad you feel that way. I always worried you thought like Dad."

"Shit. You had a better understanding than I did of what was going on over there. Anyone with a lick of sense would've stayed out of that jungle."

They continued to talk, moving inside as the cool became cold. Dean shared with Tony some of his experiences, which he only loosened up about with the addition of whiskey. He told him of his unit's long hump across the Long Ho Valley and up the Quang Ho ridge. Told him about Lee and Rider and Stitch and Paxton. How they had marched and macheted their way from map point to map point, directed by commanders who seemed to have no sense of the reality of the terrain, of how hard and long it took to march a mile.

He told him of the battle of Quang Ho, on a hill designated 425. It was a battle like so many battles, but it was his battle. And all along, as he was telling Tony, he could not think of why, after all these years, his brother would be the first family member to hear this story. He had shared it a number of times with other Vietnam vets, ones who had been in the thick of things, knew what combat in those jungles and on those hills meant. Not Cindy. Not his dad. No, his brother Tony, the one who had deferred service.

Dean had never been more alive than during that battle. An army company had been ambushed as they were in the valley between hills 425 and 427. The company had established a perimeter to hold off the attacks. More importantly, low cloud cover prevented any air support. Only the marines were close enough to come to their aid until the Hueys and Phantoms could fly in.

And so Dean and his pals, Kilo Company, marched and then charged hill 425, which turned out to have an entrenched ring of NVA bunkers. Machine gun by machine gun they grenaded and shot and stabbed their way to the top. Losing Stitch and Paxton and others. Dean's platoon, the first, and was told to hold the mountain top while second and third platoons worked their way to the army guys still down in the valley. Before they got there, the cloud cover lifted—at least long enough for the helicopters to evacuate the army and drop off artillery on hill 425 while the napalm burned the enemy on 427. Dean's platoon had blown the top off the mountain to flatten it for that artillery.

Kilo Company held the hill for two days against counterattacks, were bombed mercilessly with mortar fire, watched jets—two times the cloud cover lifted to allow them—napalm again the NVA lines, and heard the screaming of burning men alive above the roar of jets and fire. Dean held the hands of his comrades dying before the helicopters could swoop in and save them.

Drunk, the two brothers eventually wearied themselves into silence. When Dean woke the next morning, heart throbbing and mouth dry, Tony was gone. A small note on the kitchen counter read, "Thanks."

CHAPTER 25

March 21, 1979

Drizzle dropped from the nearly uniform gray clouds. Tall maples, birches, and ashes were just budding, and the scenery alongside the road would have been desolate had it not been for the green of the firs and spruces. He flicked the wiper button every so often to wipe away the dots of water that piled up. He had just left the home of Gary Swan. Reggie had driven by for a check in when Gary's manager at Adamson's had reported him absent and did not know who else to call. Reggie had kicked in the door and radioed Dean the moment he was inside.

Gary had died in his recliner, the TV still on. When Cotton arrived, both Dean and Reggie agreed with the coroner that Gary had passed due to natural causes. The three of them put Gary into the coroner's van. After Cotton left, Reggie and Dean searched the house for any information regarding next of kin. Dean knew Gary's parents had died a few years before, but he did not know if he had any siblings or cousins. The effort proved fruitless. The probate courts would have to figure out what to do next. They boarded up the door before leaving.

Dean drove aimlessly through town and then back. He found himself on Route 23. He stopped at a 7-11 and picked up a cold ham and cheese sandwich with a small bag of Fritos and a six-pack of cold Pabst Blue Ribbon. He drove out to the Pratt farm and pulled off to the side of the road across from their driveway. The call with the Nimitz's that morning had been the same depressing conversation. No new leads. No new evidence. He could not bring himself to tell them the case was due to be shelved into cold case storage next week. After the conversation, he had opened the case file. He was halfway through it when the call from Reggie had come in.

He shut off the car and rolled down the window. He unwrapped the sandwich and freed a can of the beer, opening it. From beneath the rest of the six pack, he pulled out the Nimitz case file.

Dean pulled out his notebook from his front pocket and a pen. He flipped to a blank page. He wrote down the short list of evidence. Twenty thousand in cash and a copy of *The Communist Manifesto* in Billy's closet. Why both? He added a question mark next to both items. He thought of Renard's quip. He wrote spy next to both and added yet another question mark.

The thirty-eight with six bullets in it that once belonged to Corey and his grandfather.

That left the Remington M1911A pistol. Last known owner was Dennis Kowlowski who died in 1963. He bought it in 1952. What happened once he bought it was unknown. He scratched his head and took a drink.

The sandwich was dry, so Dean tore open the mayonnaise and mustard packets and squeezed their contents to the underside of the top bun. They did not save the sandwich, but he ate it anyway. The sandwich mirrored his list: lots of promise but not much living up to it. He went back to the case file and his notebook. The passports were confusing, for no one had ever mentioned Billy traveling, and they were not in his possession. And drug dealers did not usually resort to that kind of passport forgery, at least those bringing their haul across the Canadian-U.S. border.

He flipped to another blank page and divided it up into a set of columns, a task he had done a half-dozen times already. On the far left, he wrote "Time" and then added columns to the right for each of his suspects: Sarah, Carlos, Alex, Corey, Josh, McCord, and Zorn. He added yet a final column next to Zorn and put a question mark there.

Billy was at the Shambles from six to about eleven-thirty, so he wrote "11:30" in the far right. He noted Sarah, Carlos, Alex, and McCord all claimed to be home, but only Carlos and McCord had anyone to vouch for them, albeit, their wives. Corey and Josh both said they left Billy walking and went home immediately, but they did have not alibis saying when they arrived home. Zorn claimed to be at the club with fellow Grim Devils member Quentin Trask, which Trask had confirmed to Guthrie. At midnight—according to the phone records it was 11:58 p.m.—Sarah received a call from Billy. They talked for a few minutes, and that was the last known interaction with Billy before his death. Dean scratched his head. On the previous page, he wrote "Drugs?" next to the cash.

He looked at his watch: 4:13. He wadded up the sandwich and chip packaging into a bundle and drove back into town. At the 7-11, he threw them away and called Sadie from a pay phone. She was free until seven, and she would be happy to see him.

⚬⚬⚬

As he buckled his belt, she smiled at him and held a Virginia Slim in her right hand. She inhaled. The rain began slashing in from the southwest, drenching the window in sheets and thumping the roof.

He smiled back, but she noticed the weakness of the smile. "What's wrong, baby?" she asked.

"Huh? Oh, nothing. Just thinking about this case."

"That's why you're here, to not think about work."

He winked at her. "I wasn't while." He turned on the lamp on the nightstand.

"Is it that Billy kid again?"

He nodded as he pulled out a cigarette and lit it. "Yep. Reviewed the case again today."

"And?"

He looked at her and considered if he should tell her anything. He would have told Cindy everything, even though she hated it. "It's just bothering me. That we haven't solved it yet."

"It was months ago though."

"Yeah, that's what's eating at me. So little information. And contradictory. You know, the Canadian police found some things in Montreal that don't make a lot of sense. Unless you're a drug dealer or a spy. And I don't get the sense this kid was capable of being a spy. And no one thinks he was into drug trafficking. And what the hell's to find in Zion?"

She slid her long legs over the side of the bed and stood up, smiling as she did so. She grabbed the thin robe on the chair next to the bed and pulled it on, her nipples still visible through it. "Spy? In Zion?"

"I know, right?"

"Drink?"

He nodded, and she walked out. He buttoned up his shirt. He sat on the edge of the bed, and as he reached down to grab his shoes, he used the nightstand for balance. His grip slipped, and he clutched at the handle on the drawer to the stand, which he pulled out a little as he sat back up, left shoe in his right hand. Through the gap of the drawer, he saw a notebook. He looked at it. He knew what it was without opening it. He thought about pulling it out and looking at it, seeing who else visited her. If she had other regulars like him. But he did not. He knew she did. He knew he was not special. He slid it closed and started putting on his shoe.

Sadie walked in and handed him a drink. Bourbon with two large ice cubes.

"Thanks." He took a drink and set it on the table. "It's probably drug stuff. Everything these days seems that way."

She held a vodka tonic in her hands. "Seems that way."

"I figure if we can find out who Billy was transporting drugs for, we'll find his killer."

"You think he was transporting?"

"I don't see him running a dealing business. Not with Zorn in town. I could see him driving the stuff from Canada down for some extra cash."

She smiled, but it was a smile he had rarely seen on her, one that allowed a glimpse beyond her facade into the woman she really was. "You know, more than Zorn and his goons transport drugs in this town."

"Yeah, like who?" He asked it without thinking, just a normal question, but he could tell immediately that it cut through something, like he had crossed a threshold not meant to be crossed between a hooker and her john, especially when her john was a cop. "Nevermind. Sorry."

She nodded once and took a drink.

He downed the last of his bourbon quickly, setting the glass down on the table, the ice tinkling.

CHAPTER 26

Dean pulled into his parents' driveway deep into the evening. They were probably having dinner, but he needed to talk to someone about the case, and his dad was someone he could talk through theories with, no matter how crazy, and someone who would understand his desire to answer the questions still unanswered. As he walked up to the front door, he looked back to the street and recognized Tony's car. He pulled open the storm door part of the way and knocked and then opened the door.

"Hello?" said Eric.

"It's me, Dad." Dean closed the doors behind him and walked toward the sound of his dad's voice, which seemed to flow along the smells of steak and au gratin potatoes.

His mom and dad and Tony were all sitting around the dining room table. Small pool of bloody oil on Tony's plate. Eric jamming the cut side of a roll onto the plate and mopping up the grease and leftover cheese. The fat of the steak separated and piled off to the side on Jessica's. She smiled and stood up. "Let me get you a plate."

He nodded. "Thanks." He sat next to Tony, patting him on the shoulder as he did.

The t-bone was extra well done, as his parents had always made it—except for Tony—crispy on the outside with a distinct, thick char. Tony and Eric had already collected the crispy parts of the au gratin, a prized portion of the meal since he had been a kid. Enough so fights often erupted for the last bit, forcing Eric to claim it for himself or Jessica. The spinach was plain, so Dean added salt and pepper. The whole meal was reminiscent of the early Sixties, down to their seating. Only the empty chair across from Dean reminded them that it was not.

With beers in hand, the men remained at the table as Jessica cleared the plates.

Dean pointed back and forth between Eric and Tony. "So you two mended finally?"

"A work in progress," said Tony. "A work in progress."

Eric nodded.

"Good. Good. So, Dad, I wanted to pass some things by you about the Nimitz case."

"It's been a while."

"Yep." Dean looked at Tony.

Eric said, "It's all right. He can listen."

Tony gave him a thumbs up.

Dean shrugged. "So after the busted interviews, I keep going over things. Trying to find a new angle."

"Who are the players?" asked Tony.

"A lot of them, but we've got Alex Smith."

"The DA's kid?"

"That's the one." Eric gulped his beer.

"Yeah, well, he's one of them," continued Dean. "He and William's girlfriend, Sarah, had a few nights together. Plus it seems Alex is somehow involved in the drug trade. Not sure. You've also got Charlie McCord. Definitely making his money beyond what the body shop is bringing in. Then you have Paul Zorn—the other end of the drug trade stick. And maybe the girlfriend's father. For evidence, we've got the pistol that fired the shots, with its dead end in the Sixties. Twenty thousand in cash and *The Communist Manifesto* in Billy's closet. And the trove of passports and cash found with the body in Montreal."

Tony gave him questioning look, so Dean told him about his trip to see Renard.

"Billy a spy?" Eric's voice was incredulous. He set the can of Budweiser on the table.

Dean nodded his agreement. "I know. Doesn't make much sense. In Zion at least."

Tony leaned in. "Yeah. I studied *The Communist Manifesto* in college. Lots of people did."

"Yeah, but Billy seemed to have no inclination towards study, if you know what I mean?"

"What about his friends? What did they say about him?"

"Generally, nice guy and all that. He seemed like a good employee. Showed up. Did the work. One of his buddies made comments that Billy wasn't all that happy with the work situation. And we know he wasn't putting in overtime, which is what he was telling his parents."

"He was still young, though, right?" asked Eric.

"Twenty-five."

"So maybe he was learning about this stuff. Was getting pinko or something."

Dean took a drink of his beer. "Maybe, but that seems like the convoluted answer. He's a spy. There's not much to spy on here in Zion. I mean, drugs make more sense. Maybe the dead guy in Canada was moving drugs and Billy was one of his drivers. Had passports to help move beyond driving between Canada and the U.S. Flying them in. Or—Billy had mentioned getting out of here with his girlfriend. Heading to Puerto Rico. Maybe he had other ideas. Thought he needed a passport to help him out."

Tony rubbed the back of his neck. "It's not unheard of having someone on the State-side funneling Soviet spies across the border. Someone on this side to give them a bus ticket and stuff."

Dean shook his head. "I don't know. Maybe. But I prefer the simpler answer."

"Occam's Razor you."

"Yeah, that."

"What about his friends and family the day of his disappearance?"

"Two friends alibi each other. One was at home alone—though we know he showed up after Billy left the bar. Shortly after that. Don't know why. His dad stopped us before I could get an answer. His girlfriend was at home alone. Says she talked to Billy around midnight. His parents alibi each other. And Zorn. Well, it's Zorn. Trask alibis him."

"You think the Grim Devils are a part of this?"

"It was a stab in the dark."

"Hell, it was desperation," said Eric. "Mind you, we didn't have anything. Still don't."

"Yeah," said Dean. "We figured if drugs are involved, it's Zorn. But we pressed on the two friends Corey and Josh. They were with Billy the night he disappeared. Josh was acting weird. So we pushed. And Zorn suggested that the other friend, Alex, was not pristine. Which we know, but he made it sound bigger."

"And then Henry blocked everything."

"And then there's McCord."

"I don't buy it, son. I've known Charlie for a while. Seen him at the council meetings. A nice house doesn't mean he's a drug dealer. And why would he kill the kid anyways?"

"Look, I—"

Tony stood up. "Could've seen something he wasn't supposed to." Tony stretched his arms by grabbing his elbows above his head. "Maybe Billy is clean. Works a bit late one night or shows up to pick something up after hours and sees his boss up to no good. Charlie pops him."

Eric grunted. "So you've got a list of suspects, hardly any evidence, and what are you wanting?"

Dean nodded. This is where he wanted to get to the entire evening. "I want to do the surveillance we talked about. I want to sit on Alex. I think he's the key. We sit on him, and we watch him, and he leads us to information. It's our best shot at cracking this. But I need Guthrie at least so we can do twelve-hour shifts."

"Dead ends?"

"Yeah." Dean downed the last of his beer. "His parents call every Wednesday. I can't even tell them we're doing anything actively now."

Tony said, "Makes sense to me. If that doesn't lead you anywhere, you'll have to button up the case."

"It was about to go into cold storage anyways. Just a week. Give me and Guthrie a week of overtime. I'll work it on my own time for my hours."

Eric twisted his lips and pulled at the Budweiser bottle's label. "Screw it. We got nothing else. You and Guthrie can keep an eye on him for a few days. See if he does anything fishy."

Dean said they would start the next day. They all cracked open another beer and the conversation drifted to the goings-on about town, the chief's tolerance of the mayor, and memories of better times. They even toasted to baby-brother Nolan, killed in action, proving the belief that living or dying in a combat zone was often more a matter of luck than skill. Dean had been lucky by that measure of things. Nolan not. But Dean could not let go of the idea that good luck in war meant bad luck at home.

CHAPTER 27

March 22 - April 4, 1979

Parked across the street from Adamson's, Dean and Guthrie had Alex Smith's car in clear sight. Guthrie had left his car nearby and sat with Dean in the chief's personal car, a light gray Caprice Classic Landau Coupe. Dean had borrowed it, knowing Alex had seen Dean's car. He may well have seen the chief's, but not that Dean specifically knew of.

Guthrie handed Dean a black coffee in a styrofoam cup with a plastic lid on top. Dean lifted the lid, took a sip, and set the cup in the plastic cup holder hanging on the door.

"I've never done surveillance before, so what's the drill?" Guthrie looked around for someplace to place the plastic lid on his cup, gave up, and held it in his free hand.

Dean smiled. "Pretty boring really. Sit and watch. Stay awake. Stay alert. If he moves, follow. Be discreet. I'd rather lose him than let him know we're following. Keep track of everything." He tapped the notepad sitting on the seat between them, a pen hooked to its spiral binding. "Have an extra pen?"

Guthrie shook his head.

"Here." Dean had three in his coat pocket, pulled out a blue Bic at random, and gave it to Guthrie. "Record time and people. And if he's driving, include the vehicle make, model, and license.

I'm guessing he'll be driving his own. And note any other things that seem relevant. We're hoping he goes someplace of interest to us. It's only the two of us, so one of us gets the night shift."

"I'll take it." He looked at Dean. "I need a few nights off from the wife. She's on me about fixing stuff around the house. Jesus, I'm just too lazy to do it."

Dean nodded. He looked out the window. He thought Guthrie was seeking a response from him, but he was not sure he wanted to go there. Marriage conversations meant he had to talk about his failed one. In the end, he could not leave his fellow detective hanging out there. "How long you been married?"

"Fifteen years. She's a saint."

Dean chuckled. "Okay. We'll keep her off your back. I'll radio you my location at nine so you can take over."

"I bet you never had that issue."

Dean gave him a closed lip smile. "We had others." He rubbed his fingers across his lips. "Cindy was a saint too. Remember that. They're the saints and we're the morons." He patted Guthrie on the shoulder, who nodded and left the car to go home and sleep in preparation for that night's watch.

And so began a week's long surveillance operation watching Alex go from home to work to the Shambles to home to repeat it all the next day, except on the weekends, when Alex left his parents' home on Saturday night to go to the Shambles. Josh and Corey showed up at the Shambles on Thursday, Friday, and Saturday, but no other days. Sarah never made an appearance. The logs the detectives kept were monotonous. An alternating set of black—Dean's notes—and blue ink—Guthrie's notes. Beyond boring.

After a week, Dean called a temporary halt to the surveillance. The next day, he decided they instead should watch Josh. His behavior previously, his weird statements, added up to something, so Dean thought. Without consulting the chief, they resumed their alternate shifts with a new notebook. Guthrie agreed to work it on his own time, so they did not watch over him during his normal working hours or in the small hours of the night. Guthrie would watch Josh go into the store and report to the station. Dean would arrive around lunch and sit on Josh until the evening. Guthrie would then watch until he was certain the target had called it a night.

Josh worked longer hours and went out less frequently. More boring. After five days, Dean was about to call the whole thing quits, but he decided to give it one more day. He would never know what intuition told him to stick it out one more day. In the end, he was not sure he welcomed it, bittersweet as it turned out to be.

However, Dean did decide to give it that extra day. Josh left work at 2:02 p.m., alone, and in his '76 blue Mercury Cougar, license plate 406-BPH, with a 1978 re-validation sticker.

Josh pulled out of the Bridewell's parking lot and headed north toward High Street, turning east onto it. Not his normal route home. Dean followed a ways behind. As Josh came up to the short jog that split it into two one-way streets—High Street and Clemson Street—he took Clemson. Then past the grain mill's beige and grey siding, where the freight train tracks ran on the southern side, and out beyond town—where Clemson turned into Route 43, into the countryside where the occasional house loomed from a long driveway and fields not yet planted dominated the landscape.

Dean dropped farther behind, worried that being out of Zion exposed him more. A Buick came up behind him, paused, and passed, and he sped up to regain some ground.

Josh drove on Route 43 for ten minutes before turning south onto a small paved road with a leaning, rusting road sign that read 100S. Dean drove past the turn off and double-backed after a mile, turning onto 100S. He drove slowly down the road, past a two-story farm house. A truck was parked in the gravel driveway. After that, the paved road narrowed to a single lane that had not been re-paved for years. The fields gave way to trees, a tall, thick forest of virgin wood: maples, ashes, and birches.

After ten minutes of driving slowly, he saw Josh's car pulled off to the side of the road, in the grass. Dean stopped his car, eased it in reverse, and backed up a quarter of a mile. He pulled off the road and maneuvered the coupe into the woods, hoping it would not be visible should Josh decide to leave.

Dean stayed in the woods but followed the road back to Josh's car. He listened for any sounds beyond the rustle of the trees in the breeze, dropping down from the canopy. With every loud crack, he stopped and looked around. Some animal somewhere, he told himself. About twenty-five yards from Josh's car, he crouched behind a large maple tree.

Josh was not in the car. Dean looked around trying to guess which direction he would have gone, looking for some clue. He reasoned Josh had not walked too far, but what did that mean? By the way Josh had driven out here, he had some purpose and had done it before. Dean retreated back toward his car fifty yards. He would wait for Josh, but he needed to be sure he was out of sight from whatever direction he would return. He leaned against the tree, briefly the image of Billy's body flashing across his mind. He pulled out the flask and took a pull, but he forced himself to not light a cigarette. The old Marine discipline kicking in.

After two hours huddling against the tree and pulling his sport coat around him tight to ward off the chill, he heard voices and then footsteps, though he could not tell from what direction. Crouching behind the tree now, he looked behind him to ensure they were not coming up on him.

The more steps they took and the more they talked, the more he knew his position was secure. He thought back to the car and wished he had camouflaged it better, but too late now. He recognized Josh's voice. The other, a man's voice but just barely audible, he could not make out. Josh and the other man were on the same side of the forest as Josh's car. Wherever they were coming from, it was from the southwest.

"I'm not liking this," said Josh.

The other responded but not loud enough for Dean to make out the words. He peered around the edge of the tree, but they were not yet visible. The sun was getting low in the sky. In the forest, it seemed even darker.

"But what if he does that to us too?" asked Josh.

A reply.

"You don't think so?"

Dean looked toward Josh's car. He saw two men, one of which he knew was Josh though he could not make him out in the dimming light and shadows. One of them opened the trunk and the sound of something—not hard, not heavy but not light either—landing in it.

"You're sure it'll be all right?" asked Josh.

The companion did not reply, but he put his hand on Josh's shoulder and patted it.

"Fine."

Both of them got into Josh's car, who conducted a three-point turn and sped back toward Route 43. As they passed, Dean did not risk exposing himself to see who the passenger might be. Josh did not slow down as they passed his car.

Tempted as he was to head off in the direction Josh had come from, Dean figured it was a fool's errand at this time of day with night approaching and only an initial direction. Josh and his companion may very well have taken many turns. No, better to come back in the morning, with daylight, Guthrie, and a couple from patrol. He walked through the woods back to his car, hugging the edge of the road.

As he drove back to Zion, he contemplated the scene that had just unfolded. He would have bet Josh's companion was Alex but perhaps Corey. And he would have bet they were moving drugs. Perhaps their storehouse was in the woods. Hunches all, but they thrilled him. The chase. The waiting in the darkening woods. The deducing of actions, motives, and people. All of it felt like a wonderful high. He had felt this before. In battle. In New York. If not for this case, he might have forgotten altogether that feeling, a dim memory sinking backward into some daze of a different self.

CHAPTER 28

Sadie dragged her finger down his chest, touching his light chest hair, sending tingles into his shoulders. She took a drag off her cigarette from her other hand as she lay on her stomach with the bedspread covering her legs.

Dean lay on his back and looked at the orange cinder at the end of his cigarette flaring brightly in the room. Frank Morgan's saxophone in "The Nearness of You" filling the space around them. Sadie let her hand rest on his chest.

"You had quite a day."

He raised his head. "Huh?"

"You don't normally take command like that, but you did. You walked in and took me."

"Hmmm."

"I'm serious. I mean, you pay for it, so it's not like you can't take command any old time, but you don't. But today, you did." She turned her head and smiled at him, a glint in her eyes. She was pleased, even proud.

He let his head fall back onto the pillow. "I guess I did. And, yeah, it was a good day."

She sat up and dragged most of the bedspread with her, leaving him exposed. She giggled, grabbed the bottle of Wild Turkey, and sat back down, throwing the cover over him. She patted his crotch and smiled. "There, all covered up again." She offered him the bottle.

He took it and drank some and handed it back to her.

She took a drink. "So don't just sit there and say, 'It was a good day.' What was good about it?"

"I spent the day in the woods." She stared at him. He smiled and then could not hold the laugh back. "I was doing some surveillance. The person went out of town and led me to something. I think it'll be important."

She stabbed the cigarette out in the ashtray on the nightstand. "Like what? What could be that exciting to bring the tiger out of Dean Wallace?"

"I think they've got a drug stash out there." He waved vaguely in the air. "Just a hunch. I'll find out more tomorrow when I go back out there. But that's, that's not what's exciting. It's the—shit. It's what makes this job so exciting at times."

She leaned over and kissed him on the chest. "Well, tiger, we've still got time. Wanna play?"

He nodded and took control.

⚬⚬⚬

When Dean returned home, he opened the refrigerator, hoping to find something he could make to eat. With limited options, he made a sandwich of Wonder Bread, three slices of generic brand bologna, and liberal spread of Miracle Whip. He downed it with a Pabst Blue Ribbon.

He cracked open a second beer to wash the last of the bread down. He picked up the phone and dragged the cord behind him to the kitchen table. He called the station and asked Jim for Guthrie. Jim set the receiver down, shouted at Guthrie, and then transferred Dean without saying a word.

"Hey, I was wondering about you," said Guthrie.

"Sorry I didn't call earlier. Josh actually moved today beyond the normal."

"And I missed it. Damn."

"It was in the afternoon. He left the store and took Forty-Three out to road One Hundred S. Drove past a farm house and beyond where the paved road ended. He disappeared for a couple of hours and came back with somebody I couldn't ID, and then left."

"What do you think it is?"

"I'm guessing they have a drug stash out there."

"They need two hours to get to and from? They're probably growing it."

"Maybe. But I think we need to check it out. Let's you, me, and maybe Etheridge go out there tomorrow." Dean rubbed his finger along the edge of the telephone's case. "See if we can find it."

"You don't know where it is exactly?"

"No idea other than a general direction. But I think we'll find it."

"Who do you think it was with Josh?" The sound of a lighter.

"I couldn't ID him."

Guthrie let out the smoke. "Yeah, but you have a guess."

Dean smiled. "Yeah. I do. I'd bet it was Alex."

⚜

Dean took a shower and put on a pair of jeans and a t-shirt. He lit a cigarette as he flipped through his records, wondering what he wanted to listen to. He decided to stick with jazz. He debated between Sonny Rollins and John Coltrane. He decided on Sonny's *Saxophone Colossus*. The Caribbean vibe of "Saint Thomas" filled the room. He sat down on the couch and cracked open another beer.

As the drum solo hit the cymbals, a knock on the door took Dean out of his reverie. He left the music on and loud as he opened the door to his brother.

"Hey there," said Tony with a smile.

Dean turned sideways and gestured for Tony to come in. As Tony walked past, Dean said, "Welcome." He followed his brother in, stopped by the fridge, grabbed a beer, and tossed it to Tony. He sat down on the couch as Dean turned down the stereo.

Tony tapped the top of the can. "I thought I'd swing by. My continuing efforts."

Dean raised his beer. "To continuing efforts."

Tony opened his, raised it, and quickly drank the froth that came out of the top.

"How's that going, by the way?"

Tony slumped into the couch beside his brother. "Pretty well actually. I think Mom has a lot to do with that. Buttering him up and whatnot."

He had been making an effort to visit them once a week, and when he was unable to do so, he made sure he called. They had never, of course, gotten to the root of their long disagreement. But that was like his family. Just bury any unpleasantness, any strife as if it had never happened, though the tense words, the sullen quietness all showed through nonetheless. In this case, the years had done much of the work of burying the painful memories.

Dean said, "I understand not speaking to Dad all those years, but why didn't you ever come around here? You just disappeared."

Tony was silent for a while, scratching the front of his chin. "I always thought Dad's response to Nolan's death was over-the-top. Not in terms of his grief. No. Not that. I'm talking about his response to those around him. He shunned me. Practically disowned me. I was easy to deal with from his perspective. I'm the son who didn't do his duty. You." He wagged a finger at Dean. "You, though, were an entirely different issue for Dad. You're the good son. Served your country. And then Nolan gets killed, and you're the reminder. The son who lived who every day reminded him—Dad—of his sacrifice. You were the scab that never healed. I was the scar."

"Great. I never thought of myself as the scab. No one likes a scab." Dean drank the last of his beer. "I'm a reminder to myself. I can't escape this skin."

Tony smiled. "So my banishment was from the family. Not because you wanted it, but because Dad wanted it. He wanted me to feel the shame, to feel his disgust." Tony's eyes began to well up. "And because of that, I never forgave myself for having skipped the war. I couldn't face you. I was too ashamed."

Dean nodded and got up and grabbed two more beers. He sat back on the couch and handed his brother one of them. "You didn't skip the war. No one did. You just lived a different horror." He thought of their youthful years, thought of the evening when they played kick-the-can with a bunch of the neighborhood kids. Sometime in the Sixties, not long after Kennedy was killed. The Wallace brothers had always played as a team, and that night was no different. Huddled under a copse of pines at the Jordan house and about a hundred yards from the can, a duo from the "it" team had left behind a sole protector and a half dozen other kids were in jail—the Copley's front porch.

The brothers had formed a plan: Dean and Tony would be the bait and Nolan would race to kick over the can and free a prisoner. The two older brothers darted from beneath the pine trees, startling the "it" team, who ran after them. Dean and Tony sprinted straight for the can—an empty Folger's tin— hoping to get the guard to commit chasing after them. Nolan darted out from cover.

Tony glanced behind him and saw only one pursuer and called out to Dean to continue on. And the sound of four footsteps behind Dean dropped to two, but he did not know if his brother was behind him or the opposing player. He dared not glance back. He later learned Tony had saved Nolan from capture by doubling back to Nolan, who was almost caught. As Dean led the guard away, Tony and Nolan circled back to the can. A few yards ahead of the youngest Wallace, Tony threatened the jail, forcing the pursuers to divert their attention to him again, giving Nolan the valuable seconds and space to free a prisoner, kicking the can with a ferociousness that permanently ended its career.

In Dean's memory, Tony had always seemed to be the protector. Dean had done what was needed to be done. Dutiful. More than once, Tony had dealt with a couple of guys who bullied Nolan. Dean had reported them to the principal, expected the system to administer justice. Nothing out of the ordinary, but then, the Wallace boys were a force.

Dean shared the kick-the-can memory with Tony, who remembered it as Dean being the hero. Tony shook his head as he recounted from his vantage point how Dean had burst out at full speed from beneath the trees and screamed to get the pursuers' attention. How he sprinted and in that wake took the bulk of the risk, allowing Tony to retreat back, save Nolan, and let them free the prisoner.

They drank their beers and listened to the last notes of "Blue 7" and then silence.

With Nolan gone, they felt like a diminished version of themselves without any way to recover.

CHAPTER 29

April 5, 1979

Dean drove the Nova with Guthrie in the passenger seat down 100S. He found the approximate spot where Josh had parked his car. Etheridge, along with Reggie, pulled to a stop behind them.

A rain storm had rolled through overnight. The first thunderstorm of the spring. The thunder had sounded distant even with the thumping of the rain on the roof and the flashes of sheet lightning strobing the rooms.

A dampness hung everywhere in the forest, still dripping off the leaves, making stepping a squishy endeavor. The temperature had dropped along with the rain, and all four were wearing Zion Police jackets. Dandelions had seeded overnight.

Dean told them they were looking for anything that looked like it could stash drugs. Containers, trash bags, a hole beneath a large rock, whatever. But he thought it would be obvious. So they fanned out with Dean taking a leading spot to get them going in the direction he believed Josh went to and came from. As they started walking, the four drifted apart, eventually losing sight of each other, so much so, Dean felt as if he were all alone.

The forest floor heaved with leaves and tall grasses and brush. Thrushes and sparrows sang and bounced from tree to tree.

He even saw a bright red bird he thought was a scarlet tanager. It darted from one limb to another and disappeared in the throng of branches.

The family cabin on Lake Tonga had long been a place with pleasant memories for Dean, but it had been years since he had been there. Of all the bad decisions he had made in life, he had almost made his worst that last evening. He had taken a boat out to fish that day. His number was coming up in the draft. The choice, for him, had not been one of evading the dreaded lottery by any of the legitimate deferments available to him—the path Tony took just two years later. For Dean, the choice was between serve or flee. He had taken the boat out to fish not thinking—at least not consciously—of the Canadian border that cut across the lake. He may have crossed into the country without knowing it. But when he had realized how close it was, that Canada was within reach, that he could avoid the war he did not want to fight in, he almost took it. It would have been an easy out, even a way to avoid his parents.

He must have sat on that lake for an hour, staring at Canada before rowing back to the cabin on Lake Tonga. He joined the Marines the next day.

Guthrie's shout of "Over here" awoke Dean from his memories.

He worked his way over to Guthrie, with Etheridge and Reggie catching up. "Well shit," said Dean. Two school buses, still yellow beneath the dirt and leaves that had fallen on the roofs and hoods, sat in a V—one along a southwest-northeast axis and the other on the southwest-northwest axis—beside two large trees, the bark thick from their decades of growth. The Zion High School lettering was visible along the side of each bus. Bus numbers 22 and 40.

"This what we're looking for?" Guthrie smiled, holding out his hands and gesturing to the buses.

The four of them circled the buses, checking the surrounding brush for anything out of the ordinary. Reggie found what looked to be a dump site with trash bags of beer and Coke cans, empty bags of chips, cigarette packs, and so on. Etheridge had been smart enough to bring a camera, and he took several photos, and they left the dump site, knowing they would return later to gather it.

"We need to get a forensics team out here," said Guthrie.

Dean agreed and had Guthrie head back to the car to radio it in. Reggie put on a pair of driving gloves and pushed open the front door of the bus on the southwest to northeast line. The creak crescendoed through the forest, startling a flock of birds from a nearby oak, adding their pounding wings and songs to morning.

Reggie stepped aside to let Dean step in. Etheridge followed him. The smells—sweet, corrosive, dangerous—of a variety of chemicals filled the place despite the cracked windows. All seats but the driver's, which had packages of rubber gloves and surgical masks stacked, had been removed. A set of small card tables—not one matched the other—and a short bookshelf lined the side of the bus to the back, where an old claw-foot bathtub sat.

Glassware that looked like it came from the high school chemistry rooms, tubing, milk bottles filled with what looked like water, jugs of white, brown, and gray bottles with chemical names. A brown, well-used couch, and a small generator, with a hose from the exhaust taped and stretched to one of the open windows.

Etheridge looked at him and shook his head. This was bigger than just distributing drugs. Josh and company were making them. And not growing a few marijuana plants. This was a serious operation. Dean rattled off the drugs he knew about and nothing correlated with what he was seeing, but that did not necessarily mean much. Dean had smoked marijuana a bit in Vietnam before the military cracked down and opened the way for heroin. The crime lab people would have to tell him what he was dealing with.

"Let's leave everything and check out the second bus," said Dean.

The first bus was the lab and the second bus the warehouse. Dean stopped just inside the door with Etheridge and Reggie standing outside. More bottles and jugs. And three boxes of canned Green Giant Green Beans filled with sandwich-size Ziploc bags of yellowish powder. Dean picked up one of the bags.

He heard the grunt before he heard the shot. Heard it before one of the bus's windows shattered. Then the sound of the bullet being fired. He ducked, pocketed the Ziploc bag, and moved as fast as he could to the door. Outside, Reggie was holding his stomach and stumbling back. Etheridge, standing next to the front wheel, looked back at Reggie.

The third shot kicked up grass at Reggie's right foot. Etheridge had his pistol out and was scanning the woods. Reggie fell over, his eyes wide with fear, his hand to his gut, where blood came out.

Dean landed on the grass next to Etheridge. A fusillade came. Two guns. One with the familiar pop of the M16. Grass kicked up, bark splintered, more windows shattered. The shots were coming from the other side of the buses, through the gap at the base of the V they formed.

Reggie's heels kicked at the ground. Dean nodded at Etheridge, who nodded once back. Both lifted their pistols over the hood of the bus, fired several shots at random. A pause in the fusillade. Etheridge reached over and fired again as Dean crouched low and jogged for Reggie. He grabbed his foot and pulled hard, dragging him to the cover of the bus.

"Jesus," shouted Etheridge.

Dean looked down at Reggie, whose eyes were clenched shut and his hands, covered with blood, clutched at his stomach. "We'll get you out of here. Hold on." He looked back at Etheridge. "We have to get out of here."

Reggie let out a scream.

More gunfire. Two guns again.

"No disagreement. How?" Etheridge raised his pistol around the side of the bus and fired off two shots in the general direction he thought the shooting came from.

The sound of breaking glass. A flash of light and fire in the first bus. An engulfing inferno almost immediately. Orange and yellow flames whipping out of the windows. Tinges of blue. Dark, thick smoke churning out of the windows. More glass cracking and breaking—as if all the world's glass were blasting apart at that very moment.

"We run. I've got Reggie."

Dean holstered his pistol, reached down and grabbed Reggie's arms, pulling them over his left shoulder. He bent down and got Reggie's torso over his back and stood up with his legs.

Reggie's blood flowed down Dean's back as he jogged, weaving back and forth in the hopes of making a more difficult target. Etheridge followed and turned around and fired a few covering shots as they retreated. The second bus lit up like a torch after they had moved about fifty yards. The gunfire had let up, but they did not slow down.

When Dean had carried his comrades like this, he had been much younger and much more fit, but the adrenaline kept pumping now just as it did then. Guthrie ran into them half way back. He was sweating and his pistol was out. The gunfire had stopped some time before, but Etheridge had nearly shot their fellow officer in surprise.

"What the hell's going on?" said Guthrie. He saw then that Dean was carrying Reggie. "Shit."

At the cars, Guthrie called on the radio for back up. Dean set Reggie down against the patrol car's front passenger tire. He felt for a pulse. None. Blood soaked the officer's shirt and pants. He laid Reggie on his back and started CPR. He cracked a couple of Reggie's ribs doing so. He pushed on his chest until he heard the sirens. Guthrie and Etheridge standing over him.

Dean stopped and sat down against the car. He felt Reggie's blood on his back and legs and hands. Another body he had carried out of the forest to see go into a body bag. Another life snuffed out of existence. He wondered, again, as he took a drink from his flask, if life had any point other than pain and disappointment.

CHAPTER 30

After the ambulance took Reggie away, covered by a sheet on the gurney, Dean, Guthrie, Etheridge, the chief, and the lab guys had to wait hours for the fire to burn itself out. A band of volunteer firefighters held positions near the buses to contain the blaze from moving beyond the immediate vicinity.

The inferno served as a background as they and the state police and sheriff deputies searched the woods behind the buses for clues about the shooters. They found some Budweiser cans and shell casings forty yards away. Just looking at them, Dean knew they were from an M16.

A deputy found more shell casings—.30-30 rounds—beneath a tree some fifty yards away. More Budweiser cans. And a brown bag with a half-eaten turkey sandwich. On the bag, written with a black marker was the word, "Lunch."

The chief pulled out a pair of jeans and a Syracuse sweatshirt from the trunk of his car. "Son, you need to get out of those clothes." Dean glared at his father and shook his head. The clothes were placed in the trunk. Everything else was photographed and bagged.

"So?" asked Eric, his arms crossed and the muscle at the back of his left jaw tensing.

Dean described their walk into the woods, the finding of the buses, and then the ambush. That's how he began characterizing it. The bad guys did not just stumble into the police and start taking shots. They had waited. Drank a few beers for courage, even eaten a sandwich.

"That begs the question." Eric took off his glasses and rubbed the bridge of his nose.

"How'd they know we were coming?" asked Guthrie.

Eric nodded.

"Not many people knew we were coming out here. Josh might have caught one of us tailing him, but I don't think so. But it's possible," said Dean. And the idea of Josh sitting in the woods with a gun and taking shots at cops did not seem plausible. "But I don't think it was Josh or Alex—or the guy I think was Alex. No. Those two are making this, but I don't think they're going to shoot at us." He pulled out the Ziploc and tossed it to his dad.

Eric caught and opened it. "This looks like methamphetamine. Meth. They call it speed and crank, as well."

Dean nodded. He had heard of it. Speed was common enough in Vietnam. He knew many guys who took it to stay awake during watches. But it had always been in pill form. Not this powder.

Eric continued, "Some other New York jurisdictions have been talking about it. Popular outside the cities 'cause coke is so expensive. Cheap and easy to make. Very flammable. I guess it's hit our area."

"Used to be legal until, what, the mid-Sixties? Anyways, they're making it here and they're making it for someone."

"Zorn."

"Not sure about that. Could be McCord." Dean shrugged. "Maybe that's how McCord is making inroads. Zorn's been bringing in coke and H. McCord sees an opportunity with this?"

"Do you know Josh came here?"

"I only know he came in this general area. No. I can't say he was exactly here at the buses."

Guthrie asked, "So you think the guys who're buying this stuff from Josh ambushed us?"

"Do you see Josh shooting at us?" Etheridge stood with his legs wide and his arms crossed. "Do you?"

Guthrie shook his head. "No."

Eric handed the Ziploc of meth to one of the lab guys. He turned back to the three of them. "Go home. Rest up. Let's take this on tomorrow. I'll see what we can do to get finger-printing done faster on all that we've found."

Etheridge scratched his chin. "Reggie?"

"I'll do it. I'll let his wife know."

⁂

Dean took a long, hot shower, letting the water run down his back and keeping his eyes closed for a long time as the blood—Reggie's blood—swirled into the drain. He stuffed the bloody clothes into a black trash bag, twisted the top, and knotted it. He stared at the bag before going out to the Nova, popping the trunk, and bringing white and brown evidence bags and tape inside. He left the white bag folded and placed it at the bottom of the brown bag. He took his clothes and put them in the brown bag. Anything that dried and fell off his blood-soaked clothes would be seen on the white bag. He folded the brown bag closed and placed red evidence tape across the seal. He signed and dated the tape. His father was right. He should have let them do this at the scene. But what good would the evidence do anyways? It was his blood. The killers had gotten no where close to him. If the case ever went to court, perhaps some use could be made of it then.

Disgusted, tired, and angry, he poured himself a whiskey and drank it in silence as the afternoon sun gave way to evening. He stared at the walls. Only when he had to urinate did he realize he had been sitting, zombie-like, for two hours.

The doorbell rang. He answered to find his dad on the porch, a pizza box in one hand and a half-case of Pabst in the other. His eyes were still a bit puffy, red.

"You need to eat," he said and barged his way in, though Dean offered little resistance. "I even got you your favorite beer."

As his father grabbed a couple of plates from the counter, Dean cracked open two beers. They ate half the pepperoni and mushroom pizza before Dean said, "Sorry, Dad."

"About what?"

"Today. Getting Reggie killed."

Eric held the slice of pizza halfway to his mouth. "That wasn't your fault, son."

"I should have known. Should have sensed an ambush."

His dad set the pizza down. "This isn't Vietnam or Okinawa. You don't expect ambushes in the woods outside town. This is a tragedy, plain and simple. We'll find the scumbags that did this to Reggie. They better hope I don't find them. They better hope someone else arrests them."

Dean scratched his jaw and bit into the pizza. "It was like the war." He bounced his head back and forth. "Sort of."

Eric opened two more beers and slid one to Dean. "I get that. And we'll get them."

They moved to the couch and turned on the television. NBC had footage of a helicopter flying near Three Mile Island's nuclear plant in better days. The scene shifted to a timeline of the first reported problems to today. The broadcaster said that catastrophe was averted. In other energy news, the President had begun his deregulation of oil prices.

They drank more beers. The world seemed to be collapsing. Nuclear catastrophe. Communist totalitarianism. Meth labs in the woods. But all that mattered at that moment was Reggie. And it felt that way in Vietnam, too. Dean did not care about commies, about the domino theory, about geopolitics, about what chemicals people put into their bodies. He cared about his buddies, his soldiers. He cared if they lived or died and to hell with everything else. And Reggie had died on his watch.

"I will find out who killed Reggie." Dean's tone was laced with anger.

Eric nodded. "I know you will. The troopers wanted this one as well, but I told them it was tied up with the Nimitz investigation. But the DEA might be coming to town."

"They can deal with the drug part." Dean rubbed his temples. "Reggie and Nimitz may not be connected."

"I know. But it keeps the investigation with us. Go after this Josh guy. You said he was the weak link. You got him going out there. You got him leaving with someone. You show up the next day."

"That was my plan."

"And you have my permission."

Dean looked at his father, who sat staring at the television. "Permission to do what?"

The chief turned. "Whatever you need to to find Reggie's killer."

They let the news run into regular programming, drinking their beers. The conversation shifted into baseball. The Yankees had dropped their season-opening game to the Brewers. Eric was convinced the Yanks were doomed this season. Dean mentioned a trip to see an Expos game might be something they could do this summer, knowing the idea was stillborn.

As the evening wore on, Dean realized he had never seen his father drunk before. Now, six beers later, he was downing some of his son's whiskey. Dean called his mom and said the chief would spend the night on the couch.

The alcohol washed away the hammered edges, brought out a sentimental side. Dean learned his mom and dad met in San Diego after he had disembarked from the USS *Lejeune*. She was one of the crowd greeting returning Marines. He spotted her from the fourth deck balcony and, he said, fell in love instantly. He needed that, he said, after what he saw in Okinawa, the grim fighting, the hard lessons of fate and luck, and the brutality of man.

He sank ever lower in the couch. Dean found a spare blanket and pillow and gave them to his dad. As he started to turn to go to bed himself, the chief grabbed his son's wrist. "Did you—did you ever try to talk Nolan out of going?"

Dean crouched down, his father's hand still wrapped around his wrist. He did not know what to think of the question. When Nolan joined, Dean was humping in the bush or blowing money in the town on Johnnie Walker or prostitutes. His letters home were at best short and to the point. Only later, in a letter Dean received just weeks before his brother was killed did he understand why Nolan joined. His brother had had no illusions about the war, about the U.S.'s ability to win, about it meaning anything. He joined knowing full well that his sacrifice would still mean the Viet Cong and North Vietnam would win. And Dean did not understand that decision. It seemed noble to him, and he recalled from some distant recess of his brain snippets of a Latin poem, something about how sweet it was to die for your country. He knew it was bullshit. He hated thinking that his brother's nobleness was bullshit, but he knew he would rather have his life—as terrible as it sometimes was—than be killed by some kid in some far away jungle that no one wanted to be in anyways.

He looked at his father, the chief, who now drunk on the couch and tearing up, become a man. As vulnerable as the rest of them. "No. No, I never tried to talk him out of it."

Eric nodded and closed his eyes. "I thought about telling you boys to not join. To not go." His face seemed to relax as he moved closer to sleep. "But I was too scared."

CHAPTER 31

April 6, 1979

Dean and Guthrie waited in the parking lot outside Bridewell's for Josh. Dean flicked the cigarette out of the window when he saw Josh's car pull into its regular spot. Both detectives left the car doors ajar as they got out and walked up to Josh, who was tossing a windbreaker into the back seat. His eyes widened when he saw who was approaching.

He did not protest at all as Dean grabbed him by the elbow and escorted him to the backseat of his car. Both he and Guthrie slammed their doors, and Dean drove off.

A brief rain had wetted the sidewalks and pavement. A light mist still fell, and the sound of the wipers scraping off the water every so often broke the silence in the car.

Dean saw Josh turn his head at the police station as they drove by. He looked back to the front and caught the detective's eyes in the rearview mirror. He frowned and looked away. Dean had to hand it to him, Josh was acting far more calmly than he expected, which told him Josh knew exactly why he was picked up that morning.

They pulled off the main road shortly after leaving town and followed its bends around hills and avoiding nasty potholes. A mile back, Dean pulled over and turned off the car.

When Dean and Guthrie opened the back door, Josh fell into form. "No. No. Why are we here? You don't have to do this."

"Don't be a goddamned pussy." Guthrie grabbed one of Josh's legs.

Dean grabbed the other, and they both fought off the kicking and pulled Josh out of the car, where he landed with a thud on the crushed gravel road. As Josh winced in pain, Dean rolled him over and cuffed him, squeezing them tight.

"Those are too tight," said Josh.

The air smelled of wet, oily pavement and the wood and loam of the forest.

Dean and Guthrie lifted Josh up and stood him up with his back to the back passenger door.

"You know why we're talking to you?" asked Guthrie. He pulled out a cigarette and lit it.

Josh nodded quickly.

"Tell us."

"I didn't have nothing to do with it."

"With what?"

Josh crunched his eyes, grimaced, and opened them again. "I heard a cop was killed out by the lab."

"That what you call it?"

Josh nodded.

"His name was Reggie. He had a wife and a kid. He was just doing his job," said Dean.

"And he was gunned down like nothing. Ambushed." Guthrie pulled a long drag off the cigarette and tossed it half-finished to the road.

"It wasn't me. I just helped out making the crank. Made some extra cash. I had nothing to do with it." His eyes darted back and forth between the detectives. "Don't hurt me. Please."

Dean rubbed his chin. "Tell us."

"What?"

Guthrie plowed his fist into Josh's stomach, who doubled-over and vomited instantly. The foul smell of his breakfast and acid and bile joining the forest smells. "You don't want pain? Then don't be stupid."

Dean pulled Josh by the shoulder and stood him straight again. Tears were flowing down his cheeks. "Jesus, kid, toughen the hell up. Tell us."

Josh wiped his mouth on his shoulder. "I help make crank. And the lab is where we make it."

"Who do you help?"

"Alex." Josh looked away. "Alex."

"Is that who I saw you with two nights ago?"

Josh looked away and looked back. "You saw us?"

Guthrie punched him again, sending Josh down to his knees, coughing.

Dean could check that off the list: Josh did not know he was under surveillance. He lifted Josh up again. "Yeah, I saw you. That was Alex?"

"Yeah."

"Did he set up the ambush?"

"Ambush?" He winced when Guthrie raised his fist, but Dean held up his hand.

"Yeah, what happened yesterday was an ambush."

Josh looked back and forth wide-eyed at the detectives. His lip trembled. "I. I. Shit. I don't know. I just helped Alex."

Dean waved his hand. "Fine. How'd Alex distribute his meth?"

"Oh, he just made it for Zorn. A way to make money quick. Zorn bought all of it. I don't know what happens. I never even saw Alex sell it. He just said he sold it and did it."

"The Grim Devils are buying your meth?" asked Guthrie.

Josh nodded.

"So it was them that ambushed us?" asked Dean.

"I don't know. Seriously, I don't know."

"What happened after you left the lab with Alex two nights ago?"

"I took him home. I went home. I went to work yesterday. Usual day."

"How often did you help Alex?"

"A couple of times a week. Usually brought supplies. Sometimes he'd ask me to hand him things or watch the process while he caught a nap."

"We were watching Alex before you. He didn't go out there at all." Guthrie put his hand on the hood of the car behind Josh.

"He said we needed to cool it. That we were doing it too often and people would ask questions. He said Zorn told him to stop for a week or so. So we did."

"And Zorn said to start up again?"

"Yeah."

"Did you ever talk to Zorn?" asked Guthrie.

"No. Alex did all that. I just helped Alex out." Josh looked at Guthrie, pleading for him to understand.

"Was Billy part of this?" Dean pulled out a Camel and lit it.

"Billy?" He flinched even though neither detective moved. "No. No. Billy wasn't part of this. He knew about it. Thought it was stupid. Gave some speech about drugs being bad for society and stuff."

Guthrie took a step away from Josh and tugged at his ear. "Because they are."

"So where'd Billy get his cash from?" asked Dean.

Josh shrugged. "I don't know. But Billy wasn't part of this." "Corey?"

Josh sighed. "He wanted in, but Alex wouldn't let him. Said he was too much of a hot head."

"So just you and Alex cooking up crank for Paul Zorn?"

"Yeah, man. Yeah." Josh bent over, sobbing. "I'm sorry."

Dean sat down in a catcher's stance and put his hands on Josh's shoulder. "Why'd Alex show up at the Shambles after you and Corey and Billy left? Did you meet Alex there?"

"Yeah. Corey and Billy were already gone. I went back and waited outside after they left. Then Alex showed up."

"Why?"

"Alex needed me to help him. He had a big order due. He and I were out there almost all night."

"So Alex did all the dealings with Zorn?"

"Yes. Yes. Jesus, I'm so sorry."

Dean stood up.

Guthrie pulled Josh up by the shoulder. "Sorry about what?"

Josh could not utter the words through his sobbing, so Guthrie pushed him back, not hard but hard enough he stumbled and collapsed to his knees.

"I think you broke him," said Dean.

"Ah, fucking puke. He'll know when I break him." Guthrie pulled out a cigarette and lit it.

Dean took a pull from his flask and handed it to Guthrie. They looked at each other. Dean shrugged, and Guthrie nodded. They knew Josh had nothing to do with the ambush. He was barely able to participate in delivering supplies to cook meth. They had been right that he was the weak link. Now they had an in to Alex and even Zorn.

But what about Billy? Was the meth thing a wrong lead on Billy? Maybe Alex had gotten Billy to do something for him that Josh did not know about. How much would you tell this guy crying on the ground anyway? Alex already had his dad talking for him. Alex was the next rung of the ladder. They would have to bring him in and make it seem unrelated to Billy's murder to avoid the DA from stopping it before it starts. Alex had legal counsel for the Billy case but not this meth distribution. It might give them a slight opening, a space to talk to Alex before he wised up, if he did not do it immediately.

"Ah, come on man." Guthrie stubbed out the cigarette.

Dean awoke from his thinking. Josh was running down the road, and Guthrie was already three steps into a sprint. He fought the urge to join the chase, watching, instead, Guthrie run after the kid. When it became clear that Guthrie could not catch up, Dean threw the cigarette, jumped into the car, turned it around, and roared down the road. He watched Guthrie in the rear view mirror still running. He passed Josh on the left, hit the brakes, and swerved into a stop, flinging the door open as he did.

Josh veered right onto the grass that hugged the road and then down the small hill that led into the woods. Dean ran after Josh, half sliding, half running down the hill. He heard Guthrie behind him, panting heavily. As they tore into the woods, the sky was blotted out, and the forest darkened everything, making them feel as if it were overcast. He heard a stumble and Josh cry out in pain.

The detectives found him, reaching for his ankle and grimacing. Guthrie put his hands on his knees and breathed heavily, sweat dripping off his forehead.

Between gasps, Josh said, "Please don't kill me."

Guthrie looked at him and spat at his feet. "What do you think we are, fucking monsters?"

CHAPTER 32

They picked up Alex at Adamson's, and Dean made sure to make a show of it, ensuring all his co-workers saw and heard he was being arrested. Alex did not say a word as he was escorted out, where Paige snapped a few photographs and asked for his comments. Dean had called and told her the Zion Police were bringing in a suspect for questioning relating to drugs and the officer shooting the day before. Alex sat in silence for the ride to the station. Once inside, Dean sat him in the interview room, leaving the cuffs on. He walked out and closed the door behind him. Let the kid sit for a while.

As he walked out to the main part of the station, Guthrie handed him a typed report: A brief summary of the arrest of Josh and interview. Dean breezed through the text of how they picked him up at the store and the fiction of bringing him to the station followed by the largely accurate summary of what Josh said. Guthrie noted that the suspect twisted his ankle coming down the stairs into the station. Dean grabbed a pen out of his jacket and counter-signed the report. He handed it back to Guthrie and said maybe now the city would give them a proper station to avoid any more twisted ankles. They smoked a couple of cigarettes and then returned to the interview room, where Alex seemed intent on mimicking a statue.

The detectives sat across from him. Dean put his hands together. Guthrie wiped his nose with the edge of his index finger, leaned back, and put his hands in his pockets.

"Do you know why you're here?" asked Dean, tilting his head and smiling.

"I want to talk to my dad."

"About what?"

"He said last time I was here you needed to talk to him first," said Alex with a righteous tone.

"About William Nimitz's murder, right?" Dean let his hands drift below the table as he leaned forward.

Alex nodded.

"This isn't about your friend."

"What?" He wanted to raise his hands, rub his face, his arm, do something. Instead, the cuffs jingled. "I—"

Guthrie raised his hand. "Look, kid, you're in deep shit. We know all about your lab in the woods east of town. The one you torched yesterday morning after shooting at a bunch of cops and killing one of them."

"I don't—"

"He was a friend. Reggie. Had a wife and a kid. Five-year old kid. He was just doing his job and you had to shoot him. You think we're going to just let you get away with that." Guthrie had leaned over the table, elbows on it, arms crossed and in front of his chest.

"But I didn't have anything to do with that."

"Do with what?"

"Shooting that cop. I didn't know. I didn't."

"But the lab was yours?" asked Dean.

"Yeah, the lab was mine. But I don't know about any cop being shot."

Dean leaned back. "Your lab got torched. You didn't do that either?"

"Torched? It's gone?"

Guthrie gestured an explosion with his hands. "Boom."

Alex hung his head.

"Don't worry, we got enough evidence to bust you for making crank. You won't be needing your lab anymore. The question is about your involvement in the killing of a cop."

"I didn't do that." His chest bumped against the table. "I didn't man. I made crank. I sold it to the Grim Devils. That's it."

"Why use Josh in your operation, but not Corey?" asked Dean.

"That motherfucker rat me out?"

"Let's say he was inclined to talk. Why not Corey? Or did you work with him, and Josh didn't know?"

"No. Not Corey. Too hard to work with. And he bragged all over the place. Thought he knew everything. If he was part of it, he'd be telling me what to do like he was some expert. Then he'd get drunk and spill everything at the Shambles. No. Josh may be a pussy, but he takes orders and keeps his mouth shut." Alex bit down and crunched his lips together. "At least I thought he would. Shithead."

"Mostly." Dean could not help a smile. "So Josh knew about your operation. Helped you out. Who else?"

Alex jerked on the cuffs again.

Dean got up and walked behind him. As he was unlocking the cuffs, he said to Alex, "Either there's someone else who knows about the lab, or it's just you and Josh who know. And I don't think Josh did any shooting."

"Yeah," said Guthrie, "I don't see Josh being able to fire a gun at a rat, let alone a person."

Alex rubbed his right wrist and then his left. "I want to talk to my dad."

"You don't have a right to talk to your dad. And you've got only one way to avoid a murder charge. Talk."

Alex shook his head and crossed his arms. "I want to talk to my lawyer."

Dean patted Alex on the shoulders, still standing behind him. "Fine. Fine." He and Guthrie walked out of the interview room, slamming the door behind them.

༺❀༻

Dean sat at his desk, smoking a cigarette. A blank interview sheet was rolled into the typewriter, but he kept an eye on the chief's door, occasionally glancing at Guthrie, who smoked two to every one cigarette of Dean's.

Thirty minutes after Alex's dad arrived and closed the door to the chief's office, he came out, his face red and jaw clenched. Eric waved over Dean and Guthrie. All three formed a crescent in front of the Clinton County District Attorney.

Henry bit his lip and looked back and forth between the two detectives. "I'm serving as my son's attorney, so you can't talk to him without me. As the chief made clear, I can't be both my son's lawyer and the district attorney. So I've called my ADA, who'll act as the DA for this case."

Dean crossed his arms. "That's fine, Henry. We've got more questions for Alex. Has the chief told you what we've got so far?"

"I need to talk to my son." Henry cut between Dean and his dad.

Guthrie followed Henry and unlocked the interview room, letting the DA in and closed the door behind him. The detective walked back to Dean and Eric. "So now what?"

"We wait," said Eric, who walked back into his office. Guthrie shrugged and walked back to his desk, and Dean lit a cigarette and leaned against the wall of the hallway.

After forty-five minutes, Henry opened the door of the interview room, spotted Dean, and nodded that he and Alex were ready. Dean called over Guthrie, and both walked into the interview room, Dean closing the door behind him.

As Dean sat across from Henry and Alex, Guthrie drifted back to the corner of the room, rested his shoulders against the wall, and crossed his arms. Alex's eyes were red.

Henry said, "Do you want the ADA here?"

Dean said, "Do we need her here?"

"Alex is willing to talk about what he knows, but he wants immunity."

"So you know how this works. He has to tell us something, and we'll tell the ADA, and we'll see what she thinks. But I'm not—we're not giving blanket immunity."

"First, he wasn't involved in the killing of the officer. He was at home when I left for work, and that was about a half hour, forty-five minutes before the attack. He went from home to work. And he did not know the attack was going to happen and would have warned officials if he knew otherwise."

Dean nodded. Having a DA sit across from him defending himself or a relative was nothing new. He had seen it in New York a few times. Like Henry, they thought they could think their way through to safety, outwit the investigators across from them. Some could, but they were the corrupt ones, the ones the Five Families owned. The decent ones cooperated too much for their own good. An innate sense, Dean guessed, of justice, the rule of law, of not hindering a police investigation. They knew the law, but they should hire a true defense attorney, particularly when they were sitting in the interview room.

"You have a confession about Alex's role in the crank lab?"

Dean said, "Yes. The witness states he assisted Alex in making the drug and providing it to the Grim Devils. We're not inclined to believe the witness or Alex were involved or arranged the attack yesterday morning."

"My son is prepared to admit to the illegal manufacture of a controlled substance, participation in an ongoing criminal enterprise, and other minor charges. But before he tells you what he knows, he wants immunity from the murder or manslaughter charges. Anything related to the attack."

Dean looked back at Guthrie and then back at Henry. "Let's see if the ADA is here." He and Guthrie exited the interview room. The ADA was not in the main area, so Dean knocked on his father's door. ADA Clara Pond sat in the chair across from Eric. She looked up at the intrusion and smiled. Dressed in a red, long-sleeved blouse with a large bow and high-waisted, black pants that flared out from the knees down, she styled her light brown hair straight and down below the shoulders. Dean had seen her once or twice, and Henry was considered forward thinking for his hiring of her. Eric introduced them and told Dean he had briefed her. Dean, in turn, gave her a summary of the conversation he had just had.

She smiled and nodded. "Okay then. Let's talk to him."

CHAPTER 33

Pond sat across from Henry and Alex and smiled. She said she was prepared to offer immunity for Alex in the attack. She wanted to hear from Alex, however, what Dean had heard from Henry.

Alex repeated the story as she held her index finger to her lips. When he was finished, she set a leather satchel on the table and pulled out a folder. She set the satchel on the floor beside her feet and opened the folder. She flipped it around and slid it to Henry. It was a one-page document outlining the immunity in return for honest statements, including full details of his criminal activities and accomplices, and appearing as a witness.

Henry tapped at the line requiring Alex to appear as a witness. "I'm not a fan of this."

Pond frowned. "It's a requirement. You know we're not going to let Alex sing to us and then not use it. You wouldn't let that happen either, Henry."

Henry patted his son's shoulder. "You'll have to testify."

"You don't understand who you're dealing with. They won't let me live long enough to testify."

"We'll provide protection until the trial's over. I can ensure you will have a detail outside your home and work until then. Once the damage is done, I doubt they'll do anything."

"You doubt?" asked Henry.

"He's not going into some witness protection program for cooking up meth for a local biker gang. A uniformed officer was killed." She pointed a finger at Alex. "He is the one who started cooking meth. He's not innocent in this. And I'm not going to treat him that way."

Henry pursed his lips. Alex looked at his dad and back at Pond.

Henry sighed and nodded. "It's the best you're going to get. I suggest you sign it."

Alex dropped his head in defeat, took the silver pen his father handed him, and signed the document. Henry pulled the folder and document over, gently pulled the pen from his son's hand, and signed. He put the pen back in his pocket, flipped the folder around, and pushed it across the desk to his deputy. She signed and said, "Start."

"Early last year, March I think, Sam Darwish, he's with the Grim Devils, and me were sitting around drinking. I was having money issues at the time. Not enough. And I was getting ready to leave, but I was pretty far gone already. Anyways, I end up telling him why I couldn't stay. He insists I do, that he'll buy my beers. I thought, 'Why not?'

"After a while, he tells me there's a way I can make a lot of money fast. He says the Devils can pay me to cook crank for them. They'd finance me to set up, I make enough to pay off the loan, and then I can keep making and they'll buy and I get the profits. So like I'm pretty far gone, and I wasn't thinking. And I wake up at home. Head's hurting. But there's this paper bag next to my bed. It's got ten thousand in cash. I don't recall the night before well, but I remember Sam.

"I figure he's down at the Devil's garage and head down there before work. He's there. He reminds me. I say I don't want to. I mean, shit, I don't want to be doing that. Sam says fine, but because I had the money some time, I owe interest on it. I know I'm screwed then. So that's how I got into making crank. Stupid, I know, but shit, I didn't have the money to pay them back. And Sam wasn't talking like he'd really want it back anyways.

"I happened to know of a couple of buses out in the woods that were abandoned. Not very old, but not new. I think the old Pike family left them there a few years ago. Anyways, I cleaned them up a bit and started. They had some guy from California in one week, and he taught me. I think he taught a few others in the area too. They said that crank was the next great drug. And things went fine. Fine until two nights ago. Sam finds me at the Shambles and tells me he's got it on good authority the cops are going to raid the place in the morning. He tells me to keep away." Alex leaned back and raised his hands as if there were no more to tell.

Pond looked at Dean. "Detective?"

Dean nodded. "I've got a few questions. Let's start with why did Sam just ask you to start cooking crank? Seems a bit of a stretch to ask the son of the DA to do this. At a bar."

Alex pursed his lips and looked at his dad.

Henry sighed. "He's family. Not close. A cousin of mine. Son of my uncle." He scratched his chin. "He was also probably looking for leverage over me. Something he could use if the Devils got in trouble."

"So you've been cooking meth, crank, for the Devils for a little over a year now?"

Alex nodded.

"And how'd Josh get involved?"

"I asked him. Told him I was in deep shit and needed his help. He was a good friend."

"When did that happen?"

"Him helping me?"

"Yeah. When did he start helping you?"

Alex dropped his head and rubbed his temples with his right hand. "Must've been a month or two after I started. I knew I needed some help. So I asked him."

"And he agreed?"

Alex shrugged with his eyebrows. "He's a good friend."

"Did you know what the Devils were planning after Sam told you to keep away?"

"No. No I didn't."

Guthrie took two steps away from the wall. "Why should I believe you?"

Henry looked at his son. Pond looked back at Guthrie and then at Alex. Alex rubbed his hands. "I don't know. All I can tell you is that I didn't. I didn't have anything to do with it. I thought he was just warning me to keep away from the lab. Lay off. Like he did a few weeks ago. And then they told me the coast was clear."

"A few weeks ago?" Dean leaned in.

Guthrie drifted back to the wall.

"Yeah," said Alex.

"What do you mean? What happened a few weeks ago?"

"I got a call from Sam again—I mean the first time. He told me to keep away from the lab. The cops were interested in it and that he'd let me know when it was clear again."

"When was this?"

"Sometime in March. I can't remember."

"And he called you back when it was all okay?"

"Yeah. A couple of days ago. Said, get back to it."

Dean tapped his fingers on the table. "That's it? He didn't say anything more. Where's he getting the information?"

Alex shook his head. "I don't know."

Dean leaned back. The Devils knew about the surveillance. Knew about the raid. How?

Pond said, "Detective, any more questions?"

Dean looked up. He had drifted into his own thoughts for a while. "Yeah, two more. Was Paul Zorn a party to any of your conversations with Sam?"

Alex said, "No."

"And William Nimitz. Was he part of your work or was he doing something similar on his own?"

Henry put his hand in front of Alex. "Hold on. What's Billy got to do with this?"

Pond narrowed one eye and looked at the detective.

Dean said, "If he was into something similar with the Devils, it might mean we have a motive for his killing."

Alex shook his head. "All this time investigating Billy and you really have no clue who he was." He tapped his fist on the table. "Billy wouldn't touch drugs. Dude was turning all commie and shit. I couldn't stand him anymore. Asshole—"

Henry raised his hand higher. "We're not talking about Mr. Nimitz now."

Pond smiled. "Okay. So I have one last question." She clasped her hands together. "Did you pay off your debt?"

"Yes." Alex twisted his lip.

"And you still kept making these drugs, right?"

"Yes."

CHAPTER 34

Guthrie took delight in fingerprinting Alex and shuffling him out to the car, where the young meth cooker would be driven to the county jail.

Henry kept close tabs on the entire process, but even he knew he could not do much. His son was going to jail. He might get a good plea deal, but the county's chief prosecutor seemed a different man, his shoulders hunched, more lines on his face. A twinge of sympathy ran through Dean. He had been the son of a police officer, which had been challenging for both him, his brothers, and his father. Being the son of the chief prosecutor or being the chief prosecutor whose son is a drug dealer must have been difficult as well.

Pond opened the chief's door and walked out. She looked up at her boss, grimly smiled, and spotted Dean. She gestured as if she were smoking a cigarette and nodded toward the exit. He nodded once and stood up.

She waited for him as he walked to the exit. The chief came out of the office, patted Henry on the shoulder, and told him to take the day, even the next.

Dean held the door open for Clara. She pulled out a Virginia Slim. He held the light for her and then lit his own.

"So you're the chief's son, the detective from the city?" She blew smoke out of the side of her mouth.

"Yeah, that's me. Can't say I know much about you."

"Henry and Karen, his assistant, talk about you every once in a while. They think they're discreet, but, well, they aren't."

"What do they say about me?"

"Hmmm. That you're a drunk who washed out of the NYPD. Vet who saw real combat. Lucky you have a father who's a chief of police to get you a job."

Dean chuckled. "I didn't realize they had such a high opinion of me." He flicked ash off the end of his cigarette. "But it's pretty much true."

"All of it?"

"Well, I'm not sure I'd go so far as being a drunk, but let's not split hairs."

She crossed her left arm across her body, pinching her hand between her right elbow and abdomen and holding the cigarette in the air. "You don't remember me, do you?"

He inhaled on his cigarette and studied her face.

"I was a couple of years behind you."

He shook his head. "Sorry. I don't recall."

"I was in your brother's class."

"Nolan?"

"Yes. Sorry."

He shook his head and held the cigarette low.

"You were the talk of the girls."

"I was?"

She smiled. "Anyways, seems like you have a problem."

"Huh?"

"Someone's telling the Grim Devils what the police are up to."

"Oh that. Yeah, that's an issue." Who knew about the lab and the surveillance? Eric, Guthrie, Reggie, Etheridge, and probably a couple of the others. The lab raid? Essentially the same people. And. And Sadie. He had mentioned finding it. Did she know about the surveillance too? Had he been too drunk to remember telling her?

"Hey there." Pond snapped her fingers. "Back to earth."

"Yeah. Yeah. Sorry. Was thinking about that problem."

She dropped the cigarette and crushed it under her toe. "I can see that. Looks like you have a suspect."

He nodded and watched her walk to her car.

⟡

Dean, Etheridge, and Zach waited for Sam Darwish to arrive home. They waited down the street, away from his likely direction of return. Indeed, they heard first and then saw the Harley-Davidson and Sam driving toward them. He pulled into his driveway and turned off the engine. His long hair dropped to below his shoulders, but he was balding and his hair had a stringy, brittle appearance. He wore a red bandana like a sweat band. He had on the vest of the Grim Devils—their large Grim Reaper crushing skulls—jeans, and military-style black boots.

Sam had a good-sized rap sheet of drunk driving, assaults, and minor drug possession charges. He had spent a fair number of nights in the jail's drunk tank and a few longer stints in the county jail. Born in 1940, he had been a track star for Zion in high school. After, he started working for Banks's. He joined the Grim Devils in the mid-Sixties.

Dean told Etheridge to start the car and drive fast to Sam's house, hoping to catch him off guard and minimize the danger. Etheridge punched the accelerator, and the car tore toward Sam, who looked up from his motorcycle. He lifted his aviators just as Etheridge slammed the breaks. Before the car had come to a complete stop at the end of Sam's driveway, Dean and Zach were opening their doors and stepping out.

Sam started to run to his house, but he was a large man who long ago had lost his high school state finals sprinting form.

Zach, the younger and faster officer, sprinted the few yards separating him from Sam and dove toward the fleeing man, driving his shoulder into his back.

Sam grunted, stumbled forward, and flailed his arms but kept upright and running to his house. Dean was coming fast on Sam as Zach was picking himself up, when Etheridge shouted, "Freeze. I'll shoot you if you don't."

But Sam did not stop. Dean caught up with him and reached for his shoulders, but he twisted loose. Zach was beside Dean then and had his truncheon out, which he swiped across Sam's back left leg.

The big man cried out again, but this time, he fell. Dean drove his knee between Sam's shoulder blades, reaching for the big man's right hand, grabbing just inside the thumb and twisting to pull the hand back and get him under his control. Etheridge ran past and stopped between Sam and his house, his pistol leveled at the biker.

Dean cuffed the right hand, and Sam gave up and relaxed. Dean cuffed the left hand and rolled Sam over onto his back. Grass and dirt covered his mouth and nose. A trickle of blood rolled down his upper lip.

"Afternoon, Sam. We got questions for you."

CHAPTER 35

S am sat in the interview chair with a strip of tissue wadded and stuffed up his nose. Pieces of grass stuck to his beard. He was still cuffed. "Police brutality. You had no reason—"

"You ran."

"I thought you were after me."

"We were." Dean locked his fingers together.

"You know what I mean."

"I don't. Help me out. A police car shows up and you run. And I've seen what's inside your house." Dean, Zach, and Etheridge had waited on the warrant before entering to find a cache of weapons: pistols, rifles, shotguns, submachine guns. Plus several pounds of meth wrapped in plastic. Dean placed photos in front of Sam. "So you usually want to shoot any officer that comes along or were you eager to sell some of your crank?"

Sam was sweating profusely from his forehead and he kept swallowing and licking his lips. "I don't know what that stuff is. You planted it. And I've got people after me. I thought it was them."

"Ah, I see. So why are people after you? Who?"

"Just people. And I thought you were them."

"Did you tell the police earlier that you were being targeted?"

Sam laughed. "What? Hell no. Why would I do that?"

"It's what most people do when they're being targeted." Dean added air quotes to the last word. "Look, it's simple. We've got you on weapons and drug possession charges. You're looking at a good number of years. Not county jail. State prison. Worse." He pointed at Sam. "For you, it's worse. We've got a witness who says you set up the ambush that killed an officer two days ago in the woods out west of town."

"I don't know nothing about that."

"Of course not. Thing is, I don't care. We're taking those guns and checking them. I'm particularly interested in this one." Dean pointed to the M16 in the photo. "See, I know what one of those sounds like. I heard one as my fellow officer was shot dead. I'm betting this here M16 is going to match some ballistics we found out there in the woods."

Sam bit his lip.

"Yeah. And it seems like you set someone up for making crank. Encouraged him. Got him a loan. Even trained him. Do you offer health insurance too? What's the vacation policy?"

Sam rubbed his mouth. "That shithead."

"Oh, do you know something?"

Just as quickly as it disappeared, the fear, the concern came back. "You talking about Alex?" Sam squinted at Dean. "Yeah, I bet you are. Whatever he says, you can't believe a word out of his mouth. He lies just like his old man."

"Right now, all I care about is making sure you end up in prison for a long time. Weapons possession. Drug possession. Distribution. Murder. Whatever I can send you to lock up for."

Sam looked at Dean and then back down. "I didn't murder anyone. No. Not that."

"Not sure it makes much difference if you were there and shooting at us. Attempted murder? Does that sound any better? Accessory to murder? The point is, you're going away. Sit on that." Dean grabbed the photos and walked out of the interview room.

Eric was standing in the hall. "How'd it go?"

Dean gave him a thumbs up. "About ready to break." He walked to his desk, slid open the drawer with the bottle of Wild Turkey, refreshed his flask, and took a drink.

Guthrie walked up, hiking his pants when he stopped before Dean's desk. "Alex is booked and in jail. He'll have a few hours at least before his pops bails him out." He thumbed back toward the interview room. "How's Sammy boy? Heard Zach put the baton to work."

"Yep, whacked him back along the legs, sent the man down quick."

Guthrie nodded. "He about ready to spill the beans?"

Dean nodded and took another drink. "He's on the hot seat now for murder. At least he thinks he is. Based on his reaction, I think the M16 we found in his house was at the lab site."

"That's with the state now?"

"Not yet. We'll get that over probably tomorrow. Maybe this afternoon."

"Can I watch him squirm when you go back in?"

Handing Guthrie the flask, Dean said, "Hell yes you can."

They waited another hour. Dean took in a small styrofoam cup of water and set it in front of Sam, who looked up at both of the detectives. "What the hell you doing out there?"

Dean sat down and crossed his arms. "Had a good think, did you?"

Sam took the cup and downed the water in one gulp. "I was thirsty. Thanks." He tapped the cup over so that it slid across the table. "Yeah. I thought about it. I told him it was a bad idea."

"Told who?"

Sam looked at Guthrie and then at Dean. "Zorn. He set up the ambush. Knew you guys were sniffing around. He didn't mean to get anyone killed. Just scare the hell out of you. Make you think it was well defended. Keep you away."

Dean leaned back. "That's bullshit. You don't bring an M16 and, I'm guessing, a rifle with a scope, start shooting, and not expect to hit somebody. And that's not going to scare anyone off. We would've just gone back with more. More cops with more guns. Zorn's not stupid."

Sam shrugged. "What can I say? I only know what he tells me."

Dean put his elbows on the table. "I know you. You're not stupid either. This may not be the future you thought of when you were running track, but this is where you are and you're not stupid."

Sweat appeared again on Sam's forehead.

Dean stretched his arms out wide. "Fine. So Zorn says let's go into the woods and wait for the cops to show up? That about sum it up?"

Sam nodded.

"Who was with him? You?"

"No. No. I just knew it was going down. It was Zorn, Paddy, and Jimmy."

Dean recognized the names. Paddy was the Sergeant-at-Arms. Jimmy was a new member. "Was Jimmy looking for his skull patch?"

"Yeah. He was."

"When was this planned?"

"This is Friday. So it was planned on Wednesday."

"The fourth?"

"Yeah." Sam wiped the sweat from his brow. "Yeah. Wednesday night. It was discussed after the meeting. Zorn said it had to be done the next day and they needed to leave early."

"Just like that?" Dean snapped his fingers.

Guthrie, who had drifted into his familiar corner, stepped forward. "And how come the M16 used to kill a cop winds up at your house?"

"Look, now that, that—. That is not my gun. Zorn or Paddy must have left it there for me. I was not in the woods. I was at home asleep man. I knew it was going down, but I can't shoot. And like you said, I thought it wasn't very smart."

Zorn had put Sam up as the patsy. Dean knew that was why he was talking.

Guthrie said, "You know how often we get 'home asleep'? It's not an alibi. And what do you mean by 'left it there for you'?" Like a gift?"

"I don't know. Shit." Sam dropped his head. "Shit."

Dean raised his hand to stop Guthrie from continuing. "I'm just not buying this Sam. But if this is the story you're sticking to, you can be just as stupid as Paul. Answer me this."

Sam looked up at him.

"How'd Paul know about us cops showing up out there?"

A smile flickered across Sam's face. Pride coming back in full splendor, even if briefly. He had knowledge Dean did not. Sam said, "He says he has a bitch who tells him everything. Connected direct into the police."

Dean leaned back. Alex telling them this was the case was one thing. Sam was different somehow because he was a Grim Devil. "Who?"

Sam shook his head and shrugged. "Hell if I know. He kept that to himself. Always said he had himself a bitch to tell him everything."

Dean breathed in deep. Sadie. It had to be Sadie. He knew he told her things he should not, as if she were his wife. She was nice to him because he paid her. He was not under any illusions about that, but he never expected she would be pumping him for information and passing it to Zorn. He would have to deal with that later. "Fine. You don't know shit. But what do you know about William Nimitz?"

"Huh? What? He didn't have anything to do with talking to the police."

Guthrie pulled out the second chair across from Sam and sat down heavily. "No, you moron. We know that. But Billy was found in the woods, a bullet in his head, and a wad of cash in his closet. Was he working for Zorn like Alex?"

"That commie piece of shit. Hell no. He wasn't cooking. If he had showed up at the clubhouse, we'd have beat the red right out of him."

That word again, said with flagrant disgust. Dean asked, "He was a communist?"

"Yeah, man."

"How do you know this?"

"My niece's boyfriend's about the same age as Billy. Says Billy was spouting off communist crap all the time. Wanted to save people from whatever."

"Who's the niece?"

"Why do I need to tell you that?"

"The spirit of cooperation."

Sam twisted his mouth, sighed, and looked at the wall. Then he looked back at Sam. "Julie. Julie Darwish. Her boyfriend is Tim Upton."

"And where was Billy spouting this commie stuff off at?" asked Guthrie.

"I don't know. Ask one of them."

CHAPTER 36

Guthrie walked into the hallway outside the interview room, followed by Dean, who closed the door behind him. At the end of the hallway, just outside the chief's door, his father stood, pounding his fist against the door jamb. Before him stood two men. One was dressed in a black suit with a black tie and holding gold aviators in his hand as he rubbed his thick mustache with his index finger and thumb. The other wore a windbreaker and a baseball cap on his bald head that bore the logo of the DEA.

"You can't do this." said Eric. "This is our case. Our man got killed."

The man in the suit—whom Dean presumed was FBI—said, "Sir, I understand your attachment to this case, but the jurisdiction is ours."

Guthrie brushed passed the two, and Dean stopped beside his dad. "What's your jurisdiction?"

The DEA man looked at Dean. "Special Agent Tony Hayes." He extended his hand.

Dean shook it. "Detective Dean Wallace."

The FBI man said, "Special Agent David Pryce." He tapped the edge of his cap.

Dean nodded.

Hayes said, "Multiple, actually. The DEA's interested because those drugs are crossing state and international lines. The FBI's interested because there's reason to believe the Grim Devils have perpetrated crimes in Canada. The Mounties called us up. Said they found some evidence in a murder outside Montreal. I understand you've seen some of that evidence."

"We talking about the case where a guy was found murdered in his home and a bunch of fake passports and cash were found?"

"Yes. Marcel Lorrain was the victim."

"And it's connected with the Grim Devils?"

Hayes shrugged.

Eric turned to Dean. "They want to take Sam into their custody. Get copies of all our evidence on the ambush, the lab, everything. They want goddamn everything." He raised his hands in exasperation.

"But we can keep it and prosecute, right?" asked Dean.

"Maybe. But you'll have to wait. We may need that leverage to get some of them to talk, to cooperate," said Pryce.

Dean put his hands to his waist. "Shit, fellas, we want these guys for killing one of our own. Reggie Hargrove."

Hayes nodded. "We know. And we're sorry, and we don't intend to let them off for that. But there are—frankly—other priorities."

"Assholes." Eric stepped forward.

Hayes raised a finger. "You know what I meant. We're talking about bringing down the entire gang in this area. But let's not get ahead of ourselves, all right? Just give us the evidence and reports you've got."

"And Sam?" asked Dean.

"Yes. We'll take him down to Plattsburgh. You've got enough evidence to hold him?"

Dean nodded. "Yeah. We've got enough."

Pryce said, "Great. Then let's get the stuff."

Eric shook his head, waved his hand in the air in disgust, and walked into his office, slamming the door behind him.

Dean said, "Okay. I'll have Guthrie gather the physical evidence. We haven't had a chance to get the guns tested that we found in Sam's house, just so you know. I'll grab the reports. I need to type up this interview, and we'll put it in boxes for you."

Pryce placed his hand on Dean's shoulder and squeezed. "Thank you."

Ninety minutes later, Guthrie placed the last box of evidence in the trunk of the agent's car. Pryce and Hayes signed the paperwork indicating they had taken over the evidence: A box with a short stack of reports he and Guthrie had typed up, the surveillance logs, and photographs. Another box of the meth, marijuana, and heroin seized at Sam's house plus two bags with his cache of weapons.

Dean stood outside the driver's side window, looking down and in. "You know," he said to Pryce, "the Alex kid we arrested and ran that lab is the son of the county DA."

Pryce smiled. "Yeah, we know. Lucky for him, his son is small fry. And the Justice prosecutor is an asshole, so some county DA's not going to frighten him."

"All right. Please keep us informed if you can. At least about the Reggie aspect."

Hayes tapped the dash. "Let's go."

Dean only then realized the day had turned to evening. He looked at his watch: a quarter after seven. The western sky was a luminous orange and red and pink swaths of clouds a quarter of the way up the horizon. He rubbed his chin and then pulled out a cigarette and lit it.

When Cindy and he had been married, they had made a thing of watching the sunset together, except for winter. From their apartment in New York, it was not always a great view, but nonetheless, they would sit on the small balcony in cheap lawn chairs and watch the sunset wash over the sliver of sky and buildings. He smiled at the memory. Only in hindsight after the divorce did he realize the first sign of trouble in the marriage was when they stopped sitting and watching the sunset. He took a drink from his flask and watched.

A few minutes later, he went to check on his dad and Guthrie, but both had left.

His phone rang, so he walked to his desk and answered it. "Hello? Detective Wallace here."

"This is Paige McFadden."

"Good evening."

"Yeah. So want to tell me what's up? I saw a couple of FBI guys show up at the station. Well, they were at the Shambles first stuffing their face."

"One of them is DEA."

"DEA?"

"Yep."

"Gotcha. So tell me."

Dean told her. He gave her the rest of the information he felt comfortable giving. He attributed the lab to intelligence they had received to cooperating witnesses. He skimmed over the ambush and then gave her the high-level view of the evidence leading them to Alex and then to Sam. And now the DEA and FBI were interested. She thanked him and hung up.

He pulled on his coat and went to his car, leaving James and Stanley at the station for the night shift. He started the engine and sat there, rehashing the day in his mind and settling on a single thought: Sadie. He debated what he should do but realized he already knew. He hit the steering wheel with the palm of his hand. "Fuck it."

Minutes later, he was pounding on the front door of her two-story house. She whipped open the door. "What the hell Dean? You drunk?"

He thrust the door open, which thudded against the back wall, denting the red and light yellow striped wallpaper and drywall behind it in the shape of the lockset.

"Hey," she said. "What's the meaning of this? I've got someone coming over. I don't have time."

"I'm not here for the normal."

She saw the look in his eyes. Something beyond determination, beyond anger. She knew then to be frightened. "What's going on?" She put her hands to his chest.

He grabbed her wrists and twisted them away. "How long have you been informing on me?"

She held up her hands.

"How long have you been telling Paul Zorn everything I tell you?"

She knew that look in his eyes was betrayal. "Now look here." She raised up a finger and held it in the air, pointed at him. "I don't know what you're talking about. You get a grip and get the hell out."

He stepped toward her, recognizing that she had gone from light-hearted, to terrified, to strong in a few quick beats.

"I mean it. You stop right there. I don't know what you're talking about. I don't tell Zorn anything. Or any of his lackeys."

"I trusted you. I said things, and they shouldn't have gone anywhere."

"They didn't. You paid me and what happened in this house, anything you said, anything we did, no one knows but you and me." She dropped her hand. "No one."

He stood before her, in her living room, a room he never bothered to notice. She stood, dressed in black lace negligée and a light pink robe with white lace edging, next to a brown leather couch on a large, square beige rug. Matching dark wood end tables at either end of the couch with brass lamps and off-white lamp shades from which plastic diamonds hung.

A television to the right of the couch, next to the fireplace with its mantle. Framed photos of Sadie and her family and friends. A greeting card. At this distance, Dean thought it was a birthday card.

He looked back at her. And he knew he was wrong. She had not betrayed him.

"Get out." She had moved to the front door, still wide open. "Now." She gestured for him to leave.

He nodded once and grimaced.

As he walked past her and onto the porch, she said, "Fuck you, Dean. I never want to see you again."

She slammed the door behind him.

CHAPTER 37

April 7, 1979

Dean drove to the station the next morning and had Laura look up both Julie Darwish and Tim Upton. He had slept poorly and had not bothered to shave after he woke up. As he waited for the information about the niece or her boyfriend, he sat at his desk, shuffled the piled reports and memos, but barely registered their titles or purpose. Etheridge walked in after a while and sat down at his desk, tendering a wave as a hello. Dean nodded his hello.

Laura walked up to the desk and handed him a piece of notepad paper with addresses and phone numbers. "That's what we can get on those two. No arrests. Upton has a couple of speeding tickets is all."

"Thanks." Tim's address was on the south side of town, amongst the largely residential section that had built up after World War II around the now defunct piping factory. As he walked out of the station to his car, he passed Guthrie without saying a word.

The house at the address was a ranch, all brick house with white molding around the windows and a black-gray roof. The white wooden garage door needed a coat of paint.

He pulled the car to a stop in the driveway, half of which consisted of a white gravel and the other cement. He stepped out and walked up the gravel with the grass rising up in spots. When he got to the sidewalk bordered by evergreen shrubs, the front door opened. Through the screen door, Dean could make out a woman dressed in blue jeans and a Coca-Cola t-shirt. "Hello?" she asked.

"Hello." Dean stopped. "I'm Detective Dean Wallace. Is Tim Upton home?"

"He's getting ready for work. What's this about?"

"Billy Nimitz."

"Ah, I was wondering if you'd ever show up." She pushed open the screen door as her invitation to step in.

Dean walked into the entry way, where a set of light jackets hung from the wall directly across from the door. An off-white wallpaper with brown stripes and small flowers covered the walls.

She pointed to the right. "He's in the kitchen getting breakfast."

Dean walked down the hallway. It opened to a family room with the same wallpaper, a sofa, lounge chair, coffee table covered with magazines, a TV, and a basket of more magazines. To the back of the family room, the kitchen sat with a built-in table, counters, appliances, and a pantry. The small window looked out onto the driveway.

"You're looking at it like Julie does," said the man with blond hair with a part on the far left and combed over with a looping bang hanging down. He had the rudiments of a mustache. He was dressed in the blue and white uniform of the Gorman Transmission Company. They had a manufacturing center just about in Plattsburgh.

Dean held out his hand. "Detective Dean Wallace."

"Tim Upton." He took his hand and shook firmly. "That's my girlfriend Julie."

"Hi," she said as she left the room.

Dean nodded. Unmarried but living together. He rubbed his nose. He was certain they were at least the talk of their neighbors.

"Coffee?" asked Tim.

Dean said yes, and Tim poured him a cup. The detective turned down cream and sugar.

"Here about Billy? I heard you at the door."

"Yeah. I was talking to your uncle yesterday. Sam."

Tim smiled. "Talking. I get you."

"Anyway, he said you had spoken to Billy a bit. Claimed you called Billy a communist."

"I did." Tim took a drink of his coffee. "He was. He'd show up at the factory. We're non-union there. So he'd show up and agitate. Tell us we should organize, unionize. Power to the people and that kind of crap. He was a red, pure and simple. Wouldn't deny it."

"I know lots of fellas who are pro-union that don't consider— that I wouldn't consider—communists."

"Yep, I know some too. Me. Hell, the factory used to be union. But they shit-canned everyone three years ago and re-opened as a non-union plant. Most of us took the job. They can't put these transmissions together anymore and be competitive. It was either that or the factory goes some place else. I'll take the job, thank you very much. But I wish we were still union."

Dean said, "So what made Billy a communist?"

"Because he said it. And he'd pass out *The Communist Manifesto*. He didn't lead with that, but he got there pretty fast. And, boy, would he piss off some of those old-timers when he'd tell them unions were the consequence of communism. They did not like that."

"How'd others react? You?"

Tim smiled and shook his head. "I told him to leave me alone. I wasn't interested. I'm a patriot, you know, I believe in America.

The communist crap can be flushed down the toilet as far as I'm concerned. I was the nice one, though."

"Oh?"

"Yeah. I just barked. A number of guys bit. Some guys who fought in Korea and Vietnam, they didn't take so kindly to him. I know a few of them beat him up one night. Told him to not come around anymore."

"How bad?"

Tim shrugged. "Bad enough to let him know they were serious. They just told me after. Sometime last fall, I think it was."

Dean took a large drink of coffee.

"And you know," continued Tim, "that bastard showed up again. Black eye. Bandages. I'll give him that. He was a tough son of a bitch."

Until the bullet hit him. Dean nodded. He and Tim finished their coffee. Tim did not know anything else of relevance other than the guy who talked about beating Billy was George Littlefield. Shortly after, he and Julie walked him out, and Dean drove back to the station under a cloudy morning sky. Once there, he had Laura look up any information on George Littlefield she could find. She told him that Special Agent Pryce had called and wanted Dean to call back.

At his desk, Dean called Billy's parents to ask who the family doctor was and if they recalled any injuries to their son. They said he had had an accident at the shop in October, but he had not seen a doctor. Just to be sure, Dean called the family doctor, who pulled up the files on Billy Nimitz and noted no visits regarding any accidents.

Guthrie walked up to Dean after he hung up. After updating Guthrie on his conversation with Tim, they split up the hospitals from Plattsburgh to Zion and started calling to see if Billy Nimitz sought medical treatment there.

He spent a couple of hours calling the hospitals on his list, most of the time on hold. As he hung up one call, his phone rang. He hoped it was St. Francis Hospital in Plattsburgh, who said someone would call him back, so he answered. "Yep. Detective Wallace here."

"This is Special Agent Pryce." When Dean did not respond, Pryce asked, "Detective?"

"Sorry. I was expecting someone else."

"Yes. Anyways, I left a message for you."

"Yeah. Haven't had a chance to call you back."

"Obviously. Look, we've got a problem."

"What's that?"

"When we got back to Plattsburgh last night, we were inventorying the evidence you loaded up for us. We noticed a discrepancy."

"Sure. How can I clear that up for you?"

"It's a serious one, detective. I'm not sure there is any clearing this up. It might blow our whole case."

Dean sat up straight in his chair, pulling himself closer to the desk. "Excuse me?"

Pryce covered the phone and coughed. "Excuse me. Sorry about that. Yes. The photos of the weapons seized at Sam Darwish's home and the weapons we have don't correspond. Specifically, we're missing the M16."

Dean held the phone in his hand, his mind tracing the conversation the day prior with the FBI and DEA. They had not yet sent the M16 downstate for ballistics testing. The rifle should have gone with Pryce and Hayes.

"Detective?"

"Uh, yes? Is it listed in the seizure list?"

Pryce did not pause. "No. I've checked a half-dozen times. The paperwork doesn't mention it. It's not with the other weapons or any of the other evidence. It's only in the picture.

And you told me an M16 was used in the shooting. So do you have the M16 with an intact chain of evidence trail?"

Dean thought it over. Who had been in charge of gathering the physical evidence? Had he been and forgotten to do what he needed to do? Had the booze screwed him up again?

"Detective, do you have the M16?"

No. Dean was sure it was not him. But if not him…. He looked up and down the station floor. Guthrie was talking on the phone. "I don't know. I'll get back to you." He hung up.

CHAPTER 38

Tony patted his shoulder. Dean was far down a bottle of Wild Turkey, sitting on the lawn chair on his front porch. Tony's Oldsmobile popped and clicked as the engine cooled.

Tony sat in the chair next to him. The evening had slipped into night. The warmth of the day lingered, but it was fading as rapidly as the visibility of the trees sinking into the dark. Tony pulled the bottle from Dean, took a drink, and handed it back to him. "What's up?"

Dean let the question sit unanswered for a while. Why had he called Tony? Why not go directly to their dad, who would know soon enough? It was not about protecting the chief. He did not need or want that. When Dean started telling Tony about the missing M16 and Zorn's source of information, the words came out fast and quick, like he were vomiting. His body cleansing himself of disease. All the little things over the months, every word Guthrie had said, every action he had taken loomed ever larger, ever more significant. And he wrestled coming to terms, accepting that Guthrie had led him, Reggie, and Etheridge into a trap. Had walked them in and expected them to not return.

Tony took another drink and handed the bottle back to Dean. "That's messed up. They may lose leverage on Sam. Probably have. Well, they have. It's just a matter if Sam knows it or not."

"And that protects Zorn."

Tony nodded once. "Yup."

"I should've seen it."

"That's the booze and hindsight talking. Sounds like Guthrie was real careful. It's not like Dad noticed it either. Zorn's been slipping through his fingers for years. Some of that had to be Guthrie's work."

"But we've got nothing solid on him. He probably has an explanation for the M16. An explanation for everything."

Tony leaned forward and clasped his hands together. "Thing is, now you know your target. All of that stuff he was doing was in the shadows. Now you've got the flashlight."

Dean nodded.

Tony looked at his brother and then to the night sky. Only the brightest stars burnt through the haze of street and living room lights. "I know something about redemption. What it means to live with shame and to find a way, to claw your way back to something like respect. You. You are not in need of that. What Guthrie did, you didn't give him that power to do. So you can't reclaim it. You can arrest him. You can find justice for what he's done, for Reggie. But you—you do not need redemption."

Dean let a long silence rest between them. "Do you think Pryce will work with me?"

"How so?"

"Keep the missing M16 quiet for now. Help me nab Guthrie."

"I've worked with him a couple of times. He's a good agent. He's pissed as hell, I'm sure. He'll want justice, so yeah, I think he'd listen to what you have to say."

Dean nodded. "I need to talk to him."

"I'll call him. I'll tell him you'll talk to him tomorrow." Tony stood up and walked into the house.

Dean watched the Straithorn's Buick LeSabre drive past his house and into their driveway. Their daughter, Lilly, jumped out of the back seat and ran to their front door. Two years older than Jenny, she seemed a lifetime more mature. Boys meant something to her and she meant something to the boys, at least a number of them. High school was sooner rather than later. And Dean saw Jenny so infrequently, that every time he did so very much seemed to have changed. She had grown or altered her hair style or found a new favorite band. It was impossible to keep pace with her. Impossible to understand and accept what he was missing. He swirled the whiskey in the bottle and took a drink.

The screen door closed behind Tony as he took back the seat he had abandoned a few minutes before. "Pryce says he'll keep it quiet. Call him tomorrow with your plan."

"Thanks."

"Sure."

"Did I ever tell you about Stitch?"

Tony smiled. "Yes. A couple of months ago. One of your buddies that didn't make it out of Vietnam."

"Mmmm." Dean sighed. "Yep. Quang Ho. Hill 425. Lost a lot of good men there."

"Yep. Sounds familiar."

"Did I tell you I killed Stitch, that I'm the reason Stitch left in a body bag?"

Tony sat silent in the chair. He had grabbed a Pabst when he was inside.

"I take it I didn't mention that part."

"No. You did not."

"It was when we were fighting bunker to bunker. Fucking NVA knew how to build bunkers. You could drop bombs on them all day and night and those goddamned bunkers would hold together. Unless it was a direct hit, which almost never happened. Anyways, we were crawling our way up this hill. Machine guns sweeping the routes of our advance. Those assholes could set up interlacing fire as well. Don't ever believe them, when they say the NVA wasn't a good army. They were well trained. Professional. Deadly."

"I won't."

"I can't remember which bunker it was, but it was a few in. We darted from outcropping to outcropping. Wherever we could find cover. But we moved. Had to. You stopped for too long you died. Who wants to die in Vietnam?" Dean took a drink. "Shit. Anyways, it was my turn to flank this bunker and drop some grenades in it while a couple of guys provided the covering fire. I get up there. I pull the pin. I drop the grenade in. And a gook pops up on my right. I don't think. I spray the guy with my gun. The grenade goes poof. The NVA in front of me falls. He looked surprised." He rubbed the armrest's plastic. After a while, he continued. "The battle's over and we're trying to find the guys that didn't make it. I found Stitch. He was downhill from that NVA guy I killed. I shot a bunch of bullets and it killed the enemy. And it may have killed Stitch. I didn't think too much about it at the time. Just a fleeting thought. The kind like, 'Did one of my bullets kill Stitch?' But over time, over time, that begins to weigh. And then you get home. And you can't tell anyone this. No one understands except other Marines. And you can't tell them you think you killed one of your own, even if you know you aren't the first to do so because you're sitting at home on your ass drinking beer and he's dead."

They sat there in silence, watching the lights of the nearby houses turning off one by one.

"You end up hating yourself. You hate yourself for what you've done, and you wonder if there's a way to claw your way back to humanity, to even liking yourself."

CHAPTER 39

April 8 - May 28, 1979

At ten the next morning, Pryce called into the station. Laura put the phone to her shoulder and shouted, "Special Agent Pryce calling you Dean."

Dean nodded and waved to have her transfer him to the line. They spoke briefly as they had arranged, with Dean saying "Yeah," "Uh-huh," and "Thank you." He hung up the phone and walked to Guthrie's desk, who looked up from the typewriter, tapped his cigarette in the brown-glass ashtray. "So?"

"They've got all the evidence processing now. The guns will be the quickest, but even they'll be a couple of weeks at best. Sam'll be cooperative, but nothing's going to happen until all the evidence is sewn up tight. The good news is they've arrested him for drug possession and distribution, so he'll be waiting in jail."

Guthrie grabbed his cigarette and inhaled deeply. Through the smoke coming out of his mouth, he said, "Why not just test the M16 first? That's the gun."

Ballsy fucker, thought Dean. He shrugged. "I don't know. Being thorough I guess. Hell, they're the Feds. They've got plenty of money for tests. Maybe they don't believe me that it was an M16. Or they want to see if they get any hits on the other guns."

"Sure."

"Look, we spent yesterday calling hospitals. Let's hit a few today and flash Billy's picture around. See if anyone recognizes him. And did you call George Littlefield?"

"I did. He moved to Boston in November. Hasn't been back since."

"He provide alibis to prove he was in Boston the night Billy walked into those woods?"

Guthrie nodded and handed the handwritten list with phone numbers to Dean, who handed them to Zach and asked if he could call the numbers and verify Littlefield's alibi.

Dean—acting his very best as if nothing was different and wishing he had participated in the high school drama club—and Guthrie drove south to Plattsburgh and traced threads of possible return routes to Zion, pausing at the hospitals, and speaking to emergency room staff. They left their cards and photos of Billy with every hospital, asking that if anyone recognized him to call the Zion PD. Then they would see what came about.

Over cheeseburgers and fries at a place in West Chazy, Guthrie expounded on his theories of the Nimitz murder. To avoid talking, Dean let him. Guthrie liked the upset girlfriend or jealous Alex line of reasoning. Sarah Esposito was angry that Billy could not buy her everything she wanted—even though she seemed to get everything she wanted. They argued. She shot him.

Guthrie's other theory was that Alex Smith was jealous. All the talk about Alex and Billy having a falling out was true and it was around Sarah. They knew it. Alex and Sarah had slept together. Two boys liked one girl. One boy shot the other.

What troubled Dean about those two theories had remained unchanged. The money in the closet. To him, that was the central fact of importance in the case. Unless the theory of the crime could explain that money, the theory had too big of a hole. He could dismiss *The Communist Manifesto* except for the new information from Billy's cousin, Tim. Was the murder of Billy politically motivated? But the cash?

For the first time, Dean wondered if Billy's murder would go unsolved. It would not be the first time in his career. Several of his old NYPD homicides were still open. Straight up whodunits with evidence but no person to tie it to. In 1977, his last year working in New York, there had been almost two thousand murders, leaving several hundred open cases. But the idea of having this single homicide remain open was a devastating thought. He could not untangle whether he felt this way because he was less drunk than he had been in New York, because Zion had so few murders compared to the much larger city south of them, or if age and remembering Stitch and the open question of who killed him—knowing that it will never be solved.

They paid and continued their path back to Zion, leaving photos and cards and questions behind. Once back in Zion, they waited.

⁙

The Pratts celebrated every Memorial Day as if it were the biggest holiday of the year. In reality, they believed too much in the sanctity of Christmas and Easter to treat them other than the religious observances they had once started out being. Memorial Day, however, was the start of summer and deserved a grand party of a kick off. This year, Cindy, Jenny, and Spencer drove up to the Pratt farm to spend the weekend, have a cookout, and do some fishing in the stream that ran through their property.

Cindy called a week ahead and invited Dean, who was shocked. He knew he would be keeping Jenny for the week, but being invited to the cookout was unexpected. When she recommended he bring his mother and father along, he was flabbergasted. For the entire week, he contemplated if he should expect some major news. Cindy had sounded normal, but it had been years since she had asked him—let alone his parents—to do anything social with her or her family.

Eric drove them to the farm in the late afternoon. As the chief was fond of reminding everyone, summer officially would begin a few weeks later in June. As if acceding to his technical demands, the air was pleasant, still spring. But the sky was clear and that soft blue associated with delightful photos featuring the sky. Wayne Pratt had the grill already cranking at the front of the house on the lawn under the big oak tree, whose leaves had yet to reach full maturity for the season.

Smoke poured out the grill's vents. The smell of charcoal and hickory wafting over the yard. Two picnic tables covered with red-and-white checkered tablecloths, one of which was piled with paper plates, utensils, and baskets of breads, fruits, vegetables, bags of potato chips and pretzels, and containers of potato and macaroni salads. A blue ten-gallon cooler sat next to the table, full of ice and soda and beer.

As Dean stepped out of the car, Jenny ran up to him, screaming "Daddy," and they hugged. The jeans that had touched the tops of her ankles in January were now capris. She hugged her grandparents and then grabbed Dean's hand and dragged him to play a game of yard darts. The badminton net and croquet field were set up for later that day.

Spencer and Wayne worked the grill. The former, dressed in dark blue jeans and a long-sleeved yellow button up shirt, leaning in and pointing and nodding to the latter's queries. Dot hung nearby, panting and looking between the spatula in Wayne's hand and the grill. The Pratt boys played basketball in the driveway while Cindy, Dean's parents, and Eileen sat on lawn chairs, each with a can of Budweiser in their hands or on the ground beside them.

After three games of yard darts, Jenny ran off to play with the boys, and Dean walked up to the grill. Spencer nodded his hello, and Wayne asked him how he thought the burgers looked. Dean looked down. They looked too crisp for his taste, but he said they looked delicious.

Spencer stepped away from the grill when Dean did and walked alongside him toward Dean's parents and Cindy. Spencer put his hand on Dean's lower arm and stopped. "She's really growing up, isn't she?"

Dean looked at his daughter defending Cole, who towered over her. But she had, indeed, grown and was growing up. "She is."

"This is probably the last year she'll be able to spend weeks with you up here, so far from home."

Dean looked down, stuffed his hands in his pockets, and toed the grass with his shoe. And thus the reason for the invitation, with parents as a stand-by to keep him calm.

"Cindy didn't want to tell you, but with Jenny's friends and stuff, she's spending more and more time with them. Next year, she probably won't want to spend time with any adults." A thin smile crept across Spencer's face.

Dean nodded slowly. "Maybe. Maybe. Eventually for certain. I figure when Jenny doesn't want to visit, she'll let me know."

"Well, she might not. That's why I'm alerting you."

"I see. Well, thanks for the public service announcement."

Spencer patted Dean's shoulder. "Ah, don't take it like that. Just prepping you for the future."

"Sure. Sure." Desperate to change the subject, Dean said, "So you been up here all weekend?"

Spencer started walking toward the cooler. "Not all, no. Came up on Saturday afternoon. We'll leave tomorrow morning. Took the day off from the office."

After all these years, Dean still could not remember what Spencer did for a living. Something that paid well he knew. He thought about asking, but he did not care enough to ask, so he walked passed him, opened the cooler, pulled out two Budweisers, and gave one to Spencer. They both raised the can and saluted it in the air.

Dean ate a hot dog and burger, which ended up tasting better than their appearance might have suggested, and a substantial volume of mustard potato salad and carrots. The adults played croquet. Eric mastered the field the quickest and won handily, which true to form he gloated over the other players. Then the kids took on the adults in a badminton tournament. Mike, the middle Pratt boy, won in the end, beating Cindy in a sibling duel.

The kids returned to the basketball goal and the adults to their chairs and beer. Somewhere along the way, Wayne had started a fire in the fire pit, which they huddled around. Fireflies blinked away along the edge of the woods. The crackle of wood in the fire, the sound of the basketball hitting the pavement or the goal, and occasional cheers or claps from the kids wafted in and out of the conversation. The evening transitioned to night without any particular notice. During one of Spencer's trips to the house's bathroom, Cindy caught Dean's eye and gestured with a head nod to the darkness and woods away from the house—a gesture Dean understood immediately to be a request for him to walk with her.

They strolled in silence across the grassy hill to the edge of the woods. She wore tight blue jeans and a button-up blouse that hugged her figure. He wondered how she had been able to keep so trim while the rest of the world aged around her. She showed her years only at the edges of her eyes. As their vision adjusted to the darkness, the edges of the leaves caught what little moonlight there was. Dean slapped a mosquito biting into the back of his neck, breaking the silence.

Cindy slipped her hands into her pockets. "I wanted to talk to you about Jenny."

"I think Spencer already did."

"Oh?"

"Yeah, something about her not wanting to be around adults much longer and probably not wanting to visit me so much anymore."

"Yeah, that's the gist. I just wanted to prepare you. To let you know, it's not about not wanting to visit you. It's about wanting to be with her friends."

Dean smiled though Cindy did not see it in the darkness. "I know that. We were kids one time a long time ago."

"Ass." Cindy laughed. "Not that long ago."

But to Dean it felt like lifetimes. They walked in silence along the very edge of the woods. Cindy reached out her hand and grabbed the leaves.

"Look," said Dean, "I get it with Jenny. But over the past few months, I've realized—well—I always realized I think but not like now. So—"

"Spit it out," said Cindy in a kind tone that Dean long ago understood to be her form of encouragement.

"Well, I'm sorry about what happened to us. I'm sorry I couldn't give you the life you wanted."

The pause was so long, Dean wondered if she was going to ignore him. She said, "You don't have to apologize. I don't know what happened over there—not really. But I do know it changed you. Changed us in ways we can't and won't understand. In ways we couldn't have predicted. How could it not? You needed a better wife." He was going to interject, but she raised her hand. "Hold on. And I needed a different husband. At that time. We were both so young. We didn't know what to do. I just wanted a corner of life. I wasn't ambitious. Just a space, a place to call mine."

Dean hesitated in saying anything, fearing he would cut her off. So he waited and when it was clear she was not going to say anything more, he said, "I'm glad you found that space."

She stopped and looked at him. Fireflies flashed behind her. One landed on her shoulder. "Oh Dean." She stepped up and embraced him. "I'm sorry I wasn't able to help you. I'm so sorry."

"Forgive me."

"I forgive us."

He returned her embrace and cried for the first time in a long time.

CHAPTER 40

May 30, 1979

A couple of days later, with Jenny staying at her grandma's, Dean was in the station, the Billy Nimitz file on his desk. The hospital search had turned up nothing, which meant Billy had not stopped for treatment after being beaten by factory workers or the hospital people had not recognized the photo. Either resulted in a dead end.

With the Grim Devils untouchable until the FBI and DEA gave Zion PD the all-clear, which might be months at best, that path of investigation was limited. And so with all the dead ends facing him, Dean flipped open the file and started looking. He pulled out the photos. The gruesome ones and the ones provided by Billy's parents. He reviewed the coroner's report and the crime-scene report. Everything he knew about the death of Billy Nimitz summarized and ordered on sheets of paper and tucked into a folder. He pulled up the report on the gun. The Remington M1911A1 found at the scene, buried under some snow.

Purchased by Dennis Kowlowski in 1952. He died the same day JFK was shot in Dallas. And the trail stops. Dean looked at the report. Guthrie had signed his name at the bottom. Dean was already convinced his fellow detective was corrupt, handing information over to the Grim Devils, derailing investigations where he could, even helping in an ambush of police. And now, knowing that, Dean doubted every bit of Guthrie's part of the investigation. Had Guthrie done the necessary work on confirming the history of the gun?

Dean walked to the Carnegie Zion Library, a two-story brick building, five blocks from the station. Lisa Munadi smiled at him as he walked through the double-glass door entrance. She had graduated two years before Dean and washed out of SUNY-Buffalo while he was heading to Vietnam. During school, she had acted as if she were better than everyone else except for the jocks she threw herself after. Now she worked as a librarian in the town she had said she was going to abandon. Wasn't that the American reality?

"Hey Dean," she said. "What can we do for you?"

He smiled at her. "You keep archives of the paper, right?"

"Yeah. We keep it on microfilm."

"I need to see the *Zion Beacon* for 1963. November 22nd, 23rd, and 24th. Start with those."

"Doing research on Kennedy?" She walked from behind the counter toward the stairs leading upward.

"No. But a fellow in a nearby town died the same day. I want to see his obituary."

"Sure. Sure." She led him up the stairs to the single microfilm machine, patted him on the shoulder, and said she would return a few minutes later. She did with two square boxes. She turned on the machine and pulled out the tray, lifting the glass covering. She inserted the reel of film on the spindle, unspooled a bit of the film, and slipped it beneath the roller and into the uptake reel, which she rolled a few times. She set the glass down and pushed the tray in, revealing the *Zion Beacon*'s front page of the November 22, 1963. She adjusted the rotation knob to flip the image upright. "There you go."

He heard her footsteps fade away and looked at the screen. The headline for that day was, "Kennedy Shot. Johnson Sworn In." A photo of the dead president and new president alongside the article. Dean fast forwarded to the obituary section. He did not find one for Dennis, so he moved on to November 23rd. More JFK assassination coverage, including a prominent "Marxist Accused of Murder" headline.

On the bottom half of the page, a photo of Zion's mayor and Eric Wallace. Dean paused and lingered over the image. Despite his dad wearing the dress campaign hat, Dean could see that his father had grayed significantly since then. He had also gained some weight around the middle, but the image reminded him of how vigorous his dad had been. And then he thought how active and strong his dad was yet and hoped that he remained so in his later years.

He moved on to the obituaries and found one for Dennis that day. From there, Dean learned Dennis was survived by a brother and a son: Jacob and Curtis. Dean rewound the microfilm. Handed the boxes back to Lisa and walked back to the station. He had Laura call into the state dispatcher to pull the license information for both Jacob and Curtis Kowlowski.

While she did that, Dean smoked a cigarette and pulled up the day's memo on any changes to the laws and guidelines. He stuffed them into a manila folder and shoved that into a desk drawer. He walked back over to Laura, who put her hand over the mouthpiece. "I don't have the information yet."

He nodded. "My question was, 'Where's Guthrie?'"

She shrugged so he walked outside, smoked another cigarette, and walked back in. She gave him a slip of note paper. Jacob did not have a license on file. The last one issued was in 1968. Curtis's address was in Monrovia, a smaller town than Zion and to the west on Route 11 toward Chateaugay. He looked at his watch. Too early to go. Curtis was probably at work already, and Dean did not want to waste the day in Monrovia. He looked back at the reports awaiting his attention and knew he would not be able to focus on them. His mind was too hungry for an answer. So he told Laura he would be back later and drove to his mom's house and absconded with Jenny. He drove her to Montreal, where they bought tickets for the Expos-Phillies game. While downing a hot dog bathed in mustard, they watched Gary Carter hit a two-run homer in the second from their left field seats. Dean bought Jenny a hat and mitt. Carter's home run was the only score of the game. After watching the Expos, Dean thought they, perhaps, had a winning team that season. He dropped his daughter off with his mom before heading over to Monrovia. The day Jenny's dad played hooky from work and took her to a baseball game—to a foreign country even—would long remain precious and special to her.

The short drive to Monrovia along a tree-lined and farm field highway passed by with few other cars. He pulled to a stop on the street outside the home listed as Curtis's address, a split-level minimal Tudor cottage style house with olive wood siding and black shutters in need of painting. Dean walked up the driveway and the sidewalk, which was framed in a flower bed of begonias and marigolds. Standing beneath the small covered porch, he rang the bell. He started to ring again, when he noticed movement behind the lace curtain covering the front door's window.

A finger moved the lace curtain, exposing a bald head. The finger disappeared and the curtain fell back in place. A dead bolt clicked and the door swung open.

A thin, frail man stood at the entrance. An oxygen tube hung from his nostrils to a small silver tank with a red valve he had on wheels behind him. Even though he was a couple of inches shorter than Dean, the man's frailness made him seem much smaller, diminutive. Silver stubble dusted his face and he had no eyebrows above his blue-green eyes. "Hello?" he asked.

Dean flipped open his badge. "Detective Dean Wallace from Zion PD. I'm looking for Curtis Kowlowski."

"Well, you found him." He turned and slowly walked down the hallway. "Close the door behind you, please."

Dean stepped into the house and closed the door. He caught up with Curtis as he was turning into a dining room with a dark, brilliant table surrounded by six chairs. An ivory, lace table runner a foot wide cut across the length of the table, and two crystal candle holders with virgin white candles sat in the center. He started to pull out one of the end chairs with arm-rests and a floral cushion pattern. Dean grabbed the chair and pulled it out. Curtis sat down and breathed deeply. "Thank you."

Dean pulled out a chair next to him and sat down. Across from him stood a large china cabinet in a darker wood but also much older than the table. However, the cabinet seemed to hold only a few mugs and not much else.

"I'd get you something," said Curtis, "but…." He gestured to the tank and held up the tube.

"That's okay. I don't think it'll take much time."

"Mm. Francis, my wife, should be back soon."

"Sure."

"She's been good to me since. Well—"

"Can I get you something?"

"No." Curtis shook his head. "So how can I help?"

"I'm here about a gun your father purchased. It was used in a homicide in Zion. The records indicate he bought it, but nothing after that."

"My dad had several. Which gun?"

"It was a pistol. A Remington M1911A1."

A car pulled into the driveway.

"Dad had a number of rifles, but he had only one pistol. I don't like guns. Ah." The garage door was opened. "Francis is home now."

They waited in silence as the car was pulled in, the garage door closed, and the door to the house from the garage was opened. "Curt, I'm home." Keys landing on a counter.

"In here, Francis. We've a visitor."

"I wondered about the car in the driveway." She walked into the kitchen, the sounds of her shoes hitting the floor changing as she walked from carpet to linoleum. "Hello," she said when she saw Dean.

Dean stood up. "Hello ma'am. Sorry to disturb you. I'm Detective Dean Wallace with the Zion police."

Her smile faded. She wore a brown business suit with a large, silk tan scarf. Gold hoop earrings dangled along her neck. "I'll make some coffee."

"That's not necessary," said Dean.

"Maybe not for you, but after the day I've had, I need it." She pulled open a cabinet.

"Do you remember Dad's guns?" asked Curtis.

"Oh yes. I hated those."

"Me too. This detective's here about the pistol. What we'd do with that?"

As she measured Folger's into a paper filter, she tapped her right foot. "Let's see. We sold a couple of the rifles to Stephen—Stephen what's his name—Mc or something."

"McHugh. Stephen McHugh. Has the kid, Joey, who's a heck of a winger. Used to be at least, years ago."

"Right. Yep, that's him." She filled the carafe and started pouring it into the coffee maker.

"The pistol. Oh that's right. We sold it to that fella from the FBI. Remember?"

"FBI?" Dean could not hide the perplexity from his question.

"Yes, that's right."

"When was this?" asked Dean.

"So Dad died in sixty-three." Curtis looked at Dean. "Same day as Kennedy. And we took all of it. Except the guns and a few things, which my uncle took. He used them on his farm and he went turkey hunting every fall. And then he passed. Oh, last year some time. Lived to be ninety-two. Imagine that. I won't get there."

"Don't think that way," said Francis, out of Dean's sight now but in the kitchen.

Curtis mouthed "cancer" to Dean. "Yeah, yeah. Anyways, we got the stuff and we knew some people that still farm around here and asked if they wanted the guns. A few did and took them. But I knew a young man, worked down at the Webster's restaurant downtown. Good fried chicken if you're interested. He said—Taylor Parker is his name—he knew someone who was interested in the pistol. I said, 'Have him give me a call.' A couple of days later, he did. He drove out here. He's not from Monrovia. From out in your parts or more east, I think. He bought it. Gave us a hundred cash. I have no idea if it was worth that or not, but I got more out of the cash than I would've out of the gun."

The coffee maker started to drip. "That's right," said Francis, who appeared in the dining room and took a seat across from Dean. She patted Curtis's hand and smiled at him.

"Do you know his name? The one who bought the pistol," asked Dean.

Francis wagged her finger. "You know what? Since I didn't know him, I wrote his name down." She stood up and walked to the cabinet behind Dean. She pulled open a drawer, from which she pulled out a small box, the kind of which his mother stored recipes on index cards. Francis said she forgot her glasses, disappeared, and returned a few minutes later with them sitting low on her nose. She asked if he wanted sugar or cream, and he said no. He was anxious to find out who this FBI agent was that had purchased the gun, but he could not bring himself to be rude to Curtis and Francis. She pulled some mugs down.

Curtis leaned over. "She loves to have any company. So she's excited to be able to serve coffee," he whispered.

A few minutes later, each had a coffee adjusted to their liking. Francis, who splashed a bit of cream into hers, opened the box on the table and started flipping through pieces of paper.

Curtis started into a lengthy foray into his chemotherapy treatments for lung cancer. The prognosis did not look good, but Francis told him to be positive, that that was as important as the chemo. They responded to each other's cues, which Dean could not see but knew were there nonetheless. His parents had them. He and Cindy had had them.

"Ah, here it is." She pulled out a piece of paper. "That's right. He was a handsome fellow."

"Hey, now," said Curtis.

"You've nothing to be jealous of." She smiled at Curtis. To Dean, she said, "His name was Anthony Wallace."

"Is that any relation?" asked Curtis.

CHAPTER 41

Dean drove in shock. He kept spinning and tossing and tumbling the possible scenarios for Tony having the gun that killed Billy Nimitz. Did someone buy it using his name? Did Tony buy it and sell it to someone? He had not had a picture in his wallet to show the Kowlowskis. He felt like a bad brother about that and forgot it as his mind raced along with his speed east on Route 11.

Without any transition, Dean wondered why would Tony kill Billy? He was shocked at his ability to leap to that conclusion, to even contemplate his brother was a killer. He shook his head to force the thoughts away, but he could not. He accepted that Tony had bought the pistol that was used to kill Billy Nimitz. And Tony must have pulled the trigger. He did not understand why though? It did not answer for all the cash or *The Communist Manifesto*. But Dean felt the same way about this answer as he did when he was talking to Sam Darwish or Alex Smith. He knew his brother was a criminal. Knew it in his bones. He pulled over and vomited alongside the road. The sun dipping below the horizon. He rinsed his mouth with Wild Turkey before racing again along Route 11.

Now Dean had to understand why. Tony and Billy did not know each other. No connection between them had popped up during the investigation. As Dean pulled into his parents' driveway and parked next to his father's car, his right palm throbbed from having struck the steering wheel repeatedly since Monrovia.

He took a drink of Wild Turkey and lit a cigarette before getting out and walking up to the door. Even there, he hesitated but went in. Jenny ran up to him and hugged him. He told her they would be going soon but he needed to talk to Grandpa first. She made some comment about helping Grandma cook and ran off. Then the smell of onions and green peppers. His stomach quivered.

His dad sat in his recliner tapping down the tobacco in his pipe. "Hey there. Your mom's making chop suey." He looked up and paused when he saw Dean's drawn face. "What's wrong?"

Dean told his dad about tracing the Kowlowski gun back to Tony, including trying to piece together the connection between the gun, his brother, and the victim. The chief leaned back in his chair, struck a match, and lit his pipe, puffing hard to get it to stay lit. "What're you going to do?"

"What do you mean?" Dean flopped down onto the sofa. The TV was mute, but Walter Cronkite was on screen. A banner with SALT II with an image of the Soviet and American flags side-by-side.

"Not sure how to be any clearer. What are you going to do with this information?"

"I need to talk to him. Find out what happened to the gun after he bought it." That was the only explanation he could come up with that cleared his brother. Tony had bought it and then sold it or discarded it. He would take "lost it" as an answer. Dean knew he did not believe it though.

"You mean, like was it stolen or something?"

"Yeah. Something. I mean—" Dean looked over at his father, who struck another match and thrust the flame into the pipe. "You knew, didn't you?"

"Huh?" Eric looked at him out of the corner of his eye.

"You knew Tony bought the gun already. You knew—." But Dean could not yet bring himself to those final, fateful words.

Eric scratched his eyebrow. "So what if I did?"

Why would the Chief keep that information to himself except to protect Tony. And his brother would only need protecting if—. "And you've kept it to yourself? Tony killed a man, and that's okay."

His father leaned back against his chair, the wood frame creaking. He dropped his head and looked at Dean. "You and I have killed, son."

"That was war."

"And this isn't?" The Chief gestured to the TV. The map of Iran was replaced by the flag of the Soviet Union. "You don't call this a war? Them or us? Our way of life is at stake."

The Communist Manifesto. The passports in Canada. Billy Nimitz was a spy. Or involved with spies somehow. Dean still could not wrap his mind around the idea a spy would be a young kid in nowhere New York.

Dean shook his head. "Was this approved by the FBI?" He said the words, but he knew the answer already.

Eric stood up. "I'm going to wash up. I think dinner's close to being ready." He walked out of the room.

Dean sat there, staring at the TV but not seeing it. Jenny walked in and tugged his arm. "Daddy."

"Yes?"

"What's wrong?"

He looked over at his daughter. He shook his head. "Things a young girl like you don't have to worry about."

"About what? And dinner's ready."

He smiled at his daughter, who was growing up so fast but yet seemed so young and innocent still in spite of how much he had screwed up. "I can't tell you. But I'm not sure what the right thing to do is."

"But you do. You always say, 'You know what the right thing to do is.'"

He grabbed her and hugged her. He and Cindy had always said that. Whenever she had gotten into trouble at school, they had queried her about why she had punched the boy who took her Oreos or had pushed her way onto an occupied swing set. Jenny knew that she had done wrong, and so her parents had encouraged her to listen to that message in her head. Here she was telling him, and it immediately clarified what he needed to do to. He was a policeman, and Billy Nimitz had been murdered. Dean only knew of one right thing to do, even if it was painful.

༶❦༶

An hour later, Dean sat in his car across the street from Tony's two-story brick and wood siding house halfway between Zion and Plattsburgh. The house was in a small housing addition surrounded by farms. He pulled out his last cigarette and lit it before crushing the packet.

A large bay window in the family room let light from the TV pour out. Dean took a drink and shoved the flask into his coat pocket. He smoked the cigarette down to the filter, got out of the car, flicked the cigarette to the road, and walked up Tony's driveway.

When he reached the porch, Dean noticed the front door was open. "Tony?" he said in a volume close to shouting. He opened the screen door and knocked on the door jamb. Waited. He peered into the entryway, which led straight into the family room and back to the kitchen and a hallway. A lamp was on next to the tan, leather sofa. The TV, which faced the sofa and backed up against the front window, was tuned to ABC and an *Eight Is Enough* rerun. On the coffee table, a plate with a half-eaten sandwich and potato chips. "Tony?" Dean took a few steps into the family room, attempting to look down the hallway that began where the family room ended and the kitchen began.

"Hello. Dad called." Tony's voice came from the shadows of the kitchen. "And I saw you out there in your car."

"Yeah? So you know why I'm here."

"You want to arrest me."

"Come out from there." Dean leaned right to see if he could see Tony in the kitchen, but he could not. "Let's have a drink, a talk."

Tony stepped into the doorway of the kitchen. "What's there to talk about?"

"Billy was a spy, wasn't he?" He paused to let his brother respond, but when he did not, he continued. "I'm not sure what he was spying on. Nothing much up here, but then I'm not much of an expert in that area. But the FBI and the Mounties seem interested in some fake passports of a guy in Montreal who was a communist. Some of the passports had Billy's name on them. You know this, of course. Knew it before I even told you weeks ago." He watched his brother's face. No change. He continued, "Billy was going to flee, take secrets that he had been given. I'm guessing here. You found out. You aren't a field agent in the FBI, but I know you want to be. Perhaps taking him out—no, bringing him in—would get you that role. Something went wrong. It's easier if something went wrong"

Tony stood just inside the kitchen, his hands in his pockets.

Dean clenched his jaw. The anger rose up, and he shouted, "Say something."

His brother shook his head. "What do you want me to say? You want me to confirm or deny your story? Is that going to change what you do to me?"

"Tell me. Give me a reason to do something different."

"Like Dad?"

"No. I can't overlook it. But I can except something that is less than murder." Dean waited for reaction on his brother's face, but it was blank. He shouted again, "I don't understand why a gun you bought last year was used to kill a kid a few years out of high school who worked in a car-repair shop. Maybe I could live with that, with not knowing, if the killer wasn't my brother. But since I found out about the gun, I've been trying to understand, trying to figure it out. There's a reason, right? You sold the gun to someone? Lost it? Dropped the thing and it went off. Something other than you stood there and pulled the goddamn trigger."

"You'll never get it. If you get the facts, if you get what happened that night, you won't really understand. You never will."

Dean stepped forward.

"That's close enough." Tony's hand dropped to his back.

"You going to shoot me?" Dean raised his hands in front of his body. "Like you shot Billy?"

Tony took a deep breath. "Do you know what it's like being the brother who didn't serve his country? Who found a way to avoid going to war?"

"Lot's of people did that. It was a war to stay out of."

"Hmph." Tony shook his head and sighed. "Jesus, you really think that. The moment Nolan died, I was a pariah to Dad. He hated me for not going. He said I was a coward. But not now. No. Not now. I killed Billy because he was funneling Soviet agents into the country. He was in the woods that night to meet one of them crossing over from Canada. He'd give them money and a drive to Plattsburgh, where they'd take a train with the tickets he gave them to New York City. Poof, they'd disappear into the country. Show up in DC or military bases and take pictures, recruit, infiltrate. This has been going on for years. He'd help them out, too. Pick them up, bring them up here, and ensure they had a safe passage back to Canada, rich with intelligence.

"Middle of last year, they caught one of these agents heading back into Canada, laden with photos of our submarine base in Norfolk. That's when we had to figure out who was doing it. Billy wasn't smart. So we found him. The FBI wanted to keep watching him, use him perhaps."

"But you didn't?"

"No. I don't know. I don't know what got into me. I wanted to move up in the FBI. I wanted redemption in Dad's eyes. I knew from surveillance reports Billy would be meeting someone crossing the border and where he did it. So I went out day after day, waiting for him to show up. I knew where the FBI surveillance was set up. Knew that they watched Billy go in and wait for him to come out. What they wanted was to catch his contact. I knew if I went out there, I could catch them both. They weren't going to get them just by sitting in their cars.

"Billy, finally, showed up one night. I met him out there. I mean, I followed and watched him first. I was going to take photos of him meeting the agent coming into our country. Then something made a noise. I don't know what, but Billy ran. I chased him and confronted him. I announced myself as FBI. I said I was going to arrest him and take him in."

As Tony paused, Dean had the keen sense of the space between them becoming a heavy weight, a barrier and tension that isolated his brother. "What happened next?"

"Don't answer that."

Dean whipped around to find his dad standing in the entryway, his service revolver out and pointing at the floor. Dean turned and stepped back toward the doorway to the garage behind the sofa. He was able to see both his father and brother. "Dad, let me handle this."

"I'm not letting you take him in. He did this country a service. The FBI would've just given him back to the Russkies. Let him live in his communist paradise. He's better off dead. This country is better off with him dead. Tony's a patriot."

Dean looked at Tony. "Is that what you believe? Do you think you did the right thing? I've killed before. In war. And I'm still not sure it was the right thing, and it haunts me. This will haunt you. You know he didn't need to die. You could've—"

"Shut up." Tony pulled a silver automatic revolver from behind him and pointed it at Dean. "Shut up."

Dean raised his hands.

"Son, easy there." Eric took a step forward. "That's your brother."

"I know, the hero. The vet. The one who followed in your footsteps."

Dean shook his head, but he did not say anything.

"Look at me," said Eric. "Look at me, son."

Tony turned his head but kept the gun pointed at Dean.

"You think I was angry at you. Well, you're right. I was. I didn't understand at the time. I just knew your country needed you but, but you didn't need this country. And when Nolan was killed, I was just so angry. I was angry he died there in a war that we weren't going to win. Angry that I was mad at you. I couldn't face it. So I took it out on you. But you didn't deserve it."

"But you welcomed me back after I killed Billy."

Their dad shook his head. "Shit, son, I was just happy to see you after so much time. It didn't matter what you did."

Tony let his arm that held the gun drop, but Dean remained where he was. Eric looked back at Dean. "He doesn't say another word without a lawyer."

Dean's brother dropped to his knees, letting the gun flop to the floor, and began weeping. Dean quietly removed himself from the house, returning to his car, where he leaned against the hood and opened his flask. He patted his coat for cigarettes and sighed when he remembered he had smoked the last one.

Thirty minutes later, the Chief walked his son out of the house and into his car and drove off toward Zion.

CHAPTER 42

May 31-July 31, 1979

The Chief avoided Dean for the next several days, even when his son arrived at their house on Friday evening to pick up Jenny. His mom appeared briefly on the porch and nudged Jenny out, giving her a kiss on the forehead before turning and closing the door behind her. Dean walked up to the porch, grabbed his daughter's hand and led her to his car. Whether Jessica shunned her son at her husband's request or of her own volition, Dean did not know, though he chose to believe the former.

He drove Jenny down to the city on Saturday, dropping her off at Cindy's Manhattan townhouse. As he drove away, he could not help wondering if these moments he had had with his daughter in 1979 would be the last of their kind. He knew, of course, that he could never have the same experiences, but his daughter was getting older, had city friends, and he, her dad, was far away in a small town near Canada. How could that compete with New York City? How could he compete against a townhouse in Manhattan and friends?

Unable to leave so quickly, he drove by his old precinct and stopped by the cops' bar just down the street. A string of unknown faces were interrupted by familiar ones. Lance O'Shea,

Nathan Deroni, Mike Bullard, all fellow detectives. All had forgiven him long ago for his failures and mistakes. They knew enough of his story—of the many stories like his—to know Dean had been and probably was a man in pain, so they did not talk about the past. They talked as if no time had passed. In some sense, none had. People were still killing people, and they still sought the perps.

They had heard about Tony's arrest. Mike had heard it from a fellow Albany detective, who had a friend in the Bureau, who had mentioned the nabbing of an FBI lawyer who confronted an American-born Soviet spy in the woods. The chase when Billy ran. A chase Billy would have won had he not stepped into a hole or tripped and twisted his knee.

The story, of course, had gathered color along the way, but its essentials were the same, and Dean did not bother to correct. He preferred this alternate version of his brother than the one he knew. Lost in the story was a the plight of a forgotten son seeking recognition and the twisted depths he would go.

Why Tony had pulled the trigger instead of taking Billy in was left to speculation. Dean thought he had done it when Tony realized that instead of helping an investigation along, he may have hampered it, may have undercut it mortally. Dean did not particularly like that theory, but he preferred it over satisfying some familial bloodlust, to make them all killers in war.

Too drunk to drive home, he spent the night on Lance's couch, departing the next morning. On Monday, he returned to work, to pick up the next case. His dad had shown up as well but stayed behind the closed door of his office. Neither Dean nor Tony had stated that the Chief had been an accessory after the fact. That would remain undocumented. Unreported.

At noon, Dean's phone rang. "Hello?"

"Detective Wallace?"

"Yes."

"This is Special Agent Pryce. We have what we need to arrest Guthrie. Do you want to do it? I'll even let you in on the interrogation, which we can do there."

"Hell yeah."

An hour and fifteen minutes later, Pryce walked into the Zion police station. He looked at Guthrie, who sat at his desk holding a half-finished pastrami sandwich, and the detective knew the gig was up, even though he knew he would play it out to the bitter end.

Pryce and Dean sat across from Guthrie in the interview room. The FBI agent clicked the record button on a cassette recorder. "Detective Jeremy Guthrie, I am going to record this interview. Okay?"

Guthrie nodded.

"I need you to reply in the affirmative or negative."

"Yes. Yes, that's okay."

"Good." Pryce then exposed the trap he had sprung with the assistance of Dean. When Guthrie learned the weapons were being sent to ballistics, he panicked that he had forgotten to remove the M16 from the items handed over to the FBI. The M16 that tied Sam Darwish to Zorn and to the ambush at the meth lab. The FBI had set up hidden microphones in the Grim Devils clubhouse. He played the crackling tape for Guthrie.

"Yeah, what's up?" said a voice that sounded like Zorn.

"I just heard that all of Sam's weapons are being tested now by the FBI," said the second voice. One that Dean recognized as Guthrie's.

"So. I've got the M16. You got that out. That's the only thing they had on Sam."

"You have it. Shit. I thought I hadn't got it in time."

"You were pretty tanked when you gave it to me. Maybe you shouldn't drink so much."

Pryce clicked the stop button on the surveillance. "So we've got you talking to Zorn about missing evidence. The M16."

"You can't tell that's me."

Pryce pulled out a set of four photos and a journal with a time log. He pushed them toward Guthrie. "Here, we've got Paul Zorn going into the clubhouse. Here's the one of you going in. Here's you coming out. Here's Zorn leaving. Each is tied to a time, which we've listed here. Which, in case you don't get the drift, is timed to the recording. And we've got excellent chain of custody on all this. You're done, Guthrie. We've got you."

What had been beads of sweat along Guthrie's forehead turned to rivers. "Look. I don't think—"

Pryce tapped the photos of Guthrie. "We've got you. All you can do now is help yourself."

Guthrie fell apart faster than most suspects he interviewed. He had been helping Zorn for years. For cash, Guthrie tipped him off on impending raids, helped disappear evidence, and arrested rivals. He was so far in the hole with the Grim Devils, he had no way to claw his way back out. When Zorn learned of Sam's arrest, he had told Guthrie to grab the M16. It was too valuable to just toss, so the disgraced detective gave it to the club president. But first, distraught and guilty over Reggie's death, Guthrie had drunk himself into a stupor, forgetting—at least clearly enough—that he had swiped the M16.

"What about Reggie?" asked Dean, who leaned over the table.

Guthrie shook his head. "I didn't mean for anyone to get hurt. I didn't. I thought they'd clear out before we even got there. I was as surprised as you when the buses were still there untorched. I just warned them and thought they'd clear out, but I found out Zorn didn't like your meddling. He was hoping to take you out. But I swear I didn't know about that until after."

Pryce, with other FBI and DEA agents, arrested a number of the Grim Devils later that day, taking them all and Guthrie down to Plattsburgh. Dean never saw Guthrie again, something he was not too upset about.

The chief seemed unfazed by the arrests and made no mention of them to Dean. He tried to speak to his father, but Laura shook her head. He could see the sadness, the pity in her eyes as she did so.

Dean felt sadness too and then anger. He knew he had done the right thing. He knew it.

⚘

Later that summer, Dean borrowed a tent and backpack from Zach and entered the woods beyond the Pratt farm, walking a series of trails that led through a state and federal forest. He camped by streams, washing his face in the cool, shallow waters. He heated civilian versions of MCI rations. They tasted just as horrible as he remembered, the nastiness cut only by the liberal usage of Tabasco.

At night, he contemplated the sky and listened to the forests. After four nights, he was ready for why he had hiked out away from humanity. In a clearing near a stream at sunset, a fire was burning, the blue-speckled enamel coffee cup of whiskey sat by him. He pulled from his pack the journal he had kept in Vietnam. A small ovestuffed thing with torn pages, different inks and pencils, drawings, random sayings, and photos. A journal beat up around the edges and the paper often stiff and fragile from the wet, the dampness that seemed to be the single constant of the bush.

He pulled out photos. And he tossed them into the fire. Slowly, and then more quickly. And then he ripped out pages and held them as the flames licked the corner and grew. He dropped them into the fire.

He said to no one or thing, "I know this. We all die. And it is always too soon. I wish you could have had the lives everyone intended for you. As for me. As for me, I will live on. I will try to live the life intended for me, as screwed up as that is."

He tossed the journal onto the fire. And he said their names. "Lee. Rider. Paxton. Stitch. The NVA kid just outside the bunker. Nolan Wallace. Dean Wallace." He stared at the journal as it burned. "Hell. Even Tony."

The journal burned bright, crisping to a fine ash that a gentle wind crumpled into the heart of the blaze, and it captured some ash and lifted it into the air, where it hung before it floated away.

DID YOU LIKE THE CLEARING?

I hope you enjoyed *The Clearing*. If you did, I would be grateful for an honest review on Goodreads or Amazon. Thank you!

Please be sure to visit patrickkanouse.com, where you can find out about other works and sign up for my newsletter, which comes with a free short story.

You can follow me on Facebook (https://www.facebook.com/Patrick-Kanouse-143397475720205/) and Twitter (@patrickkanouse).

You can also find posts related to this book (old articles, photos, etc.) at Pinterest: https://www.pinterest.com/patrickkanouse/.

GET A FREE BOOK AND SHORT STORY

I occasionally send newsletters about new releases and special offers related to my mysteries. If you join the mailing list, I'll send you:

1. *A copy of* The Shattered Bull, *the first in the Drexel Pierce series.*
2. *A copy of "A Knock of Ransom," a Drexel Pierce short story.*

You can get The Shattered Bull *and short story for free by joining at: http://eepurl.com/b2-OCb or by scanning this QR code:*

ABOUT THE AUTHOR

Patrick is a mystery author, poet, and technical writer. His poetry has appeared in many journals and websites.

He works for Pearson Education, an educational publisher with offices worldwide, as the director of content creation and development platforms and teaches business report writing at IUPUI.

He lives with his wife, Gina, and their spoiled Yorkie, Kennedy, in Westfield, a suburb north of Indianapolis.

OTHER BOOKS BY PATRICK KANOUSE

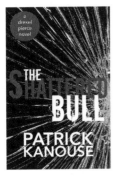

The Shattered Bull

Chicago. Murder. Justice.

As Detective Drexel Pierce, struggling to oovercome the death of his wife, investigates the murder of Hal "The Bull" Nye, a mysterious message seems to hold the clue that will expose the killer. Old friends with shady pasts, mobsters, and rivals lead Drexel towards the murderer. As the machinery of investigation closes in on the Bull's young girlfriend, Drexel risks it all to save her and save his illusions of a society that believes in truth.

Available October 2016.

An Ingenious Murder

A murder so bizarre, no one is sure what happened.

The murder of a reclusive AI scientist pits rookie Detective Terence Brotsky against the seedy underworld and high-tech future of Greater Chicago in 2102.